O9-BHK-829

Never Coming Back

ALSO BY ALISON McGHEE

Shadow Baby
Falling Boy
Rainlight
Was It Beautiful?
All Rivers Flow to the Sea

NEVER
COMING
BACK

Alison McGhee

Houghton Mifflin Harcourt

BOSTON   NEW YORK   2017

For information about permission to reproduce selections from
this book, write to trade.permissions@hmhco.com or to Permissions,
Houghton Mifflin Harcourt Publishing Company, 3 Park Avenue,
19th Floor, New York, New York 10016.

www.hmhco.com

Library of Congress Cataloging-in-Publication Data
Names: McGhee, Alison, date, author.
Title: Never coming back / Alison McGhee.
Description: Boston : Houghton Mifflin Harcourt, 2017.
Identifiers: LCCN 2017007452 (print) | LCCN 2017013821 (ebook) |
ISBN 9781328764348 (ebook) | ISBN 9781328767561 (hardcover)
Subjects: LCSH: Mothers and daughters—Fiction. | Parent and adult child—Fiction.
| Alzheimer's disease—Fiction. | Domestic fiction. | BISAC: FICTION / Literary. |
FICTION / Contemporary Women. | FICTION / Family Life. | FICTION / Medical.
Classification: LCC PS3563.C36378 (ebook) | LCC PS3563.C36378 N49 2017 (print) |
DDC 813/.54—dc23
LC record available at https://lccn.loc.gov/2017007452

Book design by Kelly Dubeau Smydra

Printed in the United States of America
DOC 10 9 8 7 6 5 4 3 2 1

Lines from "The Love Song of J. Alfred Prufrock"
by T. S. Eliot appear on page 71.

To MG

Jeopardy

Now that my mother was disappearing, I wondered when it began to happen. A few months before her neighbor called to tell me something was wrong, or maybe years ago, when I was in my nomadic twenties and home only once or twice a year? Or did something inside her change in a single moment? Quit working? Decide enough was enough?

Hard to say. Hard to know.

But happen it did, and when I left the southern wild and moved back north it was not to be with her, exactly, because where exactly are you when you begin to disappear? Where do your thoughts go, and the words you once used to express them? Are they still inside you somewhere? Not that she was ever big on words to begin with, my mother.

Was big on words? *Had ever been* big on words? Is. Was. Are. Were. These were the days of mixed-up tenses.

When Sylvia the nurse called and said, *She is/was agitated, she is/was looking for you, she is/was having a tough time,* I could get in the car and be there in an hour. They thought my presence would help, and it did. That was what they told me anyway. Which was something that surprised me.

There were many surprises.

"You're coming back north, Clara?" Sunshine said. "Why? I mean, that's fantastic, but why?"

"Have you forgotten that north is where winter lives?" Brown said. "The land of snow and ice? The season of your discontent?"

That was Sunshine, my best friend, and Brown, her husband and my other best friend. I pictured them sharing the phone next to their bed, both ears pressed against the receiver. They had cell phones but they still used a landline both upstairs and down. That was what happened when you lived in the Adirondacks, a place where cell service was spotty and things that elsewhere seemed essential, weren't. Their phones were heavy and black, like old-time phones, because that was what they were, old-time phones, bought at a garage sale for a dollar apiece. Sunshine and Brown liked weight and heft. Or maybe what they liked was permanence.

"Shut up about winter, Brown," Sunshine said. "Don't scare her away."

"If she moves back north, she has to live here," Brown said, and "Absolutely," Sunshine said. They were talking to each other in low tones, as if I couldn't hear them on the other end of the line. This was not uncommon.

"In Old Forge?" I said.

"Duh!" They were still speaking at the same time. They both put the same exclamation mark at the end of the *Duh*. I could hear it. It scrolled across the bottom of my mind, a black jumpy line with a point at the bottom. ! ! !

"Have you two merged? Become a single entity? Can you no longer speak for yourselves?"

"No, no and yes," Sunshine said, and "Old Forge," Brown said again. "Old Forge is where you should live."

They knew my mother and they had known her for a long time but I hadn't said a word to them, or to anyone, about what was happening to her, about the fact that she was the reason I was even thinking about moving back. *Tell no one,* my mother had said, and no one had I told, not even Sunshine and Brown. But it was late that night, and monkey mind had taken over and I was clutching my tiny silver hammer earring for luck and wandering around in the dark until I figured out what to do.

My mother was disappearing and I didn't know what to do, didn't know how to keep her with me, in this world, on this plane of existence, thinking and talking the way I had always known her to think and talk. Sunshine and Brown were the people I had called because they were my best friends. And because even if they were already asleep, they would answer the phone if it rang. That was the kind of people they were.

They were the kind of people who had always been there.

What happens when someone close to you starts to disappear is that they aren't always there. They are with you and then they aren't. This happens while their hearts still beat, while their lungs still breathe, while they look directly at you. They talk and laugh and sing and then they don't. They are here and they are gone, are and were, simultaneously.

"Did I wake you guys up?"

"No. Kind of. Who cares."

Each of them speaking over the other.

"Old *Forge?*" I said again, like it was a place I'd never been to before, a kind of mythical place that existed on another planet.

"Old Forge," they said. "We're here."

"We'll hike and cook and stack wood," Sunshine said. "We'll get breakfast at Walt's Diner. Brown will write his code and I'll sell my hats and you can do your Words by Winter thing—you can make a living at that, can't you?—and maybe write another book. It's been a long time since *The Old Man* was published."

"No to writing another book. And yes, I can make a living at Words by Winter."

"Good," she said, in a soothing, motherish way, "very good."

"We can all visit The Fearsome together," Brown said. "The Fearsome" was his nickname for my mother. "Serenade her with Leonard Cohen songs, eat our dinner out of jars with cocktail forks, help her chop wood. We'll protect you from her and her from you, more to the point. Unless you're planning to move in with her in Sterns?"

"Not an option."

"Didn't think so. Then Old Forge it is. Come on home."

"Old Forge isn't home."

"It's half an hour north of Sterns. That makes it home-ish."

Old Forge, where my mother used to take me once a year, in the summer. We went swimming in Fourth Lake, we had pancakes at Keyes Pancake House, we spent hours wandering through the multi-roomed palace of Adirondack Hardware. We went to the water park, where once, another mother, a mother who wasn't my mother, took a Polaroid picture of me sitting inside Cinderella's giant pumpkin and gave it to us. Old Forge was our big summer adventure. Now I thought, *Why did we go only once a year?* Since it was so close to home, we could have gone there every week if we wanted, every *day,* for God's sake.

"Old Forget," I said. "That's what I used to call it, when I was a kid. I used to think of it as this magical place."

"It *is* a magical place," Sunshine said. "We're magical, aren't we? And we're here. Come home, Clara."

"Yeah," Brown said. "Come home-ish."

So home-ish I came.

....

That particular phone call happened roughly a month after I first noticed anything. I had come home for a long weekend, opened the kitchen cupboard to get a coffee mug and beheld a carton of orange juice, tucked between the plates and bowls, both of which had been pushed aside to make room for it.

"Hey there, Mr. Orange Juice," I said. "Too cold in the fridge for you?"

I picked Mr. Orange Juice up and carried him out to the dining room, where my mother was deadheading her indoor geraniums. One October years ago she had uprooted them, transplanted them into buckets, and moved them inside to keep them safe from the cold, and then in the course of that long upstate New York winter, decided they were happier inside than outside.

"Ma?"

She looked up, her hands full of withered blossoms, and shook her head. "No. You know I don't like orange juice. Too sweet. I got that for you."

"I found it in the dishes cupboard."

"What are you talking about?"

I jiggled the carton. "This. It was between the bowls and plates."

"Stop," she said, frowning. Still shaking her head. "Put it back where it belongs. Orange juice is expensive."

It was then that a weird feeling came over me. When I remembered that moment I could still feel the heaviness of the carton in my hand, how I had spread my fingers out to hold it so it wouldn't fall, how it was room temperature and not cold the way you expected orange juice to be. I saw the frown on her face, the way she glanced from the faded red and pink flowers in her hands back to me. I felt my other hand shove itself by instinct down into the pocket of my jeans to close around the silver hammer earring, the talisman that was always with me to keep bad things from happening.

"It was in the dishes cupboard," I said again. This annoyed her.

"Stop it, Clara. If you can't say anything nice, don't say anything at all."

Had my mother ever, even once in her life, said, *If you can't say anything nice, don't say anything at all*? She had not. Plenty of other mothers said that—I had heard it from other mothers all my life, directed at their own children in that singsong mother voice—but not my own. Had you asked me, I would have bet every bit of money I had that my mother had not uttered and would not ever utter that line. What did that sentence have to do with this orange juice situation anyway? The weird feeling spread.

"Ma?"

What was I hoping she'd do? Laugh, because what she'd just said was such a non-her thing to say? Turn it into a joke? My mother was not the joking type and never had been. Was I hoping that she would come up with some kind of an explanation, maybe explain that the orange juice in the cabinet was part of an elaborate ruse, and then explain what exactly that ruse was? Yes. That was what I hoped for. Because knowledge —of wrongness, of something-is-not-rightness—was creeping up from my feet, spreading through my body, on its way to my heart and from there to my mind.

I had come home for the weekend because it was her birthday.

She was about to turn fifty.

I was thirty-one.

Yes, my mother was eighteen and a half when she had me. And she had just turned fifty years old when they told us what she had. Not old enough. Way too young. Young young young young young was how old my mother was, when we heard those words "early" and "onset."

And if I could tell you one thing, people, with regard to those clichés about the brevity of life and how fast it zips by and how it'll be over before you know it? It would be that all of them, every damn one of them, was true.

....

The cabin on Turnip Hill Road that I bought when I moved back home-ish to the Adirondacks was one room. Two hundred and fifty square feet, which, spelled out like that, looked bigger than 250. The first time Sunshine and Brown came to see the cabin, I sat in the porch chair, angled because the porch was so narrow, and waited while their station wagon picked its way around the curve and up the dirt driveway.

"But there's no room for anyone but you," Sunshine said. "You and your computer."

Her voice was full of wonder. She peered through the door as if she were in a museum looking at a diorama.

"Why so tiny?" Brown said, his eyes lit up, as if there had to be a fascinating reason.

But there wasn't. If there was a reason at all it was about excess, the existence of it and the not wanting it. It was about not having room for anything more than was physically in the cabin. Because there was already something huge in my nonphysical life, something that couldn't be wrestled down into a manageable, handle-able size.

Sunshine and Brown stepped inside the single room and stood on either side of the ladder that led to the sleeping loft and looked around. They didn't touch anything that first visit. It must have looked like a dollhouse. Like a museum. Everything perfectly in its place because there were so few places for anything. Two towels, one in use and one hung over the door to dry. Three pairs of socks in a drawer with two shirts and two pairs of jeans. No waffle iron, no hair dryer, no cupboards filled with dishes and pots and pans. A half-full bottle of Jack Daniel's sat on top of the miniature fridge next to the miniature stove next to a small blue ceramic jug that held the ashes of Dog.

"Nothing in excess, I see," Brown said.

"Except books," Sunshine said. "Books are definitely in excess."

They were talking to each other as if I weren't right there in the room with them.

"Correct me if I'm wrong, but is that coffee table made of books?"

"It is. So is that lamp stand."

"So is this dining table," Brown said. He crouched to examine the construction of my table. A piece of plywood set on four cornered stacks of books. He gave the plywood an experimental push. It slid, but not much. Plywood was heavier than it looked.

"Oh my God, Brown," Sunshine said. She had climbed up into the sleeping loft. "Get up here and take a look at her bed. She's literally sleeping with books. *On* books. Books as box spring."

"Hello," I said. "Hello? I'm right here. I can hear you."

They ignored me.

"How do I love thee, books?" Brown said. "Let me count the ways."

"Her one true love," Sunshine said. "Some things do not change."

I lifted the bottle of Jack from its perch and went out onto the porch to wait until they finished with their self-guided tour. *It's a monument to minimalism,* I heard Brown say from the sleeping loft, and *She's winnowed,* Sunshine said, *but isn't she too young to be winnowed?* Winnow, winnowing, winnowed, which was a word that sounded like "widowed." Once you started giving things up, it became easy. Or eas*ier*.

Not everything, though. Not everything could be given up.

If my mother could not remain the same, then something else must. That first little fool of a pig built a house of straw, and the second pig built one of sticks, and down they both came. But the third little pig, that little pig built a house of bricks, and it stood.

Books were something real. Books were something true. Books would be my bricks.

....

After the Mr. Orange Juice incident, things went downhill fast. My mother forgot to call two Thursdays in a row. When I called her instead, she was first surprised and then annoyed and then insistent that we had already spoken. Then, a week later, she was pulled over on top of Starr Hill, driving erratically, suspicion of DWI, but there was no alcohol in her bloodstream. Which I could have told them; she didn't drink and never had. The state trooper knew her, from back in the days when she was justice of the peace of the town of Sterns, and he let her off with a warning. Then he tracked me down on the Panhandle, via her neighbor William T. Jones, who had my phone number in case of emergency, and filled me in. And back I came, into Syracuse and from there in a rental car to Sterns, where I found her sitting at the kitchen table, an open can of olives on her right and an open jar of marinated artichoke hearts on her left. My mother had always eaten straight out of jars and cans, with a cocktail fork as her sole utensil. It was one of her peculiarities.

"Hi, Ma."

Her cocktail fork was balanced between her thumb and index finger, close to her mouth, as if it were a joint that had just been passed to her and she wasn't sure what to do with it. Getting high was something else my mother had never done.

"Clara."

"How are you, Ma?"

She looked straight at me and locked eyes. "I don't want anyone to know about this," she said. "No one."

"About what?"

She waved the cocktail fork/joint at me. A slash in the air. Zip it, Clara.

"Alzheimer's," she said. "You know it. I know it. Annabelle and William T. know it. The doctor knows it. No one else."

In the time that had passed between Mr. Orange Juice and the state trooper's warning she had taken herself down to Utica, to a specialist. She had been through multiple tests. She had gone to the library—my mother, a computerless woman—and read up on the disease.

None of this had she told me.

Her fourth doctor's appointment was the following morning. She sat silently next to me, the doctor on one side of the desk, my mother and I on the other. It wasn't an examining room, because the examination was over. She couldn't draw a clock. You had to be able to draw a clock. I willed her hand to start moving in the right direction—*Clock, Ma, clock*—but no.

"Ms. Winter," the doctor said. "I wish I had better news."

He looked straight at her when he said that. Some people looked any-where but straight at you when they had bad news, like when you had failed the exam and now you were being expelled, like when two roads diverged in a yellow wood and you, you took the third road, the un-paved road, the unplowed-in-winter road. This doctor? He looked my mother in the eye and didn't sugarcoat his words. I had to give him that.

"What about my daughter?" she said, tilting her head in my direc-tion.

"Your daughter? Well, there are resources available to her. Websites and forums that—"

"No. What about her chances?"

He nodded. Ah. Okay. I see what you're wondering about. "The chances that your daughter," he said, not looking at me, as if I weren't sitting right there, "carries a PSEN1 gene mutation, which is the most common of the gene mutations that cause eFAD—early-onset familial Alzheimer's disease—are fifty-fifty."

Fifty-fifty. Five-oh five-oh. Half of one hundred. Every molecule of the twisted strands that made me *me* simmered and pulsed with fifty-fifty-ness. I pushed the thought away. I did not let fear bubble and rise inside me. Yet.

She was quiet on the way back to Sterns. Quiet and thin and straight in the passenger seat. She gazed out the window at the Utica floodplain, passing on the left, passing on the right. It wasn't until we had crested and were coasting down the longest hill of Glass Factory Road—that huge and irresistibly steep downslope—that she spoke.

"When are you going back to Florida?"

"On Wednesday," I said. "But here's the plan, Ma. I'm going to move back up here. We can figure things out together."

She nodded. Unlike her. My mother was not an acquiescent sort.

"I can supervise the wood stacking," I said. "Make sure there's enough of it for the winter. Make sure it's not tossed in a big random pile, *à la* the way you would do it."

My voice sounded false, in that fake, trying-to-sound-light way. Try-ing to act as if the only reason for me to move back to Sterns was to make sure there was enough wood for the winter and that said wood was correctly stacked. Ignoring the fact of her illness. Ignoring the fact of the distance between us, all that was hidden, all that had gone unspoken, all that was unresolved.

She nodded again.

"I figure I can be back in about a week," I said. "Give notice on the Treehouse, load up the Subaru." The Treehouse was my name for that little house, built into the limbs of an ancient live oak down on the Florida Panhandle, the forgotten coast of the Sunshine State. "It's a month-to-month rental anyway, so that's no big deal. Then zip up Ninety-five and be right back in Sterns. Poof!"

The *poof* did not come out the way I intended it. It was supposed to be light, a balloon tugging at its string, an interrobang of a word. But it fell flat. Tamar, straight and thin and quiet Tamar, nodded. Could she not do anything but nod? Who was she, the Nod of Wynken and Blynken? Anger flared inside me and my hands clenched the steering wheel. Nod, nod, nod. Was she just going to nod to whatever I said? Nod away her life?

....

Except it wasn't that way.

In the single week that it took to move myself out of the Panhandle and drive back north, my mother swept the rug out from underneath her life. Underneath our life. There was a standing cash offer on the house and the storage barn and all the surrounding land from one of the Amish families who had moved into Sterns, and she walked through the fields and woods to the too-small house where they lived with their eight children and took them up on it. I heard about this after the fact, from the neighbor William T. Jones, who along with his girlfriend, Crystal, had helped her pack everything up. Kitchen and dining and living room and Tamar's bedroom and my old bedroom. Bathroom and mudroom.

It sounded like such a long list. All those rooms. As if there would be box after box, bag after bag, truckload after truckload. But there wasn't. My mother was a woman of few possessions. You could say she was born winnowed. Ahead of the curve. The Amish paid cash for what they wanted and Tamar called the Salvation Army to pick up the rest.

"What about the books?" I said to William T. "Did she donate them too?"

Because there were hundreds and hundreds of them. The books of my childhood, all the books that had gotten me through all the years of school, when I propped them up behind my textbooks and read and read and read, the books that had gotten me through all the summers in Sterns, all those holidays where it was me and Tamar and no one but the two of us and all the other people I loved, the invisible people who lived between the pages of my books.

"Those too?" I said. "All my books, gone? My *books?*"

I kept repeating myself, as if William T. didn't quite understand English. But William T. understood both English and me. He shook his head and put his hands on my shoulders. Calm down, Clara, calm down.

"The books are safe," he said. "We've got them at our house. We'll bring them by for you."

The next night there they were on Turnip Hill Road, William T. and Crystal, the bed of the truck filled with box after box after box of books. We formed an assembly line and passed the boxes one at a time onto the porch: six high and six deep.

"She gave everything else away?" I said, once the porch was buried with books. "There's nothing else?"

"There's this," William T. said, and he held out the blue ceramic urn that held the ashes of Dog, gone now for nearly a decade. I cradled it against my heart.

"I'm sorry, Clara."

"That's okay. It doesn't matter."

Except that was a lie, because it did matter. What I wanted was not nothing else but everything else. Everything back in its place, including my mother, the way she used to be. Including me, the way I used to be, before the fear — fifty percent, five-oh, exactly half — entered my mind and my heart. William T. touched my shoulder, and Crystal gave me a hug, then they told me to call them, I had their number, and they got back in their truck and drove away down Turnip Hill Road.

Into the cabin I hauled the boxes of books, where I turned them into furniture. Like the boy in *Where the Wild Things Are,* whose walls became the world all around, who sailed away in a boat over days and weeks and months and a year, except there was no boat for me. Only books. And Dog? Dog sat in his urn on the kitchen shelf.

....

My mother didn't know that on the long drive north, while she was boxing up her life without telling me, I had made plans. I would support us with Words by Winter.

> *Looking for the right words? Unable to find them? Not sure how to get your message across?* **Words by Winter** *is at your service. In tough times, in good times, in times of thankfulness and times of loss, our wordsmiths, with their uncanny ability to craft the perfect words for any occasion, are by your side. $100 for up to 100 words, payable via PayPal. Our motto: "If it can't be said in a hundred words, then it can't be said in a thousand." www.wordsbywinter.com*

I used to run that ad here and there, in the beginning. Online, mostly. Word got around once I had happy clients, though. You'd be surprised how many people and places now recommended Words by Winter: wedding planners, funeral homes, dating sites. So yes, Words by Winter would support us, one hundred dollars at a time, and while there was still time, my mother and I would get into a routine. While there was still time, we would watch the television show *Jeopardy!* together, which in my head I always spelled with the proper exclamation mark! because that was what copyright laws were all about!, and eat dinner together and go for walks together. While there was still time, we would somehow figure out how to talk about the past, the said and the unsaid, and all that was locked up between us would be unlocked. The common denominator of each of those scenarios was the assumption of enough time before the erasure of time, that with enough time, the key to the kingdom would be yours and mine.

But that was not what happened.

See the daughter in her jam-packed Subaru, hands on the wheel, neck aching from the strain of staring straight north, I-95 unspooling before her for a thousand and more miles. See her as she takes Exit 31 off the New York State Thruway, hands the tollbooth man a wad of ones, then angles the car northward again. Up and down Glass Factory. Right, then right, then left through the town of Sterns and north to the driveway of the house where her mother lived, the house where she herself grew up, the house where her mother should be. Where her mother had always been. Would always be. See how the tenses mixed themselves up from that moment on, because who was the woman walking out the door onto the porch? Why was Tamar dressed up like an Amish woman? Why was there an outhouse in the backyard? Who was the Amish child in the bonnet pulling clothes off the clothesline? Whose horse and buggy were clopping into the driveway? Not Tamar's. Not mine.

"Ma."

That was me, standing in the place where my mother lived now, that same night. The Amish woman had given me the address. She had also given me a taped-shut shoebox, Keds, size nine—the only shoe my mother wore besides her winter boots. I had tried to give it back to her but she shook her head and turned away.

"Ma."

"Clara."

See the boxers as they enter the ring. The thin middle-aged woman stands straight in her corner, next to the drooping orchids on the plant stand. In her hand is one faded orchid blossom, deadheaded. The thin younger woman with the lavender-streaked dark hair stands not as straight in her corner. No cheering crowds. No attendants to towel them off, rub their shoulders, give them pre-fight pep talks. Theirs is a battle of posture, eyes and words. They have met before, these two, in many a previous ring, and neither has yet emerged victorious.

"Why, Ma?"

That was the younger woman. Inked black wire twining up one arm and down the other, the beginnings of it just visible below the rolled-up sleeve of her blue shirt.

"Because."

That was the older woman, the one with the dead flower in her hand. No tattoos for her. Hair still dark, mouth set, eyes unblinking. Why? Because. Asked and unanswered.

"You didn't have to do this, Ma. You didn't have to move into this place. You could have stayed in the house."

She shook her head, that quick back-and-forth Tamar shake. Definitive. Case closed. But the case wasn't closed. Everything that was gone — the house, the furniture, her clothes, her indoor geraniums, her cocktail fork, her cans and jars of food, her bird feeder, the dishes that we had eaten off of all my life, all my life, *all my life*—came swarming up inside me and turned my vision dark. My hand came up to my throat. My heart hammered, ready to stampede its way out.

"You didn't have to *do* this," I said. "I'm *here*. I moved *back*."

For *you*, was what I managed not to say, for *you* I moved back. Italicized subtitles scripted themselves along the bottom of the movie screen in my mind. Who was she, this woman? What kind of person closed down her entire life in a single week and moved herself into this place with no help, no advice, no warning? Who did this kind of thing? The couch was behind me and I sank down onto it.

"Why didn't you tell me?" I said.

My voice in the air between us was like wire, like the tattooed wire that wound itself up my arm and, invisible unless I was naked, around my back and down my other arm, so that when my arms were tight at my sides, I was bound around with wire. So that something was holding me at all times. Something that would not let me fall apart, no matter how bad things got.

"I'm your *daughter*," I said.

Something flickered in her eyes. "I know that."

"Then why would you do this? It was my house too!" Exclamation mark. **Boldface.** The words ***boldface exclamation mark*** began scrolling along the bottom of my mind in tiny typeface. ***Boldface exclamation*** *mark! Boldface exclamation mark! Boldface exclamation mark!* I mentally batted them away. But angry words spilled out anyway.

"Ma, it didn't have to be this way!"

"Clara."

Something in her voice. Something that made the exclamation marks stop. Something that made me look up at her instead of at the floor, where I was tracing the outline of the fake Persian rug with my eyes. Up one side, down the next, up one side, down the next. Rectangle rectangle rectangle.

"WHAT."

"Clara."

"You never *listen* to me. You never *did* listen to me." My voice kept coming out in italics and boldface and exclamation marks and I was helpless against it; it had taken on a life of its own and it would have its say.

"I always listened to you," she said.

"You did NOT. You wrecked things for me, Ma. You were the reason Asa broke up with me. Admit it. Admit it!"

She came toward me then. The boxer advanced from her corner, faded flower dangling from her hand, Keds silent on the floor the way she was always silent on the floor. She stood before me, my mother, my only mother, and she looked at me the way a person looks at another person when she knows there is little time left and she has little left to lose.

"Why do you say that?"

Because it's true. Because I looked through the window and saw the two of you talking that night. I saw how upset he was. And you wouldn't talk, and he wouldn't talk, and next day he broke up with me and then he was gone and it was your fault. It was your fault.

It had to have been her fault. And if it wasn't, then why did she have no explanation for me? Why had she just turned her head away? Asa wouldn't tell me what she said and she wouldn't tell me what she said and then **boom,** Asa broke up with me, and **boom,** Asa enlisted in the army, and **boom,** she forced me out of state for college, and **boom,** a whole bunch of years went by until **boom,** here we were. This was where we found ourselves. With her having just sold off, given away or packed up our entire lives and moved herself into a nursing home with the money she got from selling the house. *Ma, this can't be happening. Ma, this can't have happened. Ma, please can we go back in time, please can we do it over, please, please?*

But time was what we had run out of, and it happened so fast.

We went so wrong.

That was the sentence in my head, a snake slithering after its own tail. I pushed aside the memory of a night back then, an awful night that still lived in my mind, a night when I had screamed and screamed at her, said awful things, a night neither of us had spoken of since. Not then, and not now. She stood there waiting, waiting for an answer, an answer that never came, and she did not back down. I had to give her that. The senior boxer held her ground, her only weapons a faded flower and an unblinking gaze filled with, what? Entreaty. That was the word. Entreaty.

She was exactly as tall as me. How was it possible I had not noticed that before?

....

In the wake of that asked and unanswered nonconversation, the boxers retreated to their separate corners of the ring. Unbloodied and unbeaten on the outside, but on the inside, a different matter. Their scars were invisible but crippling.

Difficult Mothers for $400, please. Difficult Daughters for $600. If this were a real-life *Jeopardy!* game we would be the Daily Double.

Jeopardy! was the only ritual left now out of everything I had planned. The others I had thought up as I clutched the steering wheel and sped north—walking our woods, cleaning and organizing our house, stacking wood for the winter—were no longer possible. Even making dinner for my mother, that most modest of goals, was not possible, because there was no kitchen in my mother's room. No cupboard in which to arrange the cans and bottles she liked to eat from with a cocktail fork. No cocktail fork.

I ate dinner with my mother in the communal dining room at the place where she lived now—which was how I thought of it, instead of *the memory care wing of a care facility/nursing home*—exactly once. Mashed potatoes and pork roast and applesauce. She ate that dinner with a spoon and a knife and a fork, a regular-size fork. The sight of my mother sitting in a regular chair and eating from a regular plate with regular utensils and a paper napkin in her lap smote my heart. No. Not this, not for my mother, the Fearsome Tamar, who all my life had leaned against the counter with an opened can or jar, plucking out olives or marinated artichoke hearts or other bits of food one by one.

So: *Jeopardy!* A television game show was what we had left.

When I visited, we usually sat in the community room down the hall from her bedroom, watching. I arrived in plenty of time, many minutes before the show began at 7:30 p.m., because Tamar hated to be late. All her life she had hated to be late, but of late, her lateness hatred had intensified. On one such visit the television was already on, muttering low, a cooking show in which the contestants were given baskets of unknown ingredients from which to prepare a feast.

"That's not the right _____" my mother said, and turned to me.

_____ was what the look on her face meant, which was *Help me, I can't find the right word. It's here, it's near, it's just out of reach.*

"Channel," I said. I took the remote from the coffee table and clicked. "Here we go."

Jeopardy! was the most-watched television game show in history and Alex Trebek was its longest-running and most intimidating host. Contestants often seemed to cower before him. That night, a tax accountant was in the lead. He kept pressing the buzzer first, in an annoyingly fast and tense way, beating the other two contestants.

"Baseball for two hundred, please," he said.

Sometimes known as the white Josh Gibson was the clue.

"Who the hell's Josh Gibson?"

I was talking to myself, but from the look on the tax accountant's face, he was thinking the same thing. This was his second night on the show. Baseball for $200, the lowest bet possible. Most contestants started with the lowest. They thought small, confined themselves. They put themselves in the prison of tiny bets. The tax man was no different.

"I mean, I've never heard of the guy," I said.

My mother sat next to me eating fudge. Peanut butter fudge, which I had brought her as a gift from Vermont, where I had spent the day hiking. Driving back, I took Route 9 west across the very bottom of the state so that I could stop at the Hogback Mountain gift shop and buy my mother half a pound of her favorite fudge. Fudge was delicious. Fudge was safe.

She slivered off wafers with the plastic knife they included and ate them one at a time. The community room, which my mother had begun to call the Plant Room, contained a television, a plant stand full of orchids, a green couch, that fake Persian carpet and two rocking chairs. A long swatch of black paint on the floor guarded the sliding doors to the back garden. After a certain point in the progression of the disease, the black swatch was often perceived as a black hole into which you would fall and from which you would not return.

That was what they told me, anyway. "It takes a while to get to that point," they also told me, reassuringly.

But in the last month I had come upon my mother standing three feet away from that swatch of black paint, looking at those locked doors, with their view of the outdoors, the world beyond this one room. I had seen my mother's body physically leaning toward those doors, her arms reaching for them, reaching for the outdoors that all her life she had loved. And I had watched her look down at that black paint, regarding it in fear.

No one was ever in the Plant Room except her, and she was almost always in there. Once in a while someone poked his or her head around the doorway — "How you doing, Miz Winter?" — and we both nodded. We were the two Miz Winters.

"'The white Josh Gibson,'" Tamar said, in clear, calm and measured tones, just like the tax man. "Who is Babe Ruth?"

When I was a child and my mother and I used to watch *Jeopardy!* together, I would sit on the couch next to her, shouting out answers that were almost always wrong. Her? Nothing. Until now, when she wasn't even looking at the television. She was focused on the little white box of fudge, slivering herself off another delicate portion.

"Josh Gibson was a slugger," she said to the fudge, pincered between her thumb and finger. "He could catch too."

The fudge said nothing but she shook her head as if it had asked her a question.

"No," she said. "Gentleman's agreement. Criminal."

None of what she said made sense, but she was done talking. She wrapped the remaining chunk of fudge up in its tissue paper, laid the plastic knife next to it and closed up the little box. Then she handed it to me and I handed her the book I had brought. Fudge for book. An even trade-off.

"*Charlotte's Web,*" I said. "In case it looks familiar."

It was one of the books that had lined the walls of my room in our old house and spilled out into the rest of the house. One of the books I had read over and over and over. When I was growing up, Tamar had given me a book for every birthday and every Christmas and every first day of school and every last day of school, books that she thought I would like: about pioneer girls, children who lived on their own, shipwrecked families, solo adventurers. She knew the kind of book I loved and she knew that hardcovers were what I loved. When it came to books for me, my mother did not stint, and those books were all that she had saved for me from the desecration of the house. My childhood books, Dog's ashes and that single duct-taped-shut shoebox that I had not opened.

Tamar herself owned exactly one book when I was growing up: a tattered paperback of *Jonathan Livingston Seagull*. For as long as I could remember, that book—that embarrassing self-help-ish book with the picture of the seagull on the cover—sat on the shelf above the woodstove in the kitchen. Now it sat between two bookends on the windowsill of the unopenable window in her room at the place where she lived. Besides her clothes, it was the only thing she brought with her from Sterns.

When I hauled the boxes of books into the cabin, I opened them up and spread them out in the middle of the room. All the books of my childhood, each inscribed *To Clara, with love from Ma.* I stacked them up right there on the floor. 6 stacks x 4 stacks = one coffee table made out of books, with the unopened shoebox buried in the middle.

Now, week by week, I was giving them back to her. As my coffee table grew shorter, my mother's books grew taller. She piled them up beneath the window, on the nightstand, once in a while under the bed. Unruly piles, just like the firewood she used to chuck onto the porch in an unorganized heap.

"Thank you," she said, and she placed *Charlotte's Web* in the exact middle of her lap, unopened.

....

The place my mother moved herself into, the day after she handed the keys over to the Amish family, was a place where if she fell, someone would know immediately, and if she had a bad dream and was crying in the middle of the night, someone would know that too. Where if she needed medicine, someone would give it to her, and if she wanted to watch *Jeopardy!* she could. No questions asked.

Where she lived now there were few locks. She was not strapped to a bed or tied to a chair. She was free to go where she wanted within the confines of the building, and where she wasn't supposed to go she wouldn't go anyway, because of the black swatches of painted floor that she wouldn't step over for fear of the bottomless black holes.

Although how did they know if bottomless black holes were what she thought they were? How could anyone who was not her know exactly why she avoided them?

My mother was never coming back.

Sometimes I said that out loud. When I was driving I said it, to myself and the windshield and the seat belt and my two hands on the steering wheel.

"Your mother's never coming back, Clara."

A six-word sentence. A whole story in six words. Like the kind of assignment the me who made her living writing words for other people would give herself if she felt stuck. At first I tried variations, like *Ma's disappearing* or *Ma's never coming back.* But those were too hard to say. *Ma* was the word I had known my mother by my entire life. Not *Mom* or *Mama* or *Mommy.* Not even "my mother."

Just Ma.

So I went back to the original sentence, which was an exact quote from the shaven-head doctor in his white doctor coat and in whose office I sat, surrounded by diplomas and plastic plants. This was the day after Tamar and I had sat there together. I had made a solo appointment, so as to get more information. All the information I could, on my own, straight from the horse's mouth, as the saying went, although did horses talk? They did not. Not in words, anyway.

"Your mother's never coming back, Clara. Early-onset is particularly cruel because it strikes so much younger than the typical patient. It seems to go faster sometimes too, probably because early onset is often not diagnosed until the later stages. We hope that won't be the case with your mother, of course. That's rare. That would be the worst-case scenario."

He pushed a box of tissues across the table and my head filled with images of other people, dozens of them, who must have come before me and sat in the same chair that I was sitting in. *Your mother's never coming back, Clara* began a slow scrawl across the bottom of my brain. A wandering-minstrel-without-an-instrument of a sentence.

"Isn't there some kind of medication that can help?"

"To slow the progress, possibly, but stop it, no."

"Aren't there any studies she might be eligible for, clinical trials where she could get new medicine that's not FDA-approved yet?"

"Not at this time."

My mind kept coming up with reasonable questions and I listened to myself say them, one after another. Part of me admired the reasonableness of the young woman sitting across from the doctor. Look at her, her hiking boots laced with red laces, her vintage Future Farmers of America jacket, the lavender streak in her brown hair. She was so rational! Logical! Articulate! Concise! Self-restrained! Exclamation marks scrolled themselves along the bottom of my brain. Little Hitler youths out for a march. *Hitlerjugend.*

"The brain affects everything about the body, so there are physical symptoms as well. Large and small motor skills. Stumbling, falling. Et cetera."

"How long will it take?"

Until what, Clara? Until she couldn't drive any longer? Until she couldn't live alone? Until she needed a personal-care attendant? Until she was in diapers? Until she forgot how to feed herself? Until she refused food and drink? The words "care facility" exploded into huge boldface letters in my head. CARE FACILITY CARE FACILITY CARE FACILITY CARE FACILITY.

Clara.

Shhh.

I came out of that meeting and I spoke about it with no one, not even Sunshine and Brown. Not Burl Evans, the postman, who must have wondered when suddenly the name **Winter** was painted over with **Beiler** on the mailbox at the end of the driveway. Annabelle Lee, the choir director, who was my mother's only real friend, and William T. Jones and Crystal already knew, but I did not talk about it with them either.

My mother made me promise to be silent, and silent I would be.

The only ones I talked about it with were the doctor and the nurses and the aides and the therapists, because I had to. Her next of kin was me, her only kin was me, and what that meant was that it was all up to me: power of attorney, legal guardianship, health proxy. All those terms that no one wanted to hear or think about because were they ever to become necessary it would be many decades hence and only to other people. People who were not you. People who were not your mother.

"Things that you want to say to her, say now. Even if it seems like she's not there, like she's not listening. Say what you need to say anyway."

Sylvia, the kind nurse with the encouraging smile. She took me aside in the hall after the first of our monthly Life Care Committee meetings, in which we — the doctor and nurses and aides and I — went over details of my mother's care. *Clara, can I talk to you for a minute?* Words that lead nowhere good, ever, but everyone stops for them anyway. I leaned against the cool tile wall and listened as she told me that the one rule was that *While there will be good days and less-good days, over time the condition only worsens* and *If you have issues or conflicts that you need to resolve, do it now* and *The same thing applies to happiness, to joy. Share them with her, but do it now.*

How, though? Too many of the words between my mother and me were hard words, words with tall boots, stalking across the bottom of my brain in ugly uppercase.

"You mean like secrets? Secrets I never told her?"

"Maybe," Sylvia said. "But when it comes to secrets, particularly long-held secrets, consider carefully whether her knowledge of them would ease her mind or yours. You don't want to unburden yourself only to shift that burden to the listener."

Ma. Ma. Ma. Ma, look at me. Ma, remember me. Could we do it? Was it too late?

"Okay," I said to Sylvia, that dumb word *okay*, but Sylvia smiled and I smiled back at her, squashing the questions that I wanted to ask, that I needed to ask in order to get the answers that I would need in the future. The future was steamrolling down upon us — second by second we were living in a future that didn't exist a minute ago — and my mother was disappearing. Was this the way being on *Jeopardy!* felt when no matter how fast and hard you pressed and shook and clicked the buzzer, it didn't make a sound?

....

It happened too fast and it was too big — way too big — and too much was unsaid and wrong between my mother and me before she started to disappear. Too much had been left untold and now there was too much to tell, the words locked tightly within us both, tangled up with the don't-tell-anyone and the your-mother's-never-coming-back. A game of Twister gone awry. Bruises and torn ligaments and broken bones.

A year went by of this new life. Visits with Tamar, Life Care meetings, the drive back and forth from Old Forge to Utica that the Subaru and I knew by heart, evenings on the porch with me and Jack Daniel's and the solar fairy lights glimmering from the white pines I looped them around, evenings when I thought about my mother, what I had and had not done.

I had moved back in early September and now it was early September again and the light was fading. The sun came up later and went down earlier and the bitter winds of winter were nigh upon us. *Oh, don't be so filled with dread, Clara. Don't be such a monger of doom, a predictor of pain and suffering. Winter is not a time of death; it's a time of rebirth. Of hibernation. Of fallowness, that fertility may spring forth again come the thaw.* The Greek chorus behind me, full of scorn at my fear and loathing of winter.

"So how's The Fearsome?" Brown asked. "When's she coming back, anyway?"

I had told Sunshine and Brown, in the face of their repeated questions about my mother, that she wasn't around. That she had decided to travel the world, go wandering through Europe and Asia, all the places she had never been, a solo traveler on an odyssey. Lies upon lies. Once conjured, lies feed upon themselves. They get greedy. At some point they turn real and take over, tumors muttering, *Feed me feed me feed me.*

"Maybe never."

"But isn't she weary of wandering yet?"

Brown was fond not only of exclamation marks but of rhyme and alliteration. In the one literature class we had taken together back in college—Chaucer, Milton and Shakespeare, which ran together in my head, then and now, as chaucermiltonshakespeare—that class in which we all sat together next to the giant window, he used to copy down his favorite examples from the passages the professor read aloud. It was a fall of bright skies that year, and sunshine, the literal form of it, spilled through that window and set Sunshine's red-gold hair on fire, metaphorical fire. Her hair alight like the New Hampshire trees in the fall, on the mountains visible beyond the classroom.

"It's hard to imagine The Fearsome anywhere but Sterns," Brown said. "When I think of her I picture her eating out of jars and chopping down trees. Not presenting her passport to some grim Eastern European customs officer."

"She never chopped down trees, Brown," I said. "She split logs that other people delivered to us into woodstove-size chunks. Big difference."

It was a difference that Brown and Sunshine didn't care about. When they had first met my mother, lo those many years ago at college, they formed an image of her as a woodswoman who spent her days up in the Adirondacks chopping down enormous trees. A female Paul Bunyan.

That was long ago, when Sunshine and Brown were new to a rural land-scape, when they ferried back and forth from Manhattan and Boston, respectively, on school breaks. Before the three of us spent the summer before junior year together, living and working in Old Forge, which was when they fell in love with the Adirondacks. They were nothing like me, a country girl raised by a country woman.

"Semantics," Brown said.

"It is not semantics. There is a profound difference between chop-ping down a tree and splitting chunks of that tree into small pieces suit-able for a woodstove or a fireplace. Which you should know by now, seeing as you just had three full cords of fireplace wood delivered and stacked."

I was strewing conversational bread crumbs, leading them away from the forest, away from the subject of my mother. But they would not be deterred.

"Seriously, Clara. How is she?"

"Seriously, Brown, she's a year older. It was just her birthday."

"No! For real? Are you kidding?"

Brown and Sunshine were birthday people. They used to call me wherever I was, back in the nomad days, the Winter of Nomad-istry, as Brown used to say, and sing "Happy Birthday to You" into the phone. If I was anywhere within driving distance, they would have a party for me. Cake, candles, special handwritten, rhyming poems full of alliteration.

"Don't worry about it."

"But why didn't you remind us? We could've called her or something. Geez."

I shrugged. A two-shoulder shrug — quick up and quick down — which was what you did when there was something enormous you hadn't told your two best friends about and too much time had passed and all the words were locked up tight and would remain so, in this time of closed books that were slept on and eaten off but never read aloud.

"Actually I kind of forgot too."

"You *did?*"

Again the two-shoulder shrug, this time with averted gaze. But the problem with best friends, friends who had known you from day one of your first year in college, was just that: they knew you. They knew the expressions on your face, the things you did to distract. To avoid talking. They knew the two-shoulder shrug, the averted gaze.

"Why do you have such a hard time with your mother, anyway?" Sunshine said. "You've never given me a good reason."

"A good reason for what?"

Pretending you didn't know what she was talking about. That was another way to stall. To avoid. To redirect. To give yourself time to think up a good answer. But I did know what she was talking about, and she knew I knew. See the two friends as they were fourteen years ago, back in college, when they shared a dorm room in the White Mountains. See the slim green phone on the coffee table between their beds. Hear it begin to ring, that shrill jingle of a landline ringtone.

Brr. Brr. Brr.

See Clara close her eyes and picture a heavy black telephone in a kitchen in a house in Sterns. Her house, two states away, across the Whites and the Greens and down through the heart of the Adirondacks. See her picture Tamar sitting at the kitchen table, the receiver pressed to her ear, waiting. The every-Thursday phone call. See Clara bite back a sigh and pick up the phone.

"Hello."

"Greetings, Miss Winter speaking. How may I direct your call?"

"Ma."

"Shall I see if Ma is available?"

"**MA.**"

At this point I would quit speaking and wait. She would wait too. Then she would start speaking again as if she had just been summoned to the phone.

"Clara?"

"Ma."

"How are you?"

"I'd be better if you quit this stupid phone charade."

"Not sure what you're talking about."

The only way to break through was to surprise her. Pop a question into the conversation, *Jeopardy!*-style.

"Ma. Random Questions for two hundred. Why do you eat every-thing out of cans and jars with a cocktail fork?"

I remembered Sunshine glancing up at me from her desk. There was a look on her face, I could still picture it, of, what, dismay? Annoyance? I smiled at her and rolled my eyes, thinking we were in collusion—me and my annoying mother who called every Thursday—but now, here in the time of rejiggering of memory, I thought, *Maybe it was you she was annoyed with, Clara, for being snotty to your mother.* Silence on the other end of the line.

"Time's almost up, Ms. Winter. Why cans, why jars, why a minia-ture fork?"

"Because."

"Because why?"

But that was it. Silence.

Why didn't I talk to her? Why didn't she talk to me? Why did we leave so much unsaid, back then, and still? Now, so many years later, I felt Sunshine and Brown looking at each other over my head, which was bent. Telepathy. *She's hiding something,* they were telepathically telling each other. *We have to make her talk.*

....

"The Fearsome is so cool, though," Brown said. "So tough and so funny and so . . . herself. It's like my parents—they're the gracious hosts, the witty conversationalists, and I adore them, but when I compare them to The Fearsome and the way she talks, there's a tiny element of bullshit. Teeny tiny. But never with The Fearsome. Why the tension?"

"I've already told you," I said. "She's a secret-keeper. I'm still con-vinced she was behind Asa breaking up with me."

"Your high school boyfriend?"

"Yes. But she wouldn't talk about it. Just like when I was little she wouldn't tell me who my father was, she wouldn't answer any questions about my twin sister. I mean, I was a kid and I had a thousand questions and she didn't answer any of them."

"Well, the truth was pretty ugly, wasn't it?"

"So? It was still the truth, as opposed to lies of omission."

Neither of them looked convinced. But what would they know? Parents who adored them, parents who thought they were great, parents who were not hiding anything. Whereas Tamar was a different animal entirely.

"Everyone's hiding something, though," Sunshine said. "Everyone's got secrets. Don't you think?"

"I do. Have you forgotten how I earn my living? What is Words by Winter if not an exercise in secrets?"

You would think that people could write their own messages. You would think they could find a way to unburden their hearts to each other. You would think that in this enormous world full of words and the limitless ways to put them together, people should be able to figure out how to say what needs to be said. But you would be wrong. Words by Winter fulfilled three to five word requests per day. $100 x 3 = $300/day x 7 days a week (no days off in the world of words) = $2,100/week x 4 = $8,400/month, which was more than enough to live on, much more, at least in the places where the wordsmiths who work for Words by Winter had chosen to live thus far, up to and including Old Forge, New York.

Not that there were wordsmiths, plural. There was only one wordsmith, singular, and that singular wordsmith was me. I was the Winter of Words.

"How go the wintry words these days, by the way?" Sunshine asked.

We were sitting at their big wooden dining table. Dinner was finished. We were playing Jeopardy! and taking turns drinking thimblefuls of limoncello from actual thimbles, taken from Sunshine's needlework bag, every time someone won a round. Sunshine made her living by crocheting fruit and vegetable hats for babies, multiple hats a day, and selling them online. She had taken up crocheting the first time she had cancer, during those long hours of chemo, when she got sick of reading and sick of not moving. When the cancer came back she taught herself how to make baby hats because they were quick and cute and cheery and she could knock one out in less than an hour. When it came back again she set herself a speed goal: three per hour.

Now she was unstoppable. She was crocheting one as we played.

From the red and green look of the thing it was a future strawberry. Parents sent photos of their babies wearing Sunshine's hats: little strawberry and radish and apple and scallion hat–baby photos, magneted to Sunshine and Brown's refrigerator the way photos of their own babies would be magneted, if they had any babies. Which they didn't. Strawberries were most popular.

"Booming," I said. "The word business is to Clara Winter what baby hats are to Sunshine Rourke."

"You would think that people could write their own goddamn thank-you notes," Brown said, the same thing that he had been saying ever since I started my word business.

"You would, but you'd be wrong. And they're not all thank-you notes. Thank-you notes comprise only a small percentage of Words by Winter output."

It was my habit to use clinical-sounding terminology, like "comprise only a small percentage" and "output," when talking about the business of words. Clinical terminology kept things simple. Straightforward. Sterile. Clinical terminology avoided the messy, the painful, the please-help-me-this-is-too-hard-to-handle part of the job.

"Isn't it awful, though, sometimes?" Sunshine said. "Don't you ever feel wordless yourself and start fumbling around, trying to figure out how to say what needs to be said?"

I slammed my palm down on the table, which was what we did in lieu of a buzzer. Whoever slammed their hand down first got to answer the clue.

"Words for sixteen hundred," I said. "Answer to Sunshine's question. What is yes?"

I was cheating, giving both the clue and the answer, but there had been many thimblefuls of limoncello by then and the game had devolved into a non-game. Yes was the right answer, though. It was harder than you'd think to write one hundred perfect words, one hundred words that would convey sorrow, or sympathy, or love, or regret, or any one of a thousand other longings.

....

They had a test for it, a test for the gene mutation. What was necessary, before they would test an asymptomatic relative for eFAD, was a confirmed gene mutation in a parent or sibling. eFAD was caused by any one of several different gene mutations on chromosomes 21, 14 and 1. PSEN1, found on chromosome 14, was the most common.

Translation: before the neuroscientists would consider testing me for the genetic mutation that would virtually guarantee my developing early-onset Alzheimer's, my mother had to be tested for the mutation. Which she had been. PSEN1, you were identified in the wild, lurking in the woodland trails of my mother's body. A searchlight was shone upon you and you could hide no longer.

"Clara, I am obligated to tell you that if you are considering being tested for one of the genetic mutations, you will need pre-test genetic counseling."

Dry. Official. Formal. But the look in the doctor's eyes was none of those things. By now we were comrades, fellow soldiers on the anti-Alzheimer's footpath. He waited for me to say something. He knew me well enough by now to know that testing was something I already would have thought about, pondered, lain awake at night monkey-minding my way through the various ramifications. Maybe not the monkey-mind part. But the thinking about, the pondering—that much he had already guessed.

I nodded. He took that as a sign to continue.

"You'd first have a telephone call with the genetic counselor in order to assess if you're a candidate."

"Which I am because my mother has a confirmed mutation."

"Correct. So the counselor would explain the procedure, the cost, the challenges and logistics of the test itself"—he paused again, I nodded again, he continued—"and then, if you wanted to pursue it, you and your family members could schedule an office visit with the counselor."

All this I already knew, and more. An office visit where my family members and I would talk about our experience of the disease in my family, what we would do differently if we did in fact have a mutation, how our spouses or significant others and children and possible future children and colleagues and bosses might feel about it. The possible implications for health insurance and life insurance and long-term-care insurance. The possible loss of hope for our future if we had the mutation, and the equally possible, according to those who had been tested, relief. Because then you would know. You would *know.* If you wanted to know. Did I want to know?

"Okay," I said.

"Okay . . . ?"

"Okay and thank you for the information."

I looked at him, he looked at me, and between us passed the understanding that I had thought long and hard about being tested and that I had come to no conclusion and that if and when I did come to a conclusion — to test or not to test — I would let him know. He nodded. We stood up. I left and walked down the hallway and pushed through the double doors out to the parking lot and double-clicked the key to open the door of the Subaru and got inside and laid my head against the cool, cool vinyl of the steering wheel.

Because what part of any of it applied to me?

Spouse, children, siblings, aunts, uncles, boss, colleagues: no and no and no and no and no and no and no. There was no "our" or "we." There was only me.

....

It was early afternoon at the View Arts Center in Old Forge, an overcast September day. A poster sign was set up out front: me holding a copy of *The Old Man* in both hands with the caption SEE OUR QUILT EXHIBIT! MEET AN AUTHOR!

"There's a school field trip due any minute!" the woman at the reception desk said. Her voice was exclamation-mark-y, like Brown's when he was excited. Maybe she was the one who had made the poster. "They're coming down from Saranac just because of you. Big fans of your book, apparently!"

"How old are they, do you know?"

"Third grade. Still little and cute!"

A table was set up underneath a huge hand-stitched white quilt hung against the far white gallery wall. White on white, almost but not entirely disappeared. I sat on the table and watched as the children filed in, teacher in front and room parents behind. *Sit on the floor. Fold your hands. Shhh.* Third grade. Still little and cute, which made it worse if it was a day when it was hard to look at little, cute kids. Like the boy whose shirt was buttoned all the way up to his neck. Or the girl fingering the butterfly clip in her hair. They took you in, absorbed you through their eyes, trying to figure you out. You and your place in the world.

"Do you think that's her? The writer lady?"

"No. Her hair's different from the poster."

"It's still her, though. I'm pretty sure. Yeah. It's her."

The children talking about me were sitting three feet from me. They stared directly at me as they talked, in that way that small children did, as if I couldn't hear them.

"You're right," I said. "It's me."

At the sound of my voice they were instantly stunned into silence, eyes big and round with shock.

"What are your names?" I said. Writer Lady had spoken. I waited for them to emerge from speechlessness.

"Jamie," one finally whispered.

"Candace," a girl said, and then she said it again. "Candace with a *K*."

Candace transformed itself in my mind into Kandace. A small boy with a mullet looked up at me sadly and said nothing. Mullet Boy. His eyes were dark and unblinking.

"Tell her your name," Kandace snapped. "It'll freak her out." She poked him with her pinky. Why a pinky instead of her pointer finger? Poke.

"It's a really weird name!" Kandace said.

Mullet Boy drooped. The space around him widened a fraction of an inch. *Think fast, Clara.*

"Did you guys know that *weird* means unconventional? Which is a great thing to be."

Kandace twitched. She didn't want weird to be a good thing. Mullet Boy took a deep breath, a strength-gathering breath. He was going to do it. He was going to tell the writer lady his unconventional name.

"My name is Blue Mountain," he said, then squinched himself into a tight ball and hauled his shoulders up to his ears.

"See what I mean? I told you it was weird! His parents are hippies!" shouted Kandace. "Want to know why the hippies named him Blue Mountain? Because he was conceived there! Right on top of Blue Mountain!"

"What does 'conceived' mean?" Jamie said.

"It means that his parents did it on top of Blue Mountain!" Kandace was louder and louder and louder. One of her internal engines had spun out of control.

"Did what?"

"IT!"

Jamie looked confused. So did the boy next to him. So did Kandace, come to think of it. I stood up and raised both hands in the air, flat, and then floated them down, hoping it might work in a *Shhh, children* kind of way. And it did. The entire room went silent.

It could make me cry, if I let it. All those children, those little, cute kids — they didn't and couldn't know what was ahead of them, what life would bring their way. Did you? Did I? Did my mother?

My messed-up heart kicked into gear and began to race. From beat, beat, beat to beat-beat-beat to beatbeatbeat to *beatbeatbeatbeatbeatbeat* in a fraction of a second. A familiar faintness crept through me from the head down. My fingers stole up and pressed themselves against the side of my throat. This was a bad one. Two-hundred-plus beats a minute. Maybe more. A cardiologist had told me years ago that at the point that "the abnormality" began to "interfere with the normal course of living," then I should get it "taken care of." Quotation marks kept grouping themselves around the words as they floated by the bottom of my brain, because what exactly was an abnormality, and what exactly was a normal course of living, and how exactly did wires threaded up your veins into the middle of your heart and then killing off part of it mean getting it taken care of?

The racing and fluttering in my chest and in my throat filled my eyes with stars, but I was standing there in front of them and I had to get through this.

Fake it, Clara.

I sat back down on the table. That way I wouldn't pass out. *Breathe. Focus.* My thudding heart, the ocean sound in my ears.

"I have a question for you," I said. "Do you want to know what it is?"

"Yessssss!" they called together, in the way of small children.

"Think way back, will you? To when you were little."

When you were little made the adults look up and smile at me. We were the ones who knew that the children were still little. The kids didn't know they were still little.

Unless they weren't. Maybe little doesn't exist. Maybe we don't want to believe there wasn't a time when we weren't thinking about our place in life and what we wanted our lives to be. When we weren't wondering about the meaning of it all. Maybe we want desperately to think that we once had a few years when things were easy, when others were taking care of us, when we had no worries.

Clara, shhh.

"Can anyone remember something you were afraid of, way back when you were little?"

Hands shot up. Thunderstorms. Dogs with giant teeth. Bad guys with guns.

A small boy with a pierced ear sitting in the back raised his hand. "Can it be something I'm still afraid of?"

"Sure."

"I'm afraid of going into a store with my mom, and then I get separated from her, and I never find her again."

Jackpot. Lost Mothers for $1600. The Daily Double. The children moaned and held hands and shook their heads. The adults grimaced. The room itself began to shrink, all of us arrowing into our insides, alone with no mother beside us.

Ma.

I pictured her in the place where she lived now. I pictured her in the passenger seat of the car after our meeting with the doctor. I pictured her alone in the house she raised me in, packing up everything but the books and giving it all away.

"Kids? Can I tell you a secret?"

They all nodded. They all needed a secret, something to bring them out of the woods and into the sunlight. My heart hammered away in my chest and I knew that I would have to lie flat on the table once they were gone and wait until it reverted to a normal beat.

"I used to be afraid of losing my mom too," I said. "And guess what? I still am!"

I looked from one side of the room to the other in a we're-all-in-this-together, we're-all-scared-of-losing-our-mothers kind of way. Then a cell phone alarm went off, meaning that the writer lady half hour was over and it was on to the arts and crafts room. The adults began to shepherd the children out, but not before nodding to me, each of them, in a sober kind of way. They had seen through me. They could tell that something was happening in my life, something I had vowed not to talk about but couldn't help talking about, in a sideways kind of way.

....

The duct-taped-shut Keds size-nine shoebox was hidden in the middle of the middle stack of the books-as-coffee-table. When I pictured it, I saw the expression on the Amish woman's face when she handed it to me. I saw the way she shook her bonneted head when I tried to give it back to her. The knowledge that the box was here with me, buried by books but right here in the middle of the one room of my one-room cabin, was unsettling. An unasked, unanswered question. *Be brave, Clara.*

It took a little unearthing to get to it. Once the shoebox was out, the stacks were lopsided, which was also unsettling. Shifting *Little House in the Big Woods* and *Farmer Boy* and *The Long Winter* from their original stacks to the middle one evened things out again. Symmetry was crucial to the structural integrity of the books-as-coffee-table.

I picked up the shoebox and carried it out to the porch and set it down on the little table next to my chair. I looked at it and it looked back at me. What could be so light that it weighed almost nothing? Then I went back into the cabin and brought Jack and Dog out to the porch with me. Calling in the reinforcements.

"Let's see what we've got here, men, shall we?"

When I didn't feel brave, I sometimes spoke out loud in a hearty,

World War II movie commander sort of way and kept speaking this way
until 1) I felt braver or 2) I couldn't stand the sound of my hearty commander voice anymore so 3) I had to take action.

The tape came off in a satisfying duct-tape way. Three photos were
what the box held, photos of me. Me as a baby, me as a toddler, me as
a little girl.

In the first, I was zipped into an orange snowsuit and someone—
Tamar?—had propped me against a snowbank. The sun glinted off
snow and my eyes were squinted shut. You couldn't see my legs or my
arms or anything besides my face. I was an orange blob against a glar-
ing pile of white.

In the second, I was sitting on her lap. A birthday cake with two candles was on the table in front of us. A third candle stuck out of the side
of the cake: the to-grow-on candle. Tamar's tradition. In this photo, her
face was in shadow, but you could still see how soft it was, how long her
hair was, curving around the curves of her cheek. She had always been
a thin woman, my mother. Some might call her scrawny. But in this
photo, her face was the soft face of a girl.

Which she was. Twenty years old. Much younger than I was now.

In the last photo my face—maybe I was four? Five?—poked through
a giant wooden cutout of a strawberry. Strawberry Fields Forever, which
was a pick-your-own place north of Boonville. This photo was one I remember being taken. Tamar and I had gone up early in the morning to
pick strawberries. We and another family—a mother, a father, five or
six children—were first on the field. It was a foggy day, the kind of day
when noise came randomly, a voice suddenly clear in your ear and then
fading. The kind of day that steadied you with the blurring of outlines
and the narrowing of surroundings. I remembered crouching, holding
the green pasteboard berry box in one hand, reaching under the green
leaves of the plants to find and pluck the strawberries with the other.
My fingers stained red. I remembered looking around to see where my
mother was. She was not next to me, but out of the fog her voice came
floating, a few rows or many rows away, impossible to tell. She was singing "Hallelujah." She sang it over and over, first a little higher, then a
little lower, then a little slower.

The sound of my mother singing was not unusual. She sang when she was working, when she didn't know, or forgot, that I was around to hear. Maybe she thought she was alone now, there in the fog, so it was okay to sing, to raise her voice to the clouds come down to earth. To the berries, hiding beneath the green leaves. To the dirt, rich and dark beneath her sneakers. Maybe she didn't even know she was singing.

I crouched between rows of strawberry plants, that fog so thick that wisps of it curled around my hands and the berry box. I was alone and she was alone, and the voices of the other family, the one with all the children, came to my ears intermittently from wherever they were in that big field.

The berry box was full of strawberries and I put one in my mouth. So sweet. So red. The color red fused with the sensation of sweetness in that moment. Berry after berry, sweet-red sweet-red, listening to my mother sing the song that I didn't know yet was her favorite song from her favorite singer, and when her song came to an end I began picking again and rapidly filled another box and then another and then another, so that when we met again at the end of the rows, there in the fog, she would look at the berry boxes and know that I had not wasted my time, and she would be proud of me.

We sat together on the porch, Jack and Dog and I, thinking about that day and her song and looking out at the woods beyond the cabin. The fairy lights glimmered in their silent way.

....

The photo of me in the snowbank was more substantial than the others, heavier somehow.

"Because, hello, there's another photo stuck to the back of it, Clara," I said out loud. "Well, well, what do you know?"

This is what happens to people who live alone and who live in their heads. They carry on running conversations with themselves, or with the ashes of their departed dogs, or with the fireflies that blink among the pines at dusk, or with their bottles of whiskey. They say things like "Well, well, what do you know?" out loud to themselves. They use the royal we, like this:

"What do we have here, Clara?"

What we had here, Clara, was a small photo printed out on regular copy paper from a color printer. It was not me as a baby or a little girl. A curl of tape on the back of orange-snowsuit me had stuck to it and turned it into a twofer photo. It was not my high school graduation photo, as the minute I saw it I realized I had expected it to be. It was a photo of Tamar. My mother. Ma.

Except not really.

"Ma?" I said to the photo. I brought it up closer to my face and studied it, then tipped it this way and that underneath the lamp. I recognized the shirt she was wearing; it was one she had worn for a year or so when I was in high school, a shirt unusual for her because it was pretty. A white gauzy shirt shot through with blue embroidery, a non-Tamar kind of shirt. "Ma?"

The woman in the photo—my mother, at least partly—said nothing. Her eyes were bright.

"Who are you looking at, Ma?"

No answer.

"More to the point, what's that look on your face?"

It was not a look of *I have something on my mind* or *Hurry up, I'm going to be late to work* or *What is my strange child up to now* or *Can you just take the picture already* because *You know I hate having my picture taken.* It had not been me who took the photo, because I would have remembered that look on her face. And the look on her face was one I could not place, because I had never seen it before, this soft, young look.

Strange.

My mother's legacy to me: three photos of her daughter, ones she must have found in that whirlwind week she spent clearing out the house, giving everything away, packing up the rest and moving herself out. It was the habit of the Amish to pay cash for everything, and I imagined her walking into the place where she lived now and placing a shoebox filled with hundred-dollar bills on the reception desk. *Here. Take care of me and whoever I will become.* The image made my heart hurt. Yes, it was an image I had imagined up right then and there, but imaginings make unreal things real. See the look on my mother's face as she walked into the nursing home alone, her shoebox of money clutched to her narrow chest. Shouldn't she have had someone with her on a day like that, a day when she had just left behind her entire life? Shouldn't a family member, like a daughter, have been with her? *Ma.*

I put the shoebox with the three photos of me in it back into the cabin. The last photo, the one of my mother in her pretty shirt, I took with me into the Subaru, and out into the night we drove, me and my young mother, seeking calm and steadiness on the winding Adirondack roads.

....

It took a long time to find calm, if calm is another word for the kind of exhaustion that comes after outdriving your own mind. Call it calm, call it exhaustion, the Subaru and I were north of Long Lake when my brain finally stopped buzzing and I turned the car around. We hugged the curves of the road, headlights on high because so few others were out. A small bar appeared around the bend north of Inlet—a bar I'd passed but never been to, a twinkling-lit bar—and I put the blinker on and pulled in.

Jukebox and conversation and dinging register, the bartender busy with bottles and glasses and shaker, one server maneuvering around the tables and stools with her tray lifted high. Where did bar-in-the-middle-of-nowhere people come from? Did they live nearby? Were they just passing through? Had they come upon this place like me, out of happenstance and chance?

"Gin gimlet, please," I said to the server when she made her way over to me.

"Ice?"

I shook my head and she nodded and wove her way back to the bartender. I watched him make it, the way he upended the bottle without even looking, the way he shook and then strained it into a martini glass and placed it on the server's tray. His fingers were long. Piano player's hands, if it were a requirement that piano players all have long, slender fingers, which it wasn't. Then the server was back with the gimlet.

She put it on the table and tilted her head, squinting at my pushed-up sleeve.

"What's your tattoo?" she said, and pointed at the thin, black spiraling line.

"Wire," I said. "Holds me together when things fall apart."

I smiled so that she would think I was joking, even though I wasn't. I had gotten the tattoo seven years ago, when Asa died in Afghanistan.

"Huh," she said. "Do things fall apart a lot?"

I shrugged in an ask-but-not-answer way. Unimpartable information. I nodded at her own tattoo, black words I couldn't read on the underside of her arm. "What's yours say?"

She twisted her arm so that half the sentence was visible.

"'Everything was beautiful,'" I read, "'and—'"

"'Nothing hurt,'" she finished. "It's a quote from a Kurt Vonnegut novel."

"Why that particular quote?"

She shrugged in the same way I had—*I see your unanswer and I raise you mine*—and threaded her way back through the tall barstools to the bartender, who was waiting for her with a new tray of drinks.

A slice of lime floated in the gimlet as if the gimlet were a tiny swimming pool. I pushed it, just enough to get it sailing. *Enough of this dead man's float, little lime. Time to swim on your own.* Push. Push. Now it was bobbing around the perimeter of the glass. *Good job, lime. Remember to breathe.*

I looked up to see the bartender smiling. Had he been watching the lime and me and our swimming lesson this whole time? Probably. That was the kind of look he had on his face. An *I know exactly what you were doing* kind of look. I quit talking to the lime—the bartender had ruined things and now the little lime would never progress beyond dog-paddling—drank the gimlet and then began mushing the lime into pulp with the tiny red straw. Death by drowning. Death by pulverization. The server started in my direction once the glass was empty but the bartender said something to her and she shrugged and he came around the end of the bar.

No tray, no order pad, just him and a black T-shirt and jeans and boots like the boots my high school boyfriend used to wear. Don't look at the boots, Clara. Look up. No, don't look up. Look at the empty gimlet glass with the mushed-up lime pulp. Don't say anything. But the bartender was as good at silence as I was. He knew its power. He knew I would break eventually, and eventually I did. I dragged my gaze up from the drowned-lime pulverization at the bottom of the glass and looked him in the eye.

"Another one?"

I nodded. He picked up my glass and went back behind the bar and mixed and shook and strained and poured. Bartenders were dancers, dancing three-square-foot, tightly choreographed bartending ballets. Then he returned with a bowl of buttered popcorn and the drink, two slices of lime this time. The limes could keep each other company in their gimlet swimming pool. They could sink or swim together. They would not be alone either in life or death. I didn't try to smile or talk. I didn't do anything other than be what I was, a tired gimlet-drinker who wanted to sit on a high stool and prevent a lime or two from drowning.

"Long day?" he said, and I nodded. The bartender gave off the same feeling as the bar itself had when it had appeared, twinkling-lit, around the curve of Route 28. Kind. Was that the word? Warm. The photo of my bright-eyed mother with that look I had never seen before on her face rose up in my head, my mother who was never coming back. Everything I had not said to her, everything she had not said to me. Yes, a long day. A pushing-back-the-lump-in-my-throat day. A willing-myself-through-it day.

The bartender put his hands on the tabletop, just the fingertips. As if the tabletop were a piano and he was getting ready to play a prelude. A soft, slow prelude. Maybe a Chopin prelude, the one I used to play to myself late, late at night in college to end practice, in one of the soundproof piano rooms in the basement of the music hall. Me and the piano and lamplight and the heavy door with the small, square-paned Triplex-glass panel. Sunshine and Brown knew where to find me late at night, if I wasn't in my room and no one had seen me. Me and my piano and my piano hands, smoothing the keys up and down, one foot keeping the beat. The bartender's hands reminded me of those days. They reminded me of my own hands.

"Drink slow," he said, "and drive safe."

I ate the popcorn and I drank slow and I drove safe, twelve miles from Inlet to Old Forge, the oldies station coming in and out in flashes on the radio. Static was all right sometimes, like the white noise you might hear from outside a closed door to a room where a small party was happening, a party of people who knew one another and loved one another. Comforting.

My hands on the steering wheel remembered the feel of the piano keys in that practice room and the one Chopin prelude that always ended my nights. The cool touch of the shining keys under my fingers. The sound of the giant stringed instrument filling the tiny room with its cinder-block walls and ceiling made of acoustic tile. *Why music?* was the question sometimes asked of me. *Why music when you don't ever play in front of anyone? When you don't even* want *to play in front of anyone?* That tiny room. That enormous instrument with its hidden strings, the enormous sound that poured forth from my fingers. *You seriously never played any instrument until you got to college?* That was another question, to which I used to shake my head and smile and shrug the way I had smiled and shrugged at the tattooed server tonight.

My hands on the steering wheel. The bartender's hands on the bottles and glasses. Tamar's hands stretching forth into the air when she searched for a word. Drink slow and drive safe. The car and I crested a steep hill in the darkness and the Tug Hill Plateau spread out below us with a sky filled with stars. For a minute it felt as if we might fly.

....

What went wrong between me and my mother had gone wrong a long time ago, and the beginning of the wrongness could be boiled down to Conversations Late at Night in the Kitchen Where Clara Is Finishing Her Mohawk Valley Community College Application for $400. It was January, and the application was due. Asa had broken up with me in September. MVCC was half an hour away. My broken heart and I could live at home and go to school part-time and work part-time.

Tamar, suddenly: "Clara, you're not going to school in Utica."

Clara, confused: "What are you talking about, Ma?"

Tamar, resolute: "No."

Clara, bewildered: "Ma?"

Tamar, finale: "New Hampshire is where you're going to college. Two states away."

That was her. That was a Tamar remark. She was a say-it-once kind of person. I looked up at her in disbelief. She was standing next to the kitchen table with her hands jammed into her jeans pockets. The application's pages were strewn around me, nearly complete. I had filled the boxes in, one by one, in my neatest all-caps printing. I had written and rewritten the essay.

"Ma? Is this a joke?"

She shook her head, a violent back-and-forth, her hands still balled up in her jeans pockets, big lumps halfway down her thighs. Then she pulled them out and swept the pages of the application together, and before I could rise up from my chair and stop her, she was ripping them. Tearing them up, in halves and quarters, torn paper drifting down from her ripping hands.

"Ma!"

"You've been accepted already," she said. "It's something called early decision."

She showed me an envelope, from a college in New Hampshire, a *Dear Clara Winter, We are delighted to inform you that* letter, dated a month prior. Grants and work study and scholarships.

What? How? Who? I shook my head in bewilderment.

"I didn't apply to this school," I said. "There's a mistake."

"There's no mistake," she said. "I filled out the application for you. Annabelle and I did it together, last October."

She turned and walked out of the kitchen. It was late. The table was strewn with torn paper. I remembered the sound of her footsteps going up the stairs, the littered table, my galloping heart. I sat there for a minute, fingers pressed on my neck, trying to slow the beats by pressure alone, which did not work now and did not work then. A feeling like lava rose from my gut and streaked down my arms and legs, filled

my head with molten rage. Wild heart trembling, I tore out of that
kitchen and through the dark living room, pounded up the dark stairs
and shoved open the door of my mother's dark room.

What I remembered after that was screaming, mine, words ripped
out of my heart and flung at Tamar, who was invisible in the darkness between us but whose caught breath I could hear. When I thought
about it now, which I tried never to do but couldn't help, all I heard in
my head were fragments. *Who are you, what are you, Asa is good, Asa is
kind, Asa loved me, what did you say to him to make him go away like that?
What kind of mother doesn't want her daughter to be happy, doesn't want
her daughter around, what kind of mother throws her daughter out.* That
kind of thing. That was what came back to me. I didn't know if those
fragments were real.

"You know what kind of mother does that kind of thing? *Your* kind
of mother. The kind of mother who didn't want me in the first place
and now can't wait to get rid of me. The kind of mother you are. The
kind of mother who only wants to hurt the daughter she didn't want in
the first place. A nothing kind of mother. A nothing. You're a *nothing.*"

That was real. Those words happened. They spat themselves out of
my mouth and into that dark, invisible air and I didn't know how many
more would have followed them except that there was a *click,* a tiny
click, and then lamplight pooled on my mother's face. She was sitting
straight up in bed, that narrow twin bed she slept on as long as I could
remember, and she was staring at me. Her eyes were dark lakes and her
hands were hovering in the air, palms turned to each other, rising to
cover her ears and then lowering. Trembling. I had never seen my mother's hands tremble. I had never seen my mother with that look on her
face. I had never seen my mother's hands lift to her ears like that, trying
to fend off words, sounds, rage, hurt

Because she had never had to.

I had never spoken to her like that.

That was the image I couldn't get out of my head. Those were the sev-
enty words—I wrote them out once and counted them, like a Words
by Winter assignment from hell—I could never take back. My mother,

her trembling hands, the stricken look on her face that not once before or after that night did I ever see again.

....

Next morning she was gone before I got out of bed. In the kitchen there was no trace of her: no coffee mug, no bowl rinsed of Cheerios, no spoon laid to dry on a dish towel. The truck was gone too. None of this was unusual—sometimes, if the Dairylea trucks they wanted her to un-decal were hours away, she had to head out at dawn—but I crept through the house, all senses alert, like a detective at a crime scene.

Because that was what it was.

Once words have been raged at someone, they can't be taken back. They enter into the body and heart of their victim, and they change the victim forever. What is not as commonly acknowledged is that they do the same to the one who screamed them out. Nothing was the same after that. We never spoke of what had happened between us on that dark night. Not then, and not ever.

From school that afternoon I walked into the village and headed south a mile out of town. Whenever a car approached I stepped carefully onto the narrow shoulder of the road, trying to avoid the ditch, which was deep and filled with snow and ice. My boots were heavy and I clutched my silver hammer earring in my mittened hand. It took a long time to reach the choir director's trailer, where her Impala was parked in the driveway, which meant that she was home, and it took a while to get up the courage to knock on her door.

"Clara? Is everything okay?"

Which meant that she didn't know what had gone down the night before. My mother hadn't talked to her. This was clear from the easy worry on her face, the way she leaned against the doorframe and held the door open for me.

"What's going on? Did something happen to Tamar?"

At that, I nodded. Yes. Something had happened to Tamar. The light-weight had come flying out of her corner, a demon of a fighter who hadn't known she had it in her.

"What is it, Clara? Tell me what happened. Something to do with those goddamn decals? Did she fall off the ladder?"

I shook my head. She was losing patience, I could see. Worry and fear flitted across her wide face. "Clara. Talk to me."

"Annabelle!" I cried, my voice strangled, and she caught me in her arms. It was the first time I had ever called her by name instead of Miss Lee. She held me, and I cried, and she asked me over and over what was wrong, what had happened, but all I said was that my mother was okay and that I was sorry, my mother was okay and I was sorry. Sorry, sorry, sorry. The smell of fried potatoes filled the air of her trailer. The miles back north that I walked later that afternoon were long and cold. Tamar didn't look up when I walked into the house. She had already eaten, an empty can of SpaghettiOs filled with water and sitting in the sink.

Nothing could take those memories away. Facts for $2000, the Daily Double, bet small or bet it all.

The night I raged at my mother, the night that something broke inside both of us, was something that Sunshine and Brown didn't know about. They knew that my mother had been resolute that I leave home, that I go far away for college, they knew that my high school boyfriend and I had split up and he had joined the army and died later in Afghanistan, but they didn't know about that night. It was buried inside me, a shame too great to let surface.

．．．．．．．．．．．．．．．．．．．．

I knew Asa Chamberlain from age twelve on, when he and his family moved to Sterns from Vermont. I knew him the way you knew someone who lived nearby, someone you rode the school bus with. We weren't friends. He was two years older, and when you were growing up that was an unbridgeable gap a) unless you were next-door neighbors, which we weren't, or b) until you got to high school, which we did. Asa was a senior and I was a sophomore when we started going out.

The bleachers at a football game was how it started. I had jumped down to look for my tiny silver hammer earring, which had fallen out of my hand and down between the seats into the depths. That was what we called it, my friends and I: The Depths. Who knew what you would find down there: trash, chewed gum, cigarette butts, condom wrappers, empty beer cans, dead mice or couples making out.

Not me, though. I didn't make out with anyone. Not because I didn't want to. Sometimes when a couple was down in The Depths making out during a game, or when I was at a party and the basement was dark and full of friends cradled together on chairs or the couch or the floor and the air was thick with beer and lust but I was upstairs with the ones who'd come up for air, drinking in the kitchen or eating chips in the living room, my whole body would spark and tingle with want. But there was no one for me. I was an island of one.

But that day, the day of Asa, I had jumped down from the bleachers and there I was, rooting around in the mess of thrown-away cups and bottles and Doritos bags and napkins. I had to find the earring. It was my old-man earring, the earring that the old man who looked after me when I was a child, whose trailer in Nine Mile Trailer Park I went to on Wednesday nights when my mother was at choir practice, had made for me. He was a metalworker, long gone now, the person who inspired my book, *The Old Man*. If the earring wasn't in my ear it was in my pocket, the pocket of whatever I was wearing, and I wore nothing that didn't have pockets, for that reason.

I looked up from The Depths and there was Asa, working his turn at the concession stand the way the varsity did for the JV and vice versa. That was how we did it at Sterns High. Maybe every school did it that way. Maybe it was a nationwide ritual, the way making out in basement party rooms was a nationwide ritual, a ritual that had somehow passed me by. Asa was standing by the hot dog grill, half smiling, watching me.

"You lose something?" he said. I remembered his voice as quiet, but it couldn't have been. There was a distance between the concession stand and The Depths. I pointed to my ear. I was close to tears. That earring was the one physical remnant of my time with the old man, and I had to find it.

"I'll help you," he said, and then he was next to me, crouched down and looking. He was smart in the way he searched, tracing a path with his eyes and then retracing. He inched forward foot by foot, going over every bit of ugly under-bleacher wasteland.

"There you go," he said, and he plucked it up from under a foam cup that had once held coffee.

He dropped the earring into the palm of my hand. But then he did something else, which was take my fingers in his and fold them up around the tiny hammer. Unexpected. In that second, before I looked up at him, I knew that my life had just changed. A window had blown open on the island and fresh air was breezing in. A boy had touched me, was still touching me. I kept looking at his hand wrapped around mine, the tiny silver earring held tight in the darkness between all our fingers.

"You going to look up at some point, do you think?" he said, and there was laughter and something else — tenderness — in his voice. Why? He didn't even know me, did he?

"Look up," he said. "I dare you."

Up I looked. He was much taller than I was. Jeans and T-shirt and boots, like every boy I knew and like no boy I knew. "You're Clara Winter," he said, and I nodded like a toddler. Like a girl who had never kissed a boy, never gone down in the basement, let alone The Depths. Which was where we were. And which was where he kissed me, then and there.

I had not known you could meet a boy and everything could just fall into place. That I wouldn't have to think or worry or plan. Nothing about it would be easy, was what I used to think, but everything about Asa Chamberlain and me was just that. Easy. Until it wasn't.

....

"What went wrong between you and your mother?" Sunshine said. "Brown and I always thought she was cool."

"The coolest," Brown agreed. "She wasn't like any of the other parents, back in school."

From the first time they met her, that first year in college, Sunshine and Brown had loved my mother. We were from different worlds, Sunshine and Brown and I, and their fascination with my mother's physical toughness, her fearlessness in the face of winter and chainsaws and axes and life as a solo mother with no one to take care of either her or her daughter, had always struck me as suspect.

"She wasn't like your parents," I said. "I'll give you that. But you and I come from different worlds."

We were sitting at their table. This conversation about my mother was one we'd had many times over many years, and this was where it always ended: them pushing, me resisting, end of subject. It was late and dinner was long over and it was time to go home. Back to the cabin. Back to Dog in his urn and Jack on the shelf and the unreadable look on my mother's face in the photo next to it. Back to my bed of books. I still had a Words by Winter assignment due the next day, a man who wanted a birthday note in haikus to his daughter on her eighteenth birthday, one haiku for each year of her life. Haikus were not as easy as you might think. 5 syllables + 7 syllables + 5 syllables x 18 = 306 syllables exactly. Eighteen haikus were going to take me a long time, and I was tired.

But Sunshine didn't let it drop.

"Remember the first time we met her, that first Parents' Weekend?" she said. "She came bearing fudge, fudge for me and for Brown because you must have told her we were your friends."

"Peanut butter fudge, as I recall," Brown said. "From Hogback Mountain, in a little white box with a little white plastic knife inside the box."

"And remember that summer in Old Forge after sophomore year, when you were working at Keyes and Brown and I were working at the water park? She took the day off work and took us all hiking up Bald Mountain."

"She scampered right up that bare rock part at the top," Brown said. "Put the rest of us to shame, as I recall."

That was the second time he'd said *as I recall* in three sentences. It was driving me nuts.

"Also, and you might not know this," Sunshine said now, "but she used to call us when she was worried about you."

What?

"She did not."

"She did. Sometimes."

"So our impression of her is different from yours," Brown said, and the delicate way he said it made me think that he and Sunshine had talked together earlier, had decided to press the issue of my mother. "Yes, she's tough. But she's also not."

I shook my head. My mother had called them? About me? Look at the two of them, sitting across the table, remembering the fudge and the hike and the phone calls. A revised version of my mother was filling my head now, new information squeezing its way into the image I had of her.

"But Asa," I said. "She said something to Asa back in high school. She must have, because he broke up with me the next day. No explanation. And then she sent me away, she banished me from Sterns. Goodbye and good riddance to the prodigal daughter."

"Why does that still eat away at you all these years later?" Brown said, and Sunshine nodded, a nod of *You need to weigh that one specific hurt against the entirety of your life together, everything she did for you.*

Why, Brown? Because words. Words, the spoken and the unspoken, the real and the imagined conversations, pile up. Because I screamed at her, because I hurt her, because she hurt me. Words turn into walls. Walls turn into mazes. With the passage of time you find yourself deep in, winding and twisting and turning, and where is the way out?

"We never talked about it," I said. "*She* would never talk about it. And now it's too late."

"It's never too late," Sunshine said. "You're both still alive, right? Track her down, wherever she is right now, and talk."

....

It was the end of a stage of life, that night I flung those raging words at my mother. It was the first time that I saw no clear way out of something I had done. Shame filled me, on top of the hurt of losing Asa, and they fused together and seeped into my bones. I walked around that winter, the winter of my senior year, with the images of Asa the day he broke up with me and my mother the night I screamed at her rising up before me like ghosts. His head, a back-and-forth metronome of no, and her hands, trembling, rising and falling at the sides of her head. That fathomless look in her eyes. Her parted lips.

"It's strange that she would interfere with you and your boyfriend,"

Brown said. "And strange that she was against you going to school close by. Tamar seems like a live-and-let-live type."

"You would think," I said. "But you would be wrong."

The shame I felt at hurting my mother could be another Words by Winter assignment: Write a letter to your mother, apologizing for that dark night. What would I say and how would I say it? What would she say back to me? We had never talked about what happened. Parts of the story were missing.

Is it possible that parts of the whole story are always missing? Like when I was buying fudge for my mother at the Hogback Mountain gift shop and the cashier sat behind the fudge counter, crocheting something—from the round, small look of the thing it was a baby hat like the kind Sunshine made—and she refused to look up from her crocheting. *Hello, hello, fudge lady, I'm here, can you see me?*

I coughed. I jingled my keys. I coughed again, louder. I said, "Excuse me," but did she look up? She did not.

"**HI**."

Both letters uppercase, and in boldface. At that she looked up, startled. "Oh my goodness, dear girl," she said. "Have you been standing there a long time?"

That was when I saw the hearing aids, big ones. The on-a-budget hearing aids instead of the expensive, barely noticeable ones. *For God's sake, Clara, she's deaf.* The fudge lady was a kind old lady who was deaf, and she carefully cut and weighed and packed my half-pound of peanut butter fudge and then counted out my change, which I fed into the Donate to Vermont Food Shelves jar on the counter, one coin at a time, in penance, for which she smiled and thanked me.

It was so hard to know the whole story. Nigh on impossible. *Remember that, Clara,* I told myself.

....

Changes in the ability to communicate are unique to each person with Alzheimer's. In the early stages of dementia, the person's communication may not seem very different or he or she might repeat stories or not be able to find a word. As the disease progresses, a caregiver may recognize other changes such as:

- *Using familiar words repeatedly*
- *Inventing new words to describe familiar objects*
- *Easily losing his or her train of thought*
- *Reverting back to a native language*
- *Having difficulty organizing words logically*
- *Speaking less often.*

The Life Care Committee had printed out some guidelines for me, taken from the Alzheimer's Association website. In the beginning I used to read them over and over. They were mostly memorized now but I still went through them sometimes. A ritual. Familiar words and phrases used repeatedly. *She was always a strange child. She was a word girl.* Inventing new words to describe familiar objects. "The iron claw." That was the term my mother used for the hammered-metal hands that cupped the single book on her windowsill.

"You mean the bookends, Ma?"

She shook her head, annoyed, and pointed at them. "No. Them. The iron claw."

"Yeah. The bookends. That's what they're called."

She picked up the pillow next to her and threw it at me point-blank, a distance of twelve inches, because I was sitting right next to her on the couch. I caught it and laughed, a laugh of how strange, how surprising: my mother, throwing a pillow right at my face.

This was only two days after our last visit, but she was different yet again. That too was something they'd told me early on to expect. She will come and she will go, they said, and you must learn to meet her where she is.

"So," she said, nodding, when I walked in next time.

"So," I said.

She held out her hands, both hands, in a way she never had before, not now, not back then. *Don't think about back then, Clara. Meet your mother where she is.* I took her hands in mine.

"I'm glad to see you, Ma."

"I was looking for you," she said. "I keep looking."

"So they tell me. I had a bunch of work to do first, four one-day Words by Winter turnarounds—you know how it is."

She nodded. She knew how it was. Did she have any idea how I made my living? Would she have cared if she did?

"And you know how it is up in the north woods"—I waved in a vaguely northern direction, there in the Plant Room with the orchids —"there was some road work on Route Eight."

"Road work never ends," she said. "Am I right or am I right?"

That wasn't a Tamar remark. Never would she have said something like that in the olden days, which was how I was beginning to think of them. *Shhh, Clara.*

"You're right," I said. We sat down on the green couch together, she still holding both my hands in hers. She leaned toward me. Her eyes were bright.

"Is there enough wood?"

Follow her.

"There's certainly a lot of wood," I said, because there certainly was. There was a lot of wood in this world. All those trees, at least in upstate New York.

Enough wood was always something on my mother's mind, back in the olden days. Fire- and ply- and more. She cut and hauled and split and then we both stacked—in the storage barn, in the unused garage, on the porch—all summer long and as far into the fall as the weather and light let us. Enough wood to get through the winter. Survival.

"There's probably enough," I said. "I think, anyway."

We nodded, both of us. Enough wood was important. Enough to feed the stove all the way through the bitter cold of January, the bitter winds of February and the bitter snows of March. There could never be enough wood, in Tamar's world. She squeezed my hands.

"Boyfriend."

"I don't have a boyfriend."

"Boyfriend."

"Ma."

There it was, that tone in my voice. Had it always been there? Was it only now that I saw its effect on her? Because look, she was shrinking. The air around her was drawing itself in and her shoulders were narrowing and her head tilted down. Choose your words with care, Clara. Don't correct. Don't criticize.

"I've been thinking about him lately," was what I said. That was the right thing to say. She nodded.

"He died," she said.

———

———

———

That was me breathing. Making myself wait. Making myself be calm. Making myself not use the word *remember*. Because that was what she was doing, wasn't it? Remembering Asa.

"He did die," I said.

"It broke my daughter's heart," she said.

She nodded, and I was back in time sitting on a chair in the kitchen of the Treehouse in the Florida Panhandle, waiting for a pot of boiling water to turn the shrimp pink, listening to her voice on the other end of the phone. *Clara. Clara, Asa died yesterday morning. He died in an explosion in Afghanistan.* Those words had never left me. They came back to me sometimes, the sound of her voice over all those miles, the way I sat there with the phone clutched in my hands, the way the boiling water boiled itself dry, the shrimp turned to scorched rubber at the bottom of the ruined pot.

"Help her," my mother said. Her hands were still pressed against her heart.

"Maybe nothing could have helped her," I said. "Maybe she just had to get through it however she could."

"No!" my mother said. The sound in her voice was the sound of agitation. Of exclamation marks. Of breaking dishes and crashing pans. They had warned me about that too. "No!"

Follow her. Meet her where she is. But she met me instead.

"I couldn't help her," she said.

Oh, Ma.

My heart jumpstarted itself. It was happening again. Again and again, it kept happening. Too thin too dehydrated too stressed. Two of the *too*s, except these days it was all three of the *too*s. She sat quietly on the couch next to me the whole time, neither of us talking. It took an hour for my heart to go back to its normal rhythm.

....

Blue Mountain had come sidling back into the quilt room after the rest of his class had been Pied-Pipered into the arts and crafts room. By then it was just me, lying flat on the floor beneath the ghostly white quilt on the wall, waiting for my heart to stop its hammering. He came trudging back to where I lay staring up at the peaked roof of the exhibition hall. He didn't seem fazed. He didn't ask why I was lying there on the floor.

There had been space around him in the room while I was talking. An untouchable few inches that the other children didn't have. They had kept an instinctive slight distance from him, no jostling or pushing or reaching out to touch his flyaway hair or tickle his feet or hold his hand, the way children of that age do.

"I have a question," he said.

"Go ahead."

"Is your mother proud of you?"

I could have deflected, said, "That's an interesting question. Why do you ask?" or "Is *your* mother proud of *you*?" or I could have not said anything.

"I don't know," was what I said.

He nodded. So little, he was.

Did Blue Mountain feel alone in this world? Did he walk through it wondering where his place was? Why had he asked me that question, and why had he asked it when he knew that no one else would hear him ask it, he who returned when everyone else had left?

Unanswerable questions, all of them.

Children like Blue Mountain brought Asa back to me. Blue Mountain was the kind of child that Asa would look out for at the summer camp where he worked. Asa would watch over a child like Blue Mountain, protect and defend him by helping him learn how to do things he was afraid of. The monkey bars, maybe, or double Dutch. Or even the unicycle, his own unicycle, which he brought to camp and kept in reserve for the most tender children. The most fragile.

Asa had taught himself to ride the unicycle. Once, on the way to his house, I came upon him in the middle of a clearing off one of the trails through the woods. He turned slowly, around and around, with his hands off the handlebars and the sun glinting down through the pines onto his hair. When I thought about the way Asa looked on that afternoon when I watched from behind the birches on a nearby trail but never told him I was watching, how that day and that image and that memory was burned into my heart, sometimes it felt as if I might float off the edge of the world and never come back.

Too bad there wasn't an early-warning system for moments like that, moments you could never forget even if you wanted to. Only after the fact did you realize that a certain time in your life was over, and you would never get it back. You once had been whole, and now you weren't.

This was why the little, cute children were so hard to look at. The youngest ones were the ones most likely not to know that they were still whole. They walked around in their soft skins, with their backpacks and their messy hair and their clompy Velcro shoes. They scratched their mosquito bites or sucked a strand of hair, they gazed around the room with their enormous eyes. Moments like that, I wanted to put my arms around them, all of them, and tell them to watch out. A fifth grade bully or a nasty teacher or a bad priest, oh God the whole damn world was going to get them, one of these days, and they didn't even know it.

They were nearly skinless, these tiny children.

The skinless walked among us.

. . . .

On Tuesdays twice a month, Asa used to drive up to the Fairchild Continuing Care Center and sing to the residents, which was what the people who lived there were called. Never patients, never old people, never senior citizens. Residents. He took me with him a few times. The difference between Asa and me could be summarized in the way we entered the Fairchild. Asa bounded up the walkway and spread his arms wide, pushed both double doors open at the same time and was already past the reception desk before he turned to see where I was. Still by the car, usually. He would pinwheel his arms in a *Come on, Clara!* motion, and my feet would begin the trudge.

Once inside, I would be overwhelmed by the smell, the smell that only places like the Fairchild Continuing Care Center had. The smell of oldness, yes, and cleaning supplies, and cafeteria food, but so much else. Memories. Longings. So much stored up inside, never to be let out. I smelled it every time I walked into the place where my mother lived now, and every time, my heart beat faster. *Let them out. Let them out.* That was the feeling that filled me, and whether it was the wanting to leave or the wanting of all the stories trapped inside to be let out, I couldn't say. I didn't know. They were linked in my mind and in my heart.

Not so for Asa. Asa was light and I was not. Asa was there to sing to the residents, and sing he did. They lit up when he walked into the Fairchild community room. The music stand would already be set up for him, for the hymnal or sheet music he had brought with him or not brought with him. Asa didn't need sheet music. Those songs came pouring out of him: "Amazing Grace," "A Mighty Fortress Is Our God," "I Danced in the Morning."

How? Where had he learned all those hymns?

"Nobody learns those hymns, Clara. And nobody calls them hymns either. They're just songs. They're everywhere. You know them too."

And he was right. I did. The day came, not long after I had stopped going to the Fairchild with him—I was not Asa, I could not bound in and bound out the way he did, I could not stand in front of the residents and fill them with light and music the way he could—when I heard myself singing "Amazing Grace." Standing there at the kitchen sink, washing dishes, singing. The way Asa did, and the way my mother did.

Asa sang to me too. Songs from *Oklahoma!,* that old musical, when we were driving around. He would open all the windows and spread his arms wide, steering with his knees, and sing about a place where the wind came sweeping down the plain. He sang other times too, soft songs when my heart kicked into high gear and I had to lie down. He would curl himself around me and stroke my hair and sing to me, meandering songs that he made up as he went along because that was the kind of thing Asa could do. He could make up songs that were songs, real and true, and the sound of his singing voice would weave itself into my dreams.

It still did, sometimes.

....

There were only seven stages of Alzheimer's and my mother was already in Stage 5 when she moved herself out of our house. Half a year later she had progressed to Stage 6b.

"How did she get that far without anyone noticing?"

That was one of the first questions the Life Care Committee asked me. A reasonable one too. How did most people end up in a doctor's office talking about Alzheimer's? Because someone close to them had observed any one or more of the following:

Trouble paying bills on time.
Wearing the same clothes day after day.
Trouble making meals for guests.
Difficulty going grocery shopping.
Difficulty remembering the right date when writing checks.
Difficulty recalling current address.
Difficulty recalling recent major events.

They had leveled their gazes at me, as if to size me up, the daughter who hadn't noticed her mother's decline. But they didn't know the particulars of my mother's life. The house had been paid up long ago, the electric bill came automatically out of her bank account, there was no gas or oil bill because she heated the place with wood. There were almost no checks to write because there were few bills to pay; she was a cash woman for the most part. As for clothes, she had always worn the same clothes anyway: jeans and a T-shirt and a sweatshirt or her lumber jacket or a parka, depending on the time of year. Keds or winter boots, again depending. She didn't make meals to begin with, for either herself or guests. She didn't have any guests, beyond Annabelle Lee once in a while. As for current address, Sterns, New York, was good enough. No house numbers, no street names, no apartment or condo unit or suite to remember.

As for recent major events, what would qualify? Putting the orange juice away in the cupboard instead of the refrigerator? Getting pulled over for erratic driving on Starr Hill?

Yes. Those events were, in fact, the major events that precipitated the slow topple of all the dominoes that followed.

My mother was a woman of simplicity. It took the disease a long time to complicate that simplicity. Now the complications were evident every time I looked at her. An aide helped her in the bathroom, for example. And she didn't go on the field trips anymore. No more museum. No more mall. No more library. No more Erie Canal Village, no more Dairy Queen, no more strolls around the campus of Utica College.

The day came when she looked at me and asked how she knew me.

The minute she asked me that question I tried to banish it from my mind, tried to shoo it away, because *How do I know you again?* was not a question you expected ever to hear from your mother. But too late, it was already burned into my brain. I stood there frozen in the doorway of her room, my book offering of the week in my hands.

That was the first but there had been many more since. "Daphne," she had called me, and "Mama," she had called me, and once she had called me by her grandmother's name: "Helena." By the time she called me Helena I was not surprised. I did not laugh or startle or ask who Helena was. What I did was smile and say, "Hi, Ma." Because that was what you did when you were riding the wave with your mother. You followed her.

Everything progressed. Everything kept moving on down the highway, including my mother. She fidgeted, she paced, she wandered the endless hallways.

Early-onset.

Alzheimer's disease.

Fifty-percent chance of genetic mutation.

Frontotemporal dementia.

Memory care.

Assisted living.

Independent ambulation.

Increased rigidity.

Neurological reflex changes.

Power of attorney.

AD.

eFAD.

FTD.

DH.

DW.

LO.

All the medical terminology on the official websites. All the short-hand on the caregiver forums, all the uppercase abbreviations that stood in for dear husband, dear wife, loved one. Every one of them an acronym that masked the face of a loved someone. Sometimes, in the middle of the night, when sleep eluded me, the acronyms came calling. They gathered together like bees to the hive, and I was the hive and they crawled on top of me and inside me and burrowed deep, humming and buzzing. *You,* they hummed, *you, you, you, you too? You too? You too?* Maybe the day would come when I found myself behind the wheel of an unfamiliar car, driving around a bend I couldn't recall, on my way to see someone I didn't remember. Fifty-fifty. Five-oh. Maybe the bees were already living within me.

....

Follow her.

That was what the doctor and the Life Care specialist told me to do. Follow your mother wherever she goes. Meet her where she is, not where you think she should be. She was unsteady these days, her balance off. They had given her a walker but she was "not fond of using it." She had entered a stage, "not unusual, apparently, in our experience," where she kept wandering the halls looking for something. "In your mother's case, her daughter. You, apparently."

There was that word again, their favorite word: *apparently.*

"Her daughter?" I had said, at the last Life Care meeting. "But it used to be keys. Remember? It was always keys."

They nodded. They were patient. Keys, daughter—what was the difference?

"We know it's unsettling," they said, "those times when you're sitting right next to her on the couch but she doesn't recognize you as her daughter. We get that"—which was another thing they kept saying, *we get that*—"but it doesn't mean that she doesn't appreciate your presence."

"Okay," I said. We were in this together, all of us: the doctor, the Life Care specialist, Sylvia and the aide and me and even the director, who liked to drop in once in a while to keep her "finger on the pulse."

"You're a writer," the doctor said, encouragingly. He pointed at the book I had brought for her that week, *Little House in the Big Woods,* as if to prove his point. "This assignment might not be as hard for you as it is for other people, to follow your mother wherever she goes. Writers have good imaginations, right? Isn't it part of the job description?"

The aide, Sylvia, the Life Care specialist and the director all pursed their lips and nodded. They sat in a row, all four of them, pursing and nodding as if this were community theater and they were the Greek chorus.

"It is," I said. "It's part of the job description."

At that, they nodded and pursed even harder, quickening their pace. Wind-up Greek chorus dolls that someone had just snuck up behind and cranked up a notch.

"Oh, yes," Sylvia said. "You'll be great at that, Clara."

She smiled at me. It was a real smile, a smile that said she knew I was worried about not doing a good job. As if I were a child getting ready to head to Syracuse to the state spelling bee, a child who had practiced for weeks, asking anyone—meaning Tamar—to read out the words from the practice book and use each in a sentence if necessary. As if I were my former self, Sterns Elementary spelling champ, and my mother were her former self too, Tamar Winter, the tough-as-nails mother of the champ.

. . . .

"Autochthonous."

"Could you please use it in a sentence?"

That was what I used to say to Tamar, back in my elementary school spelling bee champion days. Asking to use the spelling word in a sentence was a ploy, a stall. If you didn't know how to spell a word, staring into space while the word was used in a sentence as your brain sifted through a thousand possibilities to find the right one was an excellent strategy. I used to ask in a polite, distant, measured tone of voice, as if Tamar were an official state spelling bee judge.

"No, Clara, I can't use this word in a sentence, because I don't know what the hell this word means. I don't even know how to *pronounce* this goddamn word."

That was her usual response. A Tamar remark. But the few seconds it took her to go through the rant was usually enough time for me to take a stab at how to spell the word.

"Autochthonous. A. U. T. O. C. H. T. H. O. N. O. U. S."

"Correct. Do you have any idea what it means?"

"No. How the hell would I?"

"Don't curse."

"*You* curse."

"Do as I say, not as I do. I'm your mother."

"Who cares what it means, Ma? Why does that matter? All that matters is spelling it right. Onward."

That was a lie, though. I cared. Even back then, I cared.

"Hi, Ma. It's Clara."

I always told her who I was these days, just in case. I put my hand on the walker handle, next to hers but not touching. Tamar was never big on touching. She was pushing her walker up and down the hall outside the dining room. The hallway was decorated with removable decals. blocky branched trees with stylized birds fluttering up into the fluorescent-ceiling sky. Flowers drooping on stems. Apples and pears and cherries. Every decal was a replication of something that lived and thrived only outside.

"Hello, Clara."

"Where are you going today, Ma?"

"Choir practice."

"At the Twin Churches?"

She stopped walking and looked directly at me. "Where the hell else?"

That was Tamar. That was a Tamar thing to say. She was there, she was right there with me, the daughter who never stopped asking dumb questions. The look on her face would wither a lesser woman. *Let me not be a lesser woman.*

"I don't know, Ma. Saint Patrick's Cathedral, maybe?"

She shook her head and shooed me away with her hand. Annoyed. But I wasn't going anywhere and neither was she. It was a Wednesday night in upstate New York, and it was my job to follow my mother wheresoever she went, and where she was going was choir practice, just like she did every week for thirty-two years despite the fact that she never went to church.

It was practice only, for my mother. A lifetime of practice.

There was a time when she wanted to leave upstate New York, desperately wanted to, but she got no farther than a party in Utica.

Autochthonous was an adjective. It meant formed or originating in the place where it was found. *Autochthonous* meant native. *Autochthonous* was the definition of my mother, Tamar Winter, formed and found in the foothills of the Adirondack Mountains. I thought back to those nights when she was pretending to be the spelling bee judge and I was pretending to be the spelling bee contestant, each of us needling the other, sitting there at the kitchen table, and I thought, Was that the time in my life when everything was beautiful, and nothing hurt, and I didn't even know it?

She stopped pushing the walker and touched my arm just below the elbow, where the wire began.

"What's this?" she said, and she pushed the sleeve higher, twisting my arm, trying to see the whole tattoo.

"I got it when I was twenty-five," I said. "Right after Asa died."

"Asa," she said, and the sound of his name in her voice made my heart pound. Again. "What happened with you and Asa?"

"He died, Ma."

"I know he died. He died after. After"—she cast her hand out into the air, searching for the word or words that escaped her. "After."

"After we broke up."

"Broke up."

"Yes, Ma. It happened after that night I came home and the two of you were sitting at the kitchen table talking."

The image rose up in my mind again. In the wake of the breakup I had thought about that night, the sight of them across from each other at the table, each leaning forward. The intent look on Asa's face, the look on hers of—what? Surprise? No, something more. They must have been there for a while without me—I was out babysitting—because the air in the kitchen, when I walked up on the porch and opened the door and breathed it in, was stale. Stale and charged and full of invisible words that had been spoken without me there to hear them.

The next day he returned to the house and ended it between us.

"Do you know why he ended things, Ma?"

A calm detachment, the Buddhist way of regarding the things that make you suffer. I made my voice sound quiet and mild. There was a difference between fake quiet and mild and actual calm detachment, though. I could hear Brown in my head— *Why does that still eat away at you?*—and in my head I looked at him with fake calm detachment and said, *I wish it didn't, but it does.*

"Asa," she said again, and then, "Eli."

"Yes, Ma. Eli used to come over sometimes too. We used to play cards together, all four of us." Just in time, I stopped myself from saying the word *Remember?*, which you were not supposed to do. "Eli was Asa's father," I said. "*Is* Asa's father."

Which he was, wasn't he? You didn't stop being someone's father when the someone died, did you?

"Maybe Asa was planning to enlist and he was afraid to tell me," I said. "Maybe he figured I would want to leave Sterns and he didn't want to keep me stuck there. Maybe he didn't love me anymore."

All things I had tried out in my head, then and in the years that followed our breakup and my leaving Sterns. I heard my own voice, a thin ghost filled with question marks, strutting and fretting their time on the stage, signifying nothing, and my mother was frowning and shaking her head.

"No," she said. "No."

"Why then, Ma?"

The category was Breaking Up for $400. The contestants stood at their podiums staring into space, ghost question marks floating in the air around them.

....

My mother was right about Josh Gibson. He was a Hall of Famer who never played in the major leagues due to a "gentleman's agreement" that black baseball players wouldn't play in the major leagues. He had a baby face. Soft eyes, soft lips. 1911–1947, which meant he died when he was barely older than me, the same year they brought Jackie Robinson up from the minors.

Did I even know that my mother liked baseball, let alone knew enough about it to know about Josh Gibson and the gentleman's agreement? No.

"Ma?" I said. "You were right about that Josh Gibson question."

She gave me a withering look, an *Of course I'm right, and what kind of idiot are you?* I soldiered on.

"I never knew you were such a baseball fan. Do you have a favorite team?"

"Of course."

"Who is it, then?"

But she waved her hand at me and turned away. *Fool,* was what that shooing motion meant, and my mother suffered no fools, then or now. If the fool sitting next to her was dumb enough not to know what her team was, why should my mother tell her?

When Sunshine and Brown and I played Jeopardy! we suffered no fools either. We played it for real. We made bets, we kept score, we slammed our hands down on the table. Six categories and five clues each, just the way it was done on the real show. Our only variation was that each category had to have something to do with our actual lives. Snap out a clue and one of us would slam a hand on the table and snap back an answer.

Upstate New York Mountains We Have Climbed.

Books We Most Loved as Children.

Best Diners in the Adirondacks.

Cocktails We Got Sick on in College.

Best Drugs to Counteract the Side Effects of Chemotherapy.

Names No Child Should Be Given.

"Baseball for sixteen hundred," Brown said. Baseball was one of his favorite categories. I slammed my hand down so fast and hard that the tiny bowl of salt, with its matching tiny spoon, jumped on the table.

"Name of Tamar Winter's favorite baseball team," I said.

"What is the Yankees?" Brown said, and he looked at me for verification, but I made a your-guess-is-as-good-as-mine face and shrugged.

"It's a yes-or-no question. Are the Yankees or are they not your mother's team?"

"It's upstate New York. So they'd have to be, right?"

"You tell me. She's your mother." His eyes narrowed. "Winter," he said, which was what he called me when he was annoyed at me. "There are no maybes in Jeopardy! You know the rules. Don't pose a clue without knowing the answer."

"You're right. Sorry."

"Is she really a baseball fan?"

"Apparently."

Brown made a shooing motion with his hand, exactly the way my mother had when I asked her which team she liked.

"If your mother's a baseball fan and you don't know her team, what else don't you know about her?"

He wasn't being unkind. It was a simple question. A wonderment more than a question. A musing. But it was the kind of question that wedged itself into your chest and didn't go away.

....

Facts I Knew About Tamar Winter for $800: 1) She graduated from Sterns High School at age seventeen and 2) immediately tried to head south to Florida for adventure and 3) to get away from Sterns and her father and 4) the memories of her mother, who had died earlier that year, but 5) she was raped at a party in Utica and 6) got pregnant with me and my twin sister, Daphne, who was 7) stillborn, so 8) it had been just me and her for all the years since and 9) it was still just me and her. Me and my mother. My mother and me.

Brown's question — *What else don't you know about her?* — was not answerable. It was a situation of unknown unknowns.

"It would have to be the Yankees," he said. Still frowning. "It's upstate New York — who the hell else would she root for. Seriously, she never talked baseball with you?"

"Seriously, she never did."

But maybe she had. Maybe she had, and I just didn't remember, or didn't notice, or was so uninterested that it was as if she'd said nothing. Was there a whole part of my childhood that I had forgotten? That I was leaving out? *Memory is everything that's ever happened to you,* I would have said when I was a child. Everything, held in images and conversations and knowledge buried safely in the recesses of your brain, with *safely* being the operative word. Something that could not be taken away from you. But I was no longer sure of that.

Whatever was happening on the outside with my mother, was there a secret place inside of her that still knew everything, remembered everything, was full of pictures and conversations in which she was still herself, a self that couldn't be touched? Rooms within rooms within rooms, and all of them invisible.

At night sometimes, when I came in late from the porch wrapped in the quilt, bottle of Jack dangling from my fingers, I looked at the photo propped up on the kitchen shelf. Sometimes I talked to it. "Ma? Who took that photo of you? What's that look on your face?" She said nothing. Her face was tilted, her eyes looking past me. As if she were seeing beyond me into another room, as if something good — something wonderful, from the way her eyes were lit up — was about to happen. But the photo was taken a long time ago. It was worn and soft, Xerox color copy turning streaky with age. The place where the curl of tape had held it to the photo of orange-snowsuited me was worn almost through.

When I was with her these days we turned on the television in the Plant Room and we sat together on the couch, calling out *Jeopardy!* answers. On a recent visit, one of the categories was Iconic Singer-Songwriters of the 20th Century. Clue: The singer who penned "Suzanne" for $800. Tamar slammed her hand down on the couch.

"Who is it, Ma?"

On television, a history professor had guessed Neil Diamond. Wrong. He was back to zero now. Next to me, Tamar pounded on the couch again. She was looking at me, something angry and frantic in her eyes. Her mouth was half open.

"Ma?"

She shook her head impatiently. Furiously. She knew the answer but it wouldn't come out. She clutched the book I had brought for her that week—*A Tree Grows in Brooklyn*—and held it out like an offering to the word gods. What had the clue been again? Singer who penned "Suzanne." *Think, Clara.* "Suzanne." "Suzanne takes you down to her place near the river."

"It's your boy Leonard, Ma," I said. "Leonard Cohen. Right?"

Her face eased. She nodded. The words had gone floating by her and spun themselves up into the ether before she could grab hold and bring them down to earth. Now they were back in her hands.

"You got it, Ma. You just won eight hundred dollars."

Leonard Cohen was my mother's favorite singer. The whole time I was growing up, she sang his songs, "Hallelujah," especially. "Hallelujah" in the kitchen, "Hallelujah" by the woodpile, "Hallelujah" in the strawberry field. "Hallelujah" times a thousand.

"Nice work. You beat Mr. Professor."

She turned to regard me, her daughter, the woman who kept showing up and calling her Ma.

"What's your line of work again?"

In her real life, my mother would never have asked a question like that, because in her real life, she wouldn't have needed to. In her real life, she would have known who I was and what my line of work was. *Shhh, Clara. This* is *her real life.*

"Words," I said. "I'm a word girl."

....

To move back home-ish was to move into a new world, a world of displaced time and misplaced memories. After I walked my mother back down the hall to her room, I drove home and wrapped myself up in quilts on the front porch chair. Me and my bottle of Jack Daniel's, the fairy lights twinkling in the dark, no mosquitoes or bears, a deer once in a while. The flock of wild turkeys muttered their way over the bluff behind the cabin — they were birds of dusk — but I didn't move.

What went wrong between you and your mother? Sunshine had asked. A single moment, that was what had gone wrong, a moment that got away from us and turned into silence and walls. And now I was out of time, wasn't I? I never thought it would go so fast, did I? Was a television quiz show really the only thing my mother and I had left? Because if so, it was not enough. Not anywhere near enough. *Had we but world enough and time, had we but time enough. In a minute there is time for decisions and revisions which a minute will reverse . . . I have heard the mermaids singing, each to each. I do not think that they will sing to me.* Fragments of disconnected poems floated around me in the darkness and turned into tiny italicized word trains trundling along the bottom of my mind. *I have heard the mermaids singing, each to each. I do not think that they will sing to me.*

Sing to me, mermaids. Please sing to me.

Panic churned within, skin-prickle-heart-pound panic. I took a long pull on Jack and then another. And then another. Then I called Annabelle Lee, the choir director, my mother's best and only friend. *Don't call her Annabelle Lee,* my mother's voice sounded in my head. *She hates that name.*

"Do you even know what that name is from?" I once asked my mother. Seventeen. Know-it-all.

"Some poem," she said. "Some long poem that her father liked."

Right back at me. No backing down. She didn't know the poem and she didn't care that she didn't know the poem. Another difference between the two of us.

We were still on the porch, me and Jack in his bottle and the fairy lights twinkling in their almost-unseen way, when I heard the choir director's car grinding and moaning around the curves of Turnip Hill Road. Once heard, the sound of Annabelle Lee's car could not be unheard. It was an ancient Impala, kept running by the sheer force of Annabelle's will, her math-and-music mind, and the parts she scavenged from Ron Hubbard's car graveyard. She had insisted on driving up from Sterns when I called, said she wanted to see the Tiny, as she'd heard it referenced in town.

"Forsooth," I said to Jack, "what car through yonder woods approaches?"

The urge to uncap Jack and take another long swig overcame me; I fought it. The urge to leap out of my chair and run inside and turn off the lights and lock the door overcame me; I fought it. The urge to jump into the Subaru—the keys were already in my pocket—overcame me; I would've done it had the Impala not already been mumbling its way up the bumps and rocks and exposed roots of the driveway. Annabelle Lee slid across the vast expanse of the front seat to the passenger's side, because that was the only door that still opened, and emerged. I picked Jack up by the scruff of his neck and dangled him in the air. If battle was upon us, Jack was my ally. It would be the two of us against the one of Annabelle. 'Tis enough, 'twill suffice. A fisher cat screamed from somewhere nearby. It sounded like a girl in peril.

"Are you angry at me?" I said.

That was not what I intended to say. The sound of my voice, the childish tone of it, made *me* angry, and I was me. Annabelle Lee hauled herself up onto the porch. Hauled. Heaved. Hefted. Hove. *H* words went scrolling along the bottom of my mind. The porch planks groaned under her weight.

"A little," she said. "You've been here a year and you never returned my calls. A lot of time's gone by."

"I'm trying to make up for that. For lost time. I'm trying to fill in the *blanks*."

It seemed important to emphasize the word *blanks*. Hello, my name is Clara Winter and I am powerless over italics. Heads nodded around a table, murmuring, *Hi, Clara. Hi, Clara. Hi, Clara.* Jack was still in my hand and I swung him back and forth to make the italics stop but they kept coming. Annabelle Lee — it was hard to think of her as anything but that, hard to call her by just her given name — regarded me.

"Maybe I can help fill them in, those blanks. Some of them, anyway."

"She's *my* mother, though."

"She's *my* best friend. And *you're* the one who called *me*, finally, at least tonight."

Annabelle Lee had seen my italics and raised them with her own. She shifted weight and the porch floor groaned again. Unlike my weightless mother, whose singing voice was bigger than anything else about her, Annabelle Lee's organlike contralto matched her body.

"Still the distance between you two, Clara?"

"It's not that far. I go down there every other day."

"That's not the kind of distance I'm talking about," she said, a tinge of scorn in her voice. Impatience. *Breathe in, Clara. Breathe out. Regard Annabelle's scorn and impatience with calm and detachment.*

"There was a lot of stuff back then," I said.

"There's always a lot of stuff," Annabelle said. "It's called being human."

Calm. Detachment. Fake it till you make it. "I'm trying to figure things out," I said. "Before it's too late" — she opened her mouth, about to snap out more scorn, but I held up my hand and she stopped — "and I figured you might be able to shed light."

To shed light. That sounded good. Annabelle nodded, wary but willing. *Okay. Good job, Clara.* Begin with small questions, such as why had my mother gone to choir practice every Wednesday for more than thirty years but never sung in church, not once? Why had she always eaten out of cans and jars? Those kinds of questions. Mild questions. Beginner questions.

But that was not what I did.

"For example, do you know what happened between her and Asa that night?" I said. "Why he broke up with me the very next day? Why she literally, physically, ripped up my MVCC application? Why she didn't tell me that whole fall that the two of you were plotting and scheming to get me out of the state? And what about the house? Why didn't she tell me she was selling the house?"

My voice was rising. There was nothing calm or detached about it. Annabelle Lee shook her head.

"The *house*," I said. "*Our* house. Who would do that, Annabelle? Tell me, what kind of person does that?"

She was still shaking her head. Then she turned and lowered herself off the porch, one step at a time. Bracelets jangled on her wrists. Rhinestones shone on her loafers, rhinestones she had no doubt glued on herself. There could not be two more different friends than my mother and Annabelle Lee, the choir director.

"Call me when you grow up," she said. "Call me when you want to *talk*."

She opened the passenger door and slid back across the seat to the driver's side and coaxed the engine to life again. Then she rolled down the window. Her white face loomed in the darkness, a pale moon. "It's a two-way street, Clara."

....

"Ma, I saw Annabelle Lee last night."

Across the polished floor beyond the Plant Room doorway, Sylvia raised her head and smiled at me. She loved Annabelle Lee, who visited once a week, before choir practice. Everyone at the place where my mother lived now loved Annabelle Lee. They thought she was great. So funny, so in-your-face, so stalwart and strong. My mother tilted her head at me.

"Where?" She looked around, as if Annabelle Lee might be hiding somewhere in the Plant Room.

"In Old Forge. At the cabin."

My mother looked confused. Old Forge? The cabin? I plowed on anyway.

"Ma, can I ask you something? Why did you never sing in the choir?"

Sylvia was looking at me again, wary now. *No, I will not meet your eyes, Sylvia. I'm talking with my mother. Yes, there's a weird tone in my voice.* The force of Sylvia's gaze was strong. She was impelling me to look at her, doing everything in her power to drag my eyes to hers, but I would not. My mother shook her head. She held both hands up in front of her, as if to stop me.

"I never asked you that question and I figured I should," I said. "There are a bunch of things I never asked you."

Sylvia's powers were too strong. I had to look at her. There was a warning in her eyes, a *Don't upset the patient* kind of warning, not that she would have put it that way. *You were the one who told me to say what I had to say now.* I beamed that sentence to her telepathically, but the warning in her eyes stayed. How should I do this, then, Sylvia? How should I ask my mother the questions I never asked her? My mother held aloft the book I had brought her that week — *Heidi* — as if it were a remote, and aimed it at the Plant Room television.

"I'm sorry, Ma," I said. "You don't have to answer anything you don't want to answer." From the corner of my eye I saw Sylvia relax and turn back to the desk. "Let's watch our show."

She nodded and I pressed the orange *on* button on the remote. It was time for the *Jeopardy!* contestant interview, an excruciating segment in which Trebek pried a little background information out of each one. The contestants must have been coached to act peppy and interesting, which made them the opposite: dull and stiff. An optometrist began with a story about his daughter's birthday and how, instead of whacking a piñata with a baseball bat, she whacked him on the butt.

"Oh, my," Trebek said. "Well!"

That was the Trebek method. He ever so slightly cut off each contestant with that abrupt *Well!* and moved on to the next. The second contestant, a former-teacher-now-stay-at-home-mother-of-seven, told the tale of how she once accidentally locked herself into a bathroom stall overnight. The third contestant, a man who wrote a "Single Dad Cooks" column in his local newspaper, told how he once rode a horse blindfolded and facing backward in order to impress a date.

"Oh, my!" Trebek said, and "Oh, my!" Tamar said, in exact imitation.

"This is the painful part of the show," I said.

"This is the *insufferable* part of the show," she said, and she aimed *Heidi* at the television again. She sounded exactly like the old Tamar, back when she lived full-time in the same world as I did, the Tamar who would correct me, who would speak her mind. I turned to her—what could I say, quick quick quick, to keep her here with me?—but just like that, she was gone again.

Jeopardy! was not a game of chance. It was a game of knowledge and skill and quickness, of how fast could you press the buzzer, and how fast could your mind whisk through possibilities to settle on the right answer, and how fast could you calculate a bet? When it came to the Daily Double, and again in Final Jeopardy!, contestants had a choice. Bet small and safe or bet it all. Most didn't bet it all. Betting it all was risky. Bet it all and there was a chance you would lose it all.

But there was a chance you would win it all too.

If we were the Daily Double, my mother and I, what might we lose, and what might we win, either of us, both of us, if we talked, if we really talked? If we un-ambered ourselves, un-armored ourselves, and hashed it all out, with *it* being our life together? It was late in the day for that, but was it too late? Behold the baffled kings, side by side on the green couch, remote control pointed at the television, composing nothing.

....

Brown's legal name was Court Brown—Court Jefferson Brown, to be precise. We were up late, drinking gin with apple cider and talking, when I learned that fact. We were in the college-freshmen-trade-secrets-late-at-night phase of our lives.

"Samantha Lacey Rourke," Sunshine said. "Irish on my father's side, German on my mother's."

"Clara Winter," I said. "No middle name. British and French Basque on my mother's side. Not sure of the other side."

Saying "the other side" meant I could avoid saying the word "father" or "dad."

"Court Jefferson Brown," Brown said. "No clue on either side."

Sunshine looked from him to me and back again. "Ask your parents," she said. "It's a simple question."

"No it's not," Brown and I said, exactly at the same time. Something passed between us, a flash of understanding. *There is more to the story,* was what the look he gave me said, even though neither of us knew what the more to the other's story was.

Sunshine saw the look and tried to catch up. "Why not?"

Brown shrugged. So did I. Her eyes went from him to me. She knew she was missing out, but on what? Many people in that situation would withdraw. They would feel shunned and turn bristly, peeved at the silence. I sensed her wavering. Should she press on? Should she drop the matter and know that already an invisible wall was up that wasn't going to come down from here on in? We were three days into our first year of college. I pulled my knees up to my chest and wrapped my arms around my legs. Something flickered across Sunshine's face. She had made her decision.

"You guys are telepathically saying something important to each other right now. I can feel it. So fill me in. Both of you."

I laughed. It was the kind of laugh that was about surprise. And relief. It was the no-bullshit-ness of her statement. In the three seconds that it took Sunshine to articulate what she saw happening between Brown and me — to decide that she would press on instead of retreat — I saw the kind of person she was. She would not take it personally, she would not feel left out, and she was intent on finding out the whole story. She wanted to know me, and she wanted to know Brown. She was not a surface person. From that moment on, I trusted her.

Brown must have trusted her too, because I still remember how he looked down at his knees — we were all sitting on a braided rug that I had bought for eight dollars at a garage sale — but he spoke.

"I'm a foundling."

Foundling. *Found. Ling.* A beautiful and terrible word. A baby in a blanket, left on the steps. A baby in a basket, floating down the river. A baby with dark, unblinking eyes.

"A *foundling?*" Sunshine said, and the way she said it was just like the way it was scrolling across the bottom of my brain. "Like an orphan? That kind of foundling?"

"Yeah. I was found on the steps of the courthouse in Jefferson City,

Missouri, when I was a baby. Maybe a day old. My foster parents ended up adopting me."

"And they never found your"—I could tell she was about to say "real" but stopped herself—"birth parents?"

"No."

We sat for a minute, absorbing. It was like the beginning of a fairy tale, except that this wasn't the Middle Ages and *foundling* was a rare and seldom-used word. It was hard to imagine a baby left on the steps of a building. But there was Brown, Court Jefferson Brown, alive and breathing and sitting on a braided rug in a dorm room in New Hampshire.

"So you could be, like, anything?" Sunshine said.

"Or nothing."

"Everyone's something."

"Yeah, but what? A mix of brown, I guess. Brownish."

That was the moment when his nickname was born. Brown *was* brownish. His eyes were brown and almondish, his hair was dark and curly, his skin was golden brown. He was beautiful in that muscled way that some boys are. Most lose it by their late twenties, but Brown hadn't. He was still beautiful at thirty-two, not that he seemed to know it, or had ever known it.

Then it was my turn.

....

"Okay, so your mom is French Basque and British. What about your dad?"

I remembered thinking that Sunshine must have a father who loved her with that easy kind of love you saw sometimes. The kind of love where, when she was little, he must have picked her up and put her on his shoulders and carried her around that way. Where he taught her how to play catch, tossing a tennis ball back and forth until she graduated to a mitt and a softball. Where he used to sing "You Are My Sunshine" to her, until she was known as Sunshine instead of Samantha. Where he went to all her recitals and games and cheered her on. Where he cried when he dropped her off at college. Kids who grew up that way called their fathers "Dad."

"I don't have a dad," I said. "Some guy raped my mother at a party and I'm the result."

I had not ever told anyone that. I had never said those words aloud. The words came out as if that was the way I thought of myself, a product of something bad, something evil. *Some guy. Rape. Result.* They were harsh words and they hung ugly in the air of the small room. Just the sound of them made me close my eyes, as if somehow that would make them less harsh. My mother at my age, at a party like the kind I was going to all the time, back in those days. It wasn't something I could bear to think about, the thought of something that awful happening to her. But the minute I said the words and they were out there, and my new friends were absorbing them into themselves, something in me eased.

"It wasn't just me either," I said. "I had this twin sister, and she died when we were born. It's a bad story."

I wanted to apologize. It *was* a bad story. It took the light out of the conversation. When I opened my eyes Sunshine and Brown were both looking at me, sadness in their eyes.

"I'm sorry," I said.

"For what?"

"Being a downer."

"Well," Sunshine said, and I could tell she was searching for words. "It's not all bad. I mean, she got you out of the deal, right?"

Brown clapped his hands. "Yes! She did! And you're awesome!" he said, in that way he had back then, when suddenly something struck him as full of happiness and he lit up with the joy of it and said words like *awesome* and *fantastic* and *cool* and they all ended with exclamation marks. ! ! ! In those moments Brown was like a trick birthday candle, the kind that relit themselves by magic even after you blew them out. He could still be that way. Just not as often.

It had been fourteen years since that night, when we were all eighteen and we used to go to parties together and drink spiked Kool-Aid out of plastic-bag-lined garbage cans with enormous straws poking out of them. We used to dance together at The Excuse, the three of us holding hands and hopping around the tiny dance floor. We used to go on long bike rides to celebrate the end of exams, bought tubes of cookie dough at the grocery store and baked them late at night in the disgusting base-ment dorm kitchen, backpacked part of the Appalachian Trail for a few weeks each summer with the goal of finishing the whole thing eventu-ally, a goal that had not yet been reached.

A year or so after graduation we started going to the weddings of our college friends. We made toasts and clinked glasses and Sunshine had flings with groomsmen and Brown had flings with bridesmaids and I had flings with no one. We danced and drank and laughed and cheered. We got hotel rooms next to each other and in the mornings we got up and drank pots of coffee, cream for me, sugar for Sunshine, black for Brown.

We were all living in Boston and I was with them the night it finally dawned on them, and me, that they were in love with each other, and we laughed and laughed, in relief and surprise. I was "friend of honor" when they got married on that pretty hill by the orchard north of cam-pus, the orchard where we had picked apples every fall of our four years together. My friend-of-honor toast was structured like *Jeopardy!*, our fa-vorite game even back then: six categories and five sentences for each. It was long and complicated and everyone loved it and laughed, not because it was funny, even though it was, but because we were all so happy. They had figured it out, Sunshine and Brown, they had figured out something essential about themselves and about each other, which seemed to mean they had figured out something essential about this world, and that meant that the rest of us could too.

We didn't know that cancer would come to Sunshine so young, that she would lose all those baby-making essentials, as she called them, and that within a few years the two of them would flee Boston for the mountains—right here in Old Forge, where we had all three spent that summer before our junior year working, the summer they had fallen in love with my Adirondacks—to *live more deeply*, as they told people when asked, because if it worked for Thoreau then maybe it would work for them too. We couldn't have predicted that the day would come when I, who had not once considered moving back to the land from whence I sprang, would be living in a cabin a mile away from them, here in this tiny town perched on the edge of these old, old mountains.

That's the thing, though. You think you can predict, but you can't.

. . . .

Sunshine and Brown and I talked about flying once—the topic was the first time each of us had ever been on a plane—in another of those long get-to-know-one-another conversations our first year of college. Sunshine had been seven, an unaccompanied minor going to visit her grandparents in Florida. Brown had been a baby, moving from Missouri to Boston with his parents. I listened to them talk about those first flights and all the myriad flights they had been on since, to the Caribbean, to Europe, Brown to Africa and Sunshine to Japan, which airlines were best, which had direct flights where, which logo looked coolest painted on the side of the plane. How Sunshine always had to remember to book her flights now under her legal name, which was Samantha; otherwise it was no end of trouble at security.

I said nothing.

I had been on one flight in my life at that point, when a college in Ohio that liked my early test scores flew me out to visit in the late spring of my junior year at Sterns High School. Tamar had made me go, despite the fact that I had told her I would not go farther than a half-hour drive from Asa, who had graduated the year before. She drove me to the Syracuse airport and parked in short-term parking and she waited with me at the gate—this was before the Twin Towers—until I was onboard and looking out the tiny oval window, trying but unable to find her through the huge glass window of the concourse. Where was my mother? Had she left the minute I headed down the passenger ramp? Was she already in the station wagon, hauling exact change for the thruway toll out of the glove compartment? Or was she still there, in the terminal, waiting to make sure the plane that I was on took off safely and made it up into the clouds before she relinquished her hold and turned to leave?

I was seventeen years old.

I stared out the tiny oval window and watched the ground crew load the suitcases and duffels into the belly of the plane I was sitting in. I fastened my seat belt when the flight attendant told me to. A boy with big orange ear protectors waved the plane away from the terminal. The runway markings rolled beneath my window as we lumbered our way to the line of planes waiting at the end of the runway. It was just like waiting at an intersection for the light to change, I remembered thinking.

Then it was our turn. The engines groaned and roared as they revved up, and the plane rattled and rumbled and then smoothed out as we gathered speed down the runway. At a certain point, when I sensed we were about to leave the earth, the earth that I had never left before, the earth that I had always been firmly attached to, I held my breath for luck. And then the snub nose of the plane pointed skyward and we were borne aloft.

Helpless.

That was how it felt to me. I was a passenger on an airplane made of aluminum and rubber and steel, and the only thing that nonpilot I could do was sit with my seat belt on and look out the window. Everything was out of my hands and nothing, nothing in that world was under my control and because of that, everything felt sacred.

The plastic soda cup, the square of paper napkin that the flight attendant handed me, the barf bag that I saved to bring back to Tamar because it would make her laugh, the button that, when pressed, reclined the seat I sat in, the *SkyMall* catalog that I read cover to cover as if it were a magazine, every page filled with things I had never known I wanted or needed, things that existed in this world but had been unknown to me until just now: all of it, full of wonder.

I took my eyes away from the window, on that first flight, and searched for someone. Anyone. But they were reading their newspapers, or listening to their headphones, or their heads were tilted back in sleep and snores. The flight attendant was busy at the front of the cabin, her back to me. I turned my head halfway and met a middle-aged man's eyes. He was two rows behind, sitting on the aisle. I wanted to tell him—what? Something. Something that meant something. Something about this flight, the fact that we were two human beings breathing and thinking and living at this very moment, so high in the sky. I looked at him helplessly.

"It's a miracle, isn't it?" he said to me.

Those were his exact words. You might think, he was two rows behind her and across the aisle, the plane's engines were no doubt roaring, what makes her think he was talking to her, there is no way she could have heard what he was saying. You would be wrong. We were kindred spirits, that man in his business suit and me in my jeans, filled with a helpless wonder.

Sometimes still, when I drove the curves and hills and hollows of the land where I grew up, or when my fingers remembered the hours of music they had brought forth from that winged instrument in the basement practice room, back when I was just learning to play the piano, or when I sat in my chair on the porch and the fireflies, those miraculous creatures thought by some to live on air—*air*—were floating about me, I thought of that man in that suit on that plane. I saw his eyes, those eyes that had met mine, and I heard his words again.

Did he ever think of me? The girl I used to be, turning around in her seat looking for someone, anyone, who wasn't asleep, someone who knew how she felt.

....

There are people in this world who instinctively know how you feel. Even if they don't know *you,* they sense what is happening inside you. The man on the plane was like that, and so was Asa, Asa who came back to me still, unbidden.

Something about Blue Mountain's eyes when he looked down at me, lying on the floor of the arts center waiting for my heart to calm down, reminded me of Asa. I didn't know Asa when he was little, but maybe he was like that, skinless, growing up in that house of chronic tension. Martha Chamberlain with the suspicious eyes and the ready anger, Eli with the smile that came to his face every time he looked at his son.

Or when he looked at me. Eli was not stingy with love.

Asa grew up allowing others in, especially kids. I pictured him the way he used to be at Camp. Camp wasn't a summer camp the way they were now, with classrooms and learning goals and measurable out-comes, and it must have had a different name, an actual name, but all the kids called it Camp, and we did too. Asa and a few others ran it themselves at the elementary school, under the semi-supervision of a fifth grade teacher who needed extra money. Someone was in charge of snacks and Band-Aids, someone else was in charge of story time, and Asa cheered the kids on at the playground. That was it. That was Camp.

But by the end of each week, under Asa's watchful eye, the kid who was scared of the monkey bars could swing from one to the other like an actual monkey, the kid whose foot couldn't connect with the kick-ball was walloping them out to left field, and the kid who was scared of going down the slide was going down the slide. Maybe he was slid-ing down on Asa's lap, but he was going down the slide, right? Which counted with Asa.

Everything counted, with Asa. He collected things from the woods: a fallen pinecone, a small piece of quartzite, a double acorn, and they became the awards he handed out at the end of the week. A pinecone for Monkey Bars. A double acorn for Slide. Quartzite for Kindness. The kids loved those prizes. I watched one Friday as he leaned out the play-ground pirate ship window and made a small speech about the winner of each prize and then led the applause. Every kid got a prize and every-one cheered. Everything with Asa was simple like that. The kids loved him for it. So did I.

....

"Are there things that you two don't talk about?"

That was my question to Sunshine and Brown. I had cooked us din-ner in the fire pit at the far edge of the cabin clearing. Carrots chopped by Brown, onions chopped by Sunshine, who was one of those peo-ple immune to their crying power, potatoes and sausage diced by me, then drizzled with olive oil and sealed into foil packets and put into the coals. Now we were sitting outside the ring of rocks, on the benches I had made out of old boards nailed onto stumps, drinking the wine they had brought, and waiting for the packets to cook. It was early evening in early October, the falling sun filtering through the white pines that ringed the cabin. Just over one year since I had moved back. One year of keeping the enormous secret I had promised my mother I would keep, the secret that was too hard to keep. But a promise I had made, and keep it I would.

One year of walking around in my body, this body that might or might not be carrying a gene mutation. One year of thinking with these brain cells that might or might not already be forming plaque. One year of not knowing if the things I couldn't remember were things I couldn't remember because I was a human being or because I was a human being who carried the eFAD gene mutation.

"You mean, are there things that we argue about?" Brown said. "Subjects we disagree on so deeply that it's not worth bringing them up?"

"Like if I were libertarian and Brown were socialist," Sunshine said, "that kind of thing?"

"No. More like, are there things that neither of you talks about with anyone. Secrets."

"Small secrets, like some kind of strange toenail-clipping technique?" Brown said. "Or a big secret, like me being a serial killer?"

"Wait, are you a serial killer, Brown?" Sunshine said. "Because, as your wife, that is something I would like to know."

"No, I am not a serial killer. Although think about it. Would I tell you if I were?"

He picked up the skewer we were using to test the doneness of the foil packets, held it high in the air in both hands, then ran it straight through the packet nearest him. Creepy.

"Yeah, that kind of thing," I said. "Something big."

"We don't talk about my disease," Sunshine said. "We don't talk about survival rates, life expectancy, et cetera. We don't use the word *cancer*."

"That's true," Brown said. "We hate talking about that kind of shit."

"Do you think about it, though?"

"Sometimes," Sunshine said. She laced her hands over the place where her breasts used to be. "Sometimes I think about my boobs. I miss them."

"I miss your boobs too," Brown said. "Your boobs were gorgeous. We should have had someone paint a picture of you naked before they got chopped off. An oil painting. Then we could've hung it in the living room and said our prayers before your boobs every morning."

"If we were the prayer type," Sunshine said.

"Which we're not," Brown said.

I knelt by the coals and used the tongs to extract each of the foil packets. Done. Paper plates and forks and foil packets all around. It was the in-between time, before true darkness fell over the face of the forest and the fairy lights began to glimmer.

"So, the c-word," Sunshine said. "That's a big thing we don't talk about."

"But you *both* don't talk about it," I said. "It's not a secret. You both don't talk about it because you already *have* talked about it, talked it all the way through."

"And all the way back again," Brown said. "Put a fork in it, it's done. Overdone in fact."

"And what I'm thinking about is something else," I said. "Something like a big thing, a huge thing that you just carry around inside yourself, an awful thing that no one else in the world knows about."

They were quiet. I looked down at my paper plate. Steam rose from the opened foil. Everything was done, cooked to perfection, bits of char here and there on the roasted carrots and potatoes. Smell of onions and sausage. In my head I pictured the coyotes and fisher cats and raccoons, watchful in the brush and forest beyond the clearing.

"Clara?" Brown said. "Is there something you're not telling us?"

....

My messed-up heart saved me from answering.

"Your heart thing again?" Sunshine said, at the same time that Brown said, "Oh Jesus, again with the heart. Lie down, Clara."

I lay down on the bench by the fire pit, staring up at the crown of the nearest white pine, my heart fluttering in my chest. Above me they were talking. *It always freaks me out,* Brown said, *no matter how many times I've seen it happen,* and Sunshine was saying, *At some point she's going to once and for all get sick of having to lie down in the middle of whatever she's doing and then she'll finally get it fixed,* and Brown was saying,

It's not even that complicated a thing, right? It's not even like actual heart surgery, right? and Sunshine was saying, *It's really taking a toll on her. She might not be able to see it, but we can. And, like, what about driving? That can't be safe, right?*

"Hello. I'm right here. I can hear you."

Except that I must not have said that out loud, because neither of them heard me. They talked on, murmuring in the whispery way they did whenever my heart flared up and I had to lie down, about the first time they ever saw it happen, that autumn day freshman year, how we were sitting on the top row of bleachers at the football field and then suddenly I was lying down. *Right there on the bleacher, remember?* Brown said. *Of course I remember,* Sunshine said. *I remember thinking, Wait, I don't know CPR, why didn't I take CPR in high school, because it looks as if my roommate is having a heart attack right here on this bleacher and if I had only taken CPR then I would know what to do.*

On and on their voices went. They were used to waiting for my heart to slow down, used to telling others, *Nah, she's fine—it's just a weird heart thing. Benign.* Just then my heart reverted into its normal rhythm —*beat, beat, beat*—and I opened my eyes.

"Clara? Are you crying?"

Winter was only weeks away. My mother was disappearing and everything I should have resolved with her—everything that I must have thought there would be time to resolve, decades hence—was not resolved. Did I know my mother? Did she know me?

"She is," Sunshine said. Her voice was full of a pained wonder. "She's crying."

Brown turned to Sunshine and talked low and fast, as if I had just been hurtled into an emergency room on a stretcher and he were an emergency room nurse gathering information from the EMTs surrounding me. As if he were trying to assess the severity of the situation. Triage.

"Have you ever seen her cry? I've never seen her cry."

"Once," Sunshine whispered back. "Only once. The time she told me about her boyfriend."

"The Asa boyfriend who broke up with her and then died in Afghanistan?"

"Brown. There's been only one boyfriend. So, yes."

Then Sunshine was up and kneeling on the other side of me, holding both my hands. She smelled the way she always did, lemon soap with a side of rosemary and wool. All those baby hats.

"What's going on, honey?"

Her voice was calm, but she betrayed herself with the word "honey." Sunshine never used that word unless she was worried. She was not a sweetie honey sugar kind of person. "Tell us what's going on."

"I can't. I promised her I wouldn't. It's the least I can do."

But "Clara," Brown said, and "Clara," Sunshine said, and I could hear in their voices that they were going to sit there as long as it took, as long as was necessary, until "Spit it out," and finally I opened my mouth and out it came: How I had come north for her birthday, how I had found Mr. Orange Juice in the dishes cabinet, how my mother had stood there frowning at me, those withered geranium blossoms in her hands, how after I returned to Florida the state trooper stopped her on Starr Hill for erratic driving, after which William T. called me and said "Clara, you might want to come up for another visit," how I had flown back up and visited the doctor with my mother, and then how only a week after that I pulled into our driveway in Sterns with the Subaru loaded to the gills to find the Amish family there, Amish kids running around, an outhouse standing in the backyard where the chokecherries used to be, how recently my mother had turned to me, down in the place where she lived now, looked at me and said *How do I know you again?* And eFAD. The gene mutation, the fifty-fifty chance, the fear and terror and torment that it might be inside me too, the what-iffing that went along with that: Should I get the test? What if I carried the gene, what then? What then, what then, what then.

All of it.

I talked, they listened. It took a long time and it wasn't coherent and it all came out in no understandable order but neither of them said anything. No asking for clarification, no interruptions, no wait-a-minutes. A misshapen door on misaligned hinges to a tiny, ugly room, a lost room inside me being pried open. All the old, dead air inside leaked out right there at the fire pit, where we sat with our plates. Sunshine and

Brown were human green plants breathing it in so that out it came as regular air, air that we all could breathe.

"Jesus," Brown said, when I was done, when I'd filled them in on everything. How early-onset sometimes moved faster than the standard variety, how she was now at Stage 6b and probably on her way to 6c, and did they know that there were only seven stages total. How when I found the orange juice carton in the dishes cabinet, a lukewarm interloper among the bowls and plates, I had known what William T. Jones and Annabelle Lee must already have guessed at. How my stomach knew, my body knew, how something tiny and awful began crawling its way through me then and there. How it had not stopped crawling since.

....

"So that's the deal," I said. "And now I've broken the promise I made to her. The one promise she asked of me. All that world-traveler stuff I told you? Lies. Every bit of it."

"First off," Sunshine said, "before we go into anything else, there is something that needs to be said. Which is that if you do carry that gene, the mutation thing, Brown and I will take care of you."

Right to the chase. No recriminations for not telling them before now, no chastising, no side-eye. That was Sunshine.

"Duh," Brown said. "That's a given."

"And if I kick the bucket, then Brown will carry on and take care of you solo," Sunshine added. That was also Sunshine. Cut and dried about the c-word and its ramifications. She poked Brown with her elbow and he nodded, which meant, *Yes, I will carry on.*

"So," Sunshine said, "is there anything that can be done in the here and now for The Fearsome?"

"No. Nothing. She's not eligible for any trials — too young, which is a totally screwed-up policy — and the drug she's on helps some but can't stop what's happening and all I can do is sit with her. Everything that got messed up between us is still messed up and I don't know how to fix it. She's going someplace where I can't. She's never coming back. All I can do is sit and listen and try to follow wheresoever she goeth."

Neither of them batted an eye at *wheresoever* or *goeth*. They had known me since we were eighteen; no eyes would be batted at anything I said or any way I said it.

"Am I doing everything I can do?" I said. "I don't know."

Brown's hands were keeping my one cold hand not-cold, and I pushed my other hand into his cupped palms too. Brown was always warm.

"Tell us what you're doing," Brown said. "Start with that."

"Spending time with her is what I'm doing. I go down there a few days a week and we walk around the halls. I bring her a book. We watch *Jeopardy!* together."

"Can she"—and then he stopped, but I knew what he was going to ask and so did Sunshine, because she finished the question for him—"follow along? Does she know what's going on?"

"It depends. Sometimes it's like she's not really there and other times she's weirdly good at it."

"I don't remember her being good at *Jeopardy!* back in the day," Sunshine said. "I don't remember her ever calling out any answers."

"Me either," Brown said.

"Maybe she was, though. Maybe she knew all the answers all that time and she never said anything because we were always yelling them out. See, that's part of what makes me nuts. Like, did I even know my mother?"

"What kid does?" Sunshine said. "Show me a kid who recognizes their parents as people and not just parents, and I'll show you a weirdo."

"I was a weirdo, though. Kind of."

"And you still are!" Brown said, in his exclamation-mark voice. "Kind of!"

"Did they tell you to do anything?" Sunshine said. "Anything more than visit, be there?"

"They told me to follow her."

"Like, literally? Down the hall or whatever?"

"Like metaphorically. Wherever she goes in her mind, it's my job to follow her there. Which could be any number of places. The other night she was on her way to choir practice."

That made them smile. It made me smile too. The kind of smile that you tried to hold back because it seemed wrong to find it funny, to find a woman with early-onset Alzheimer's funny, but somehow it was.

"Sometimes I talk to Dog about it," I said. "I look at his ashes and I talk it over with him. Is that weird?"

"Yes," Brown said, "but you're weird. As you just pointed out."

"I talk to Dog because he knew her," I said. "He was the only other living creature who was there with me and Tamar, living in our house, listening to us talk. He was the thing we both loved."

"Besides each other," Sunshine said. "You both loved each other."

"Love. You both *love* each other," Brown said. "Present tense."

....

"So what's the goal now?" Sunshine said. "What is within your power to do, for your mother or for yourself?"

"Good question, wife," Brown said. "Given that it's apparently a one-way street."

We were sitting on the porch now, all three of us, lined up on the edge with our legs hanging off, me in the middle. I was a human book and they were human bookends. The fairy lights glimmered on in their silent way, and the air was cold and crisp and tinged with smoke from the embers glowing in the fire pit. Brown and Sunshine were no strangers to good questions. Long ago they had asked themselves what was within their power to do about Sunshine's cancer and their lives in the face of it, and they had decided to think of it as a chronic illness. Like diabetes. Something to be neither encouraged nor denied, but managed.

"I don't know," I said.

"Not good enough," Sunshine said. "The phrase 'I don't know' is a filler phrase, used as an excuse when someone wants to avoid answering."

"A 'filler phrase'? What are you, the urban dictionary? I mean the rural dictionary?"

She would not be distracted. She butted up against me, and so did Brown on the other side. The human book was being mushed between its human bookends.

"Come on," she said. "Talk to us."

"What I want is not within my power," I said. "What I want is her, the way she was."

Her, the simple fact of her. Her in her lumber jacket chopping up firewood and tossing it onto the porch in that haphazard way. Her leaning up against the counter eating her goddamn artichoke hearts. Her walking me down the aisle at my wedding. Her as a grandmother. Jesus! Did I want a wedding? Did I want a baby? Neither of those things did I think about — my one and only boyfriend had been dead for seven years now — but there they were, images as fully formed as photos, hanging right there inside my head. Everything I didn't know, everything I now wanted, came crushing down inside me and squeezed my heart.

"But I can't go back in time, even though I wish I could," I said. "Get some answers, maybe. Figure things out."

"Dissolve the wedge between you?" Sunshine said, she who had been there for all the impatient phone calls, all the rolling eyes, all the brushing-off of my mother.

"We messed up," I said. "And now I'm losing her and she's losing me. I feel as if I don't know anything that went on inside her, back then."

"All the more reason to try," Sunshine said.

"You used to be a reporter," Brown said. "Put those reportorial skills back in action. Talk to her. Ask her questions. Interview her friends."

"Annabelle Lee is her only real friend."

"We are too," Sunshine said. "Brown and me."

"That doesn't mean you know her," I said. "Any more than I know her."

"Then get going," Sunshine said. "If Tamar is a locked trunk, your job is to pick the lock. Tick-tock. Hop to."

....

We ringed ourselves on the floor around the books-as-coffee-table. Where to begin? A list of people to talk to, which boiled down to "Annabelle." Brown got up to get Jack and in the getting stopped to peer at the photo propped on the shelf.

"Whoa. Is this The Fearsome? When was this taken?"

"No clue."

"She looks so"—he shook his head.

"Unfearsome?" I said.

"Exactly. She also looks, I hate to say it, but kind of hot. Is that weird?"

"For you to say or for Tamar to be?" Sunshine said. "In either case, the answer is no."

She got up to study the photo too. The two of them hovered before it, murmuring in their obnoxious merged-self way. *Look at that cute shirt,* Sunshine said, and *She looks so—what's the word—soft?* Brown said, and *Yes, that's the word,* Sunshine said, *so unlike the way I always think of her, which when you think about it is kind of unfair, isn't it?*

"Who took this photo?" Brown said to me. "And what's she looking at?"

I shrugged. "I don't know. It was stuck to the back of a photo of me as a baby."

"It's well-worn," he said, which was his kind of phrase. The alliteration. "Clearly been carried about, maybe in a wallet? Maybe in a back pocket?"

Brown put the photo back on the shelf, smoothing it into place with the tips of his fingers as if it were precious. As if it were valuable. An heirloom. Which maybe it was, the mystery photo, Tamar with the soft eyes and soft smile. He lowered himself back to the floor and thunked the bottle of Jack down on the books-as-coffee-table.

"Think of it like this," he said. He picked up his phone, ready to take notes. "If she's at Stage Six-b, we're halfway through the game. We're already starting the Daily Double. All the bets are twice what they started out as, and you are the losing contestant. Every category, every clue, you've got to slam the buzzer fast and hard. Even if you don't know the answer."

Sunshine began crocheting a scallion hat. Crocheting, even the pretend crocheting she sometimes did when she'd forgotten her bag of wool, helped her focus.

"Let's think categories," she said. "What do you most want or need to know about your mother?"

"Why she only ate out of cans and jars," I said. "Why she moved herself into that place without telling me. What she and Asa were talking about the night before he broke up with me. Why she practiced with the church choir for thirty years but never went to church. Why she got a long-term-care policy. Why she made me go to college two states away. Shit, I don't know. Everything. Anything."

"Whoa," Brown said. "My thumbs can't type that fast."

"You must know the answers to some of these questions already," Sunshine said. "Right?"

"No! I told you! She wouldn't tell me anything! And now we've run out of time!"

Exclamation marks, scrolling along. Sunshine was not intimidated by them. Sunshine was not intimidated by much of anything. She had been earlier in her life, though, hadn't she? Before she got cancer? Had there been a moment in there, a moment in the chemo room, maybe, or in the middle of an unsleeping night, that Sunshine had turned a corner in her mind, grown instantly out of being intimidated by anything ever again? Decided there was no more time in her life for things like intimidation, and, *poof,* zapped it right out of herself? Look at her, shaking her head. Look how fast the crochet hook moved between her fingers, flashing in and out of the pale green and white wool.

"There is no time," she said. "There's never time. People just think there is. They plod along as if it's an endless resource. As if it'll never run out."

Brown looked up from his typing. "Wait, did you say long-term-care policy?" he said. "That's kind of weird. Wasn't—isn't—she young to have one of those things?"

I had not even known what such a thing was until that first conversation with the doctor, when my mind first began to spin with what-ifs and wheres and hows.

"Early-onset often seems to progress quite fast," the doctor said. "This perception may actually result from the fact that most early-onset patients have already been living with the disease for quite a long time, but because they are so young, it's not recognized."

That would be my mother. Check.

"But Tamar is lucky in one way," the doctor said, "which is that she's got a very good long-term-care policy."

The idea of my mother with a long-term-care policy, or a policy of any kind — she was not a woman of words, nor was she a woman of insurance forms and legal documents, not to mention money, of which she had little — almost made me laugh. A long-term-care policy? The doctor had nodded, his lips pursed, as if this were excellent news.

"Exactly how is that luck?" I said.

My mother had never had a job of any kind that gave her anything but a biweekly paycheck, which was docked if she was sick or snowed in or spent a summer day taking her daughter to Old Forge. So if in fact there *was* a long-term-care policy, she must have gone out and gotten it on her own. I pictured her sitting in a chair on the opposite side of a desk in an insurance agency somewhere in Utica, no one in the spouse chair next to her, looking at brochures that the person opposite kept pushing at her.

"I hate the thought of that almost more than anything," I said to Sunshine and Brown. "That she went out and got that thing."

"Do you know when she got it?" Brown said.

"Years ago. Six or seven."

"Too early, then, to know about the" — when he hesitated, Sunshine filled in the rest of the sentence — "situation."

"Way too early. Her mother died young of cancer and her father died of emphysema. So why'd she get one? Those things are so expensive. She never had any money to spare."

One of the gene mutation what-ifs that tormented me was a long-term-care policy for myself. Should I get one? Now, just in case? The image of me in a nursing home sometimes rose up in my mind: me with a walker, me watching a blank television, me not knowing who Sunshine and Brown were when they came to visit. *Shhh, Clara.* Sunshine and Brown were nodding. That Tamar never had any money to spare was a known fact. Not that she ever talked about money worries. Not her style.

"It's a mystery," I said, and Sunshine laughed.

"How is it possibly a mystery?" she said. "Your mother got that policy for your sake. She didn't want to be a burden to her only child, for any indeterminate reason, in some indeterminate future."

The second she spoke, in that *duh* tone of voice, I knew she was right. It must have shown on my face, because they didn't say anything. They just sat there on the floor, elbows resting on the coffee table made of books, waiting.

"Goddammit," I said. "What else am I too stupid to figure out?"

"Lots, probably," Brown said, and that made Sunshine laugh, and then I was laughing too. We couldn't stop laughing, the same way we had laughed the night they told me Sunshine had cancer. By then, they had known for a week. They hadn't told anyone, not even their parents. We were all still living in Boston then. *Cancer?* I said, *you mean, like,* cancer-*cancer?* and they had nodded, both of them. Cancer-cancer. *But we're only twenty-four!* I said, and I could hear the exclamation mark at the end of the sentence. Because we were. We were twenty-four, and twenty-four-year-olds didn't get cancer. Except that some of them did, apparently, because here was Sunshine, looking healthy as always, but there it was, cancer. I had laughed—out of the sheer disbelief of it? Shock?—and then they started laughing too, and we all laughed and laughed. We choked on it, our laughter, and then we drank two bottles of wine and talked about cancer and chemo and wigs versus hats and all that stuff we had never imagined we'd be talking about, at our age— twenty-four! Twenty-four!—or ever, maybe, but there it was.

We didn't laugh the second and third time. We didn't feel so young anymore. Or maybe we did, and it felt so unfair.

"Remember the night you guys told me Sunshine had cancer and we couldn't stop laughing?"

They nodded, because they were my best friends and they knew exactly what I meant, which was that this situation with my mother and me felt as strange and weird as the fact of Sunshine's cancer had felt, so long ago.

"No one knows me like you guys," I said. "No one in the world."

"That's where you're wrong," Brown said. "Fearsome, we're coming for you."

Double Jeopardy

The next day, I saw the bartender in Adirondack Hardware. I was signing copies of *The Old Man* at a table next to a display of Dutch ovens, near the pickles and jams. The hardware ladies had brought me a cup of coffee and a blueberry scone for sustenance. The scone was dry, and every time I took a bite, crumbs were strewn over the table, my lap and the stack of books. People kept wandering up and examining the book while I brushed away crumbs and answered questions and inscribed the book if they wanted a copy.

If x = taking a bite and y = someone talking to me then x + y = crumb strewage. But at that particular moment no one was talking to me. No one was even in sight. Quick, Clara. One big bite. Then I looked up and there was the bartender, standing in front of the table. Smiling. He tilted his head to read my name on the cover of *The Old Man* stack.

"It's you," he said. "Clara Winter, the gimlet girl."

The scone had the best of me. All I could do was nod. He kept on smiling.

"That right there is the problem with scones," he said. "Can't stand the things."

That made me laugh, which made me open my mouth, which caused a crumb explosion. The bartender was one of those people who didn't look away. Didn't pretend he hadn't just seen something embarrassing. Was willing to acknowledge a scone disaster and by acknowledging it ally himself with the scone victim. He laughed too.

"Why didn't you go for a muffin? So much easier."

"I know. But a scone is what the ladies"—I nodded at the Adirondack Hardware owners—"brought me."

"And you couldn't look a gift scone in the mouth—is that what you're saying?"

"That's exactly what I'm saying."

A father and his two daughters were now waiting behind the bartender. The smaller daughter snatched a copy of *The Old Man* out of the older daughter's hands. The older daughter snatched it back. It was a grim and silent battle. The bartender moved aside to make room, but first he put his hand on the stack of books.

"When are you coming back to the bar?"

It was a question, not a statement, but it didn't feel like one. The bartender's hand was quiet on the stack of books. He waited for me to say something and he would keep waiting. The battling sisters sensed his power and stopped battling. They and their father waited for my answer.

"When's a good time?"

"Anytime's a good time."

"Sometime, then. Sometime I will return to the bar."

"Time" words kept coming out of our mouths, words emerging from the word assembly line within. Part of me liked talking like that because it was fun, and fun was in short supply. And part of me felt guilty talking like that because of the heavy curtain behind the light words, the heavy velvet curtain of *My mother is disappearing.* The bartender smiled. He couldn't see the curtain, moth-eaten and dusty, hanging limply on the dark stage. His hand lifted off the stack of books and he was gone, past the pickles and jams, past the vintage Adirondack posters, past the hardware ladies, both of whom smiled at him.

"Is that your boyfriend?" the smaller sister said.

"That's my bartender," I said.

She nodded gravely, as if I had just told her a secret. Then she pushed the book toward me, her finger pointing at the title page. "Can you write my name in here?"

"Mine too," the bigger sister said. "My name too. It's not just your book, you know. It belongs to both of us."

"Tell you what," I said, and I lifted a new copy off the stack. "I'm going to give you girls another one. My treat. Then you'll each have your own."

The father opened his mouth, invisible waves of protest beginning to ripple outward from him, but I didn't look at him and he stayed quiet. *Sometimes you need something that's only yours,* was the thought that I telegraphed back to him, *something that belongs to you and you alone.*

The small sister clapped her book shut and clutched it to her chest and jumped up and down, as if she had just won a contest. The older sister took the copy I gave her and frowned, as if something serious had just happened.

....

That night, Sunshine and Brown and I sat across from each other at their table, the giant table that would never fit in the tiny cabin. I had brought us each a Tree Hugger sandwich from the deli at DiOrio's.

"What's going on with you?" Brown said to me. "There's something weird about you. Even for a self-admitted weirdo."

"Excuse me? *Semi*-weirdo."

"You're right, Brown," Sunshine said, as if I weren't sitting there. "The word isn't *weird,* though. It's *happy.* Or *happy-ish.*"

I looked down at the table, searching for the scorch mark, intent on finding the scorch mark and focusing on it instead of feeling happy, even happy-ish, given the situation with my mother

There it was. Down the table. *Hello, scorch mark. Give me the strength not to feel happy.*

This table had been with them ever since they moved in together, back in Boston. Neither of them had any furniture and we were driving around on garbage night to furnish their new apartment. Curbside. That was our term for everything we found set out in alleys and in front of houses and apartment buildings the night before garbage pickup. We knew all the different garbage days for all the different neighborhoods. We preferred wealthy neighborhoods for the quality of their castoffs.

The day we found the table it was I who spotted it, one corner and one leg poking out from behind a Dumpster in Back Bay. "Pay dirt!" I shouted. "Hold up, driver!" All the windows were open and I stuck my head out for a better look as Sunshine backed the borrowed pickup down the alley.

"Now this, my friends, is what we call a *table*," Brown said, once we were all out of the truck and standing by the Dumpster.

"This is a table for the *ages*," Sunshine said.

"This is a table that I am personally responsible for *spotting*," I said, because once someone has started a chain of rhythmically italicized words you shouldn't break it, "and because of that I am the *winner*, and you guys are going to have to have me over for *dinner* for the rest of our *lives*."

"No problem," Sunshine said, and "Sounds good to me," Brown said.

The table wouldn't fit in the bed of the pickup. We angled it so that most of it fit, and Sunshine puttered along Commonwealth Avenue while Brown and I crouched on opposite sides of the behemoth.

"Hold on, Clara!" Brown kept calling. "Hold on for dear life! Dear God, Clara, hold on! Are you holding on, Clara?" and after a while I was laughing so hard that all the holding-on was up to him.

Now I kept my eyes on the scorch mark, focusing on it in order to keep the bartender from appearing in my mind, but he kept appearing anyway. There he was, standing onstage, in front of a ragged velvet curtain, smiling.

"Maybe she's met a man," Sunshine said.

"She already has enough men in her life," Brown said. "Between Jack and Dog, who needs any more men?"

"How sweet. A bottle of whiskey and the ashes of her departed dog."

"Hello," I said. "Rudeness."

I willed the bartender back behind the curtain, and I willed the scorch mark not to fail me, but fail me it did. The bartender kept opening the curtains to poke his head through and smile. I wrapped my arms around myself so that the thin dark wire, invisible under my shirt, would hold me together. It had been seven years since I got that tattoo and I knew exactly where to put my hands and how to crook one forearm into the other so that the beginning of the wire would meet the end of the wire. It was a technique of last resort.

"Sunshine, she's doing the wire thing again. She's holding herself together with ink."

"I see that, Brown. But why? What's she holding in?"

"Rudeness times two," I said again. "Rudeness squared. Speaking of someone in the third person when she's right here. Demerit."

"There it is again!" Brown said. "I swear to God she sounds happy-ish."

I clutched each arm with the other but the laughter was coming on strong, and "Screw you both," I said. "I met someone, okay? This guy."

"Whoa!" Brown said. "Did you hear that? Has she ever told us she met someone?"

"Nope. But here she is. Look at her, smiling."

"Where could she possibly have met this guy? What do you think his favorite color is? Do you think he's an eggs man or a cereal man?"

"Is he a boob man or a butt man? Or a mostly-neither man, given Winter's physical configuration?"

"I bet he's a lumberjack. You know she's always had a thing for lumberjacks."

"Hellooooo," I said. "Still right here."

"Oh," Brown said. "What do you know? She's right here. So where'd you meet this guy? Did you go to a party and not tell us?"

I shook my head. "A bar. He's a bartender."

"A bartender? Free drinks!"

The bartender materialized again in my mind. He stood behind the bar, slicing limes into thin wedges. Sunshine and Brown were talking about the drinks they would order when they met the bartender. They would go big because the drinks would be free, or should be free, because weren't drinks always free if you were with the bartender's girlfriend? Wasn't that like an unwritten rule or something?

"He's not my boyfriend. I just met him."

"Can you imagine her and her boyfriend in the tiny cabin?" Brown said. "Where would she put him? Maybe she could turn him into a piece of furniture too. Or artwork! A human-size sculpture made out of a human."

"There would be room if she made room," Sunshine said.

"Are you speaking metaphorically, Sunshine?"

"I am, Brown."

Brown turned to me. "Sunshine is speaking Metaphor," Brown said, as if it were a nearly forgotten language and he a professor instructing me in its ways. "And she's also speaking Literal. Kind of like simulcast."

"Stop," I said. "It's not right to talk about this kind of thing."

"What kind of thing?"

"You know. Happy-ish things."

"Why not?" Sunshine said.

"Because. It's not the time or place. We're here to talk about Tamar, not the bartender."

"Of course it's the time and place. We can talk about Tamar *and* we can talk about the bartender."

"Simulcast," Brown said helpfully. "See?"

"Happy-ish things don't stop because Tamar has Alzheimer's," Sunshine said. "Being a cancer survivor gives me the right to say that."

She tilted her head and smiled her brave-cancer-survivor smile and we automatically tilted our heads and smiled our brave-cancer-survivor-supporter smiles back at her. Our smiles were closed-mouthed and flat-eyed. We had invented them long ago, when people started referring to Sunshine as a cancer survivor, which was a term we all hated. It put the cancer first and Sunshine second, and if we couldn't get rid of the cancer entirely we at least wanted the wording to be the other way around.

....

"But enough of happy-ish things," Brown said. He had the ability to pivot like that, and we pivoted with him. "This meeting is called to order. First order of business: other than that there was at least one moment in her life, corroborated by mysterious photographic evidence, that she was wearing a non-woodcutter-type shirt and she looked pretty, what have we learned about Tamar Winter since last we convened?"

Was that an existential statement? Or a rhetorical question? Question marks scrolled across the bottom of my brain. *????????* Curlicued little sea serpents hunching along in search of answers. Sum up what you *do* know about your mother, Clara.

"Tamar Winter is my mother. She applied and unapplied decals for Dairylea for thirty years. She was justice of the peace for fourteen. She was a choir singer who never sang in church. She is a fan of firewood, food eaten straight out of the jar and *Jeopardy!* She was also a fan of Asa. At least until the night before he broke up with me."

"Asa," Sunshine said. She always said his name wrong, with a *z* sound instead of an *s* sound. "Asa Chamberlain. I wish I'd known him. I feel as if I'd know you better, if I knew what he was like."

"You would have loved him. Everyone did."

"Why?"

"He was one of those people." Asa appeared in my head, standing in the doorway of an unfamiliar room, smiling. A lump rose in my throat. I wanted to tell them more about him, about the unicycle he taught himself to ride, about the way he used to sing me to sleep, but the words wouldn't come out. All I could manage was "He was a good singer."

"Was he?"

"Yes. He used to go up to Fairchild Continuing Care and sing to the residents. Hymns."

"So he was religious?"

I shook my head. No, Asa was not religious. Unless he was all-religious, in that way that some people are, where everything in the world has meaning, and everything and everyone is worthy. "Asa said that hymns were just songs. He had a magical ability to remember the words to any song. He used to sing Leonard Cohen songs to my mother."

"Her man Cohen? She must have loved Asa, then."

"Yes. Which is why I will never understand what went down between them that night I came back and he was so upset."

"She never talked about it? Ever?"

I shook my head. They had heard bits and pieces about Asa over the years. A little when we were freshmen getting to know one another. More when he was deployed—Sunshine had been there when my mother told me the news over the telephone—and then those blurry weeks and months years ago, after the Humvee he was in blew up. That was it, though. There had been a lot left out.

....

He was a senior and I was a sophomore, but time goes slower in high school. So the two years I was with Asa, from fall of sophomore year until fall of senior year, were long, long years. They stretched out from morning, when I woke up and lay in bed picturing him, until night, when I undressed in the dark and lay down between cool sheets imagining that he was with me.

Sometimes he was. When Tamar was asleep and the pre-Asa Clara would've been too, when it was way into the night, he'd drive over and park on the logging road and then walk up to the house and brush his hand against the screen of my window. "You up?" he'd whisper, and I'd press my hand against his through the screen, and then he'd ease open the never-used front door instead of the always-used kitchen door off the porch, and then there he'd be. In my room.

He was like a miracle. This living, breathing boy, this boy I loved who loved me back.

"Are you real?" I would ask sometimes.

"As real as the Velveteen Rabbit," he would say. His favorite book from childhood, which he gave me a copy of for my birthday and which, because of him, I tried to love too, but couldn't. Too sad. Too hard.

We were together even after he graduated from Sterns High and started driving truck for Byrne Dairy, the rival company to Dairylea. He didn't want to go to college, which made his mother angry. His parents were struggling with each other, had always struggled, according to Asa. By the end of his senior year his mother had moved out and Asa lived with his father in Sterns.

"Martha Chamberlain is a tough nut," Tamar said once.

"Takes one to know one," I said, because wasn't Tamar also a tough nut? But she just looked at me. No comeback.

What was she thinking? What was going through her mind back in those days? She loved Asa Chamberlain, that much was clear. "That boy has the voice of an angel," I once heard Annabelle Lee say to Tamar. "And the looks of one too, in a lumberjack kind of way." Tamar didn't say anything back—maybe she nodded, but I was eavesdropping from the living room so I didn't know for sure—but the choir director was right on both counts. Once he knew how much my mother loved Leonard Cohen, Asa used to serenade her with his songs. "Hallelujah," especially, because it was her favorite. I could still hear his voice in the kitchen of the house that used to belong to my mother and me, singing about those chords and that baffled king composer. She used to have this look on her face when he sang, a look I couldn't read.

Now I wondered: Was that look happiness? Did Asa make her happy in a way that I didn't?

His father, Eli, was not a tough nut. He might have given the impression of tough-nut-ness, but he was anything but. He was a tall, rough-looking, rough-speaking man, but you should have seen the way he used to pick up his dog, Miss Faraday, named after his kindergarten teacher, and smooth her already-smooth fur. Eli had found Miss Faraday in a ditch outside Watertown when she was a puppy, some kind of nameless pit-husky-boxer mix, as far as we could tell, and driven home with her on his lap.

He was the same way with his son.

"Clara, do you and Asa talk about what will happen after high school?" my mother once asked me. She had that look on her face, that same unreadable look.

"Sure. I'll go to MVCC, he'll drive for Byrne Dairy and everything will be the same."

"You've decided all that together?"

"Not in so many words. But yes."

I had already mentally rejected all the SUNY schools on a too-far-from-Asa basis. Oneonta, Cornell, Geneseo, Plattsburgh, Binghamton, New Paltz, Albany, all within three hours but still too far. I couldn't stand the thought of being farther than half an hour away from Asa, who was happy exactly where he was. Happy with me, with his job, with Sterns.

And I was happy with him.

....

"Why did Asa enlist?" Sunshine said, still with the *z* sound instead of the *s*. "You've never really talked about that."

"Asa. Not Aza. Get it straight. And I couldn't talk about it."

"But why not?"

I wanted to swat away the sound of her voice, the confusion in it. Calm down, Clara. Focus. It was a long time ago.

"Because it was right after he left me," I said. "It all happened so fast. It's still a jumble in my head. We broke up, and he enlisted, and I went away, and then he died. He's dead."

"Tell us more about Asa, then," Sunshine said, after a long pause. "About that time."

She was still saying it wrong. Could she never get it right? Could she not hear? Was there a problem with her ears? *S* instead of *z*, Sunshine. *S* for sweet, not *z* for razor. Sunshine was a word person but not enough of one, it seemed, to know the profound difference between *s* and *z*.

"Everything changed after the night I came home and they were talking," I said. "He broke up with me the next day. Then he enlisted. He was an army mechanic. And then she made me go away. And if he hadn't enlisted, then—"

"Maybe he would be alive?"

I nodded. My heart fluttered in my chest, on the verge of a stampede. Too thin too dehydrated too stressed. The three *too*s, any two of which would bring on episodes. A long-ago cardiologist's voice echoed in my mind, lecturing me on the specifics of my condition. *Shhh, Clara. Shhh.*

"Is that why you don't talk about him?"

Yes. That was why I didn't talk about him. Why I tried not to think about him. All these years. Fifteen of them, now, since we broke up. And Asa gone from the earth the last seven of them. Maybe I thought there would be time to put it back together. If not me and Asa as a couple, then the puzzle of what was broken. Understand how that time and those decisions—to do as my mother said, to leave my home and venture into a new world, to go forth without Asa— changed my life. Set pattern to it in ways that I could not have known back then.

Would we have broken up anyway? Would time have worked its sorcery on us, pulled us apart? *Probably,* the thirty-two-year-old me whispered to the seventeen-year-old former me. *Admit it. You might have made it a semester, or a year even, and then you would both have known you were headed down different paths.* But that ending would have been better than what actually happened, because it would have been natural. Sorrowful, but natural.

Even after he left me, I felt in my body that there was a force between the two of us, and I imagined that one day when I was home visiting my mother and out for a walk, he would drive by and pull off to the side of the road and turn off the ignition. Get out of the car.

We would talk.

I would tell him how sorry and sad I still felt about losing him, and he would nod and hold out his hand.

We would figure it out together. That happened in life, sometimes. The long-divorced parents of my friends growing up, who loathed each other, who hated being around each other at holidays and graduations and funerals, were suddenly glimpsed in their children's wedding photos, dancing and laughing and clinking glasses. How it happened was time, maybe. Time melting away the edges. Time making you forget the awfulness.

Asa was my only boyfriend.

When he ended things with me, on that day he kept shaking his head and saying he was sorry, something broke. Something fundamental, so that the air itself broke around us, so that ever since the air I breathed came from a different country, a country I was still trying to figure out.

....

"I think about it," I said. "I think about it more than you know. Because the world, it would be a better place if Asa were still in it."

Sunshine and Brown kept their eyes straight on me, wanting more. The width of the wide table separated us and I was the field mouse and they were the hawks, listening with their eyes, ready to plummet from a mile high with claws at the ready if I stopped talking.

"And he's not," I said. "And my mother, she's going now too. And what if I had stayed in Sterns? What if I had been close by her all along?"

"Would things be different now?" Brown said.

"Maybe."

I put my hand over the scorch mark, beacon of burn in the middle of confusion. The memory of the day we found the table, when we hauled it back to their new, unfurnished place and somehow managed to shove it up four narrow flights of stairs, and then somehow managed to jimmy it into the apartment, where we all sat on top of it and ate take-out Chinese with chopsticks, came washing back over me. It was an easy memory, a memory full of laughter and adventure and possibility. Not like the memories of my raging words, flung in darkness at my mother, and that look in her eyes when she switched on the bedside lamp, and not like the memory of the look in Asa's eyes when he broke up with me.

"What was The Fearsome's reaction to you and Asa breaking up?" Sunshine said.

"Nothing. *Nada*. Zip. On the outside, anyway. I've never been able to make sense of it."

"I can't imagine my parents saying nothing."

"Your parents are normal. Mine is not. It happened, and then she banished me to New Hampshire. She showed me the acceptance letter and the scholarship and the grant. Annabelle Lee and she had filled out the application and pretended to be me. They used an old essay I wrote for Honors English, about wanting to go to Hong Kong someday."

"Seriously?" Brown said, admiration on his face. Respect for Tamar's deviousness.

"Seriously."

Blue Mountain appeared in my mind, standing over me in the Arts Center while I waited for my heart to revert. *Is your mother proud of you?* There was no question that Sunshine's mother was proud of her. All you had to do was look at her in the photo on their wall, standing on that sun-kissed dock, a yellow cardigan tied over her shoulders, smiling down at Sunshine. She was like an ad for an affluent, white New England college mother.

"Look," I said. "I was never a bad kid. I worked so hard — at school, at everything. And she kicked me out. I screamed at her, I mean *screamed at her*, the first time I ever did something like that. The only time. And we didn't talk about that either, and then I went away to school the way she decreed, and then" — I stopped talking. Lump in my throat.

"And then what?" Brown said.

The hawk hovered above, silent and deadly, waiting for the mouse. I kept my hand pressed over the scorch mark.

"And I loved it," I said. "I loved college. It was a whole new life and I loved it and I loved you guys and after a while it was in the rearview mirror, all of it. I left her behind."

My mother and Asa had, in their separate ways, launched me into action. That was the way it felt.

"And I never went back," I said. "My life is the opposite of my mother's."

"I don't know about that," Brown said.

Sunshine was silent, which meant that she agreed. Why? How? I was nothing like my mother, my mother in her lumber jacket, raising the maul in the air, bringing it down on chunks of log. My mother, with her beautiful voice, heading out to choir practice but never, not once, appearing in church. My mother, one hand on the steering wheel, driving me to New Hampshire and then driving back again alone.

....

Sunshine and Brown and their parents were all talkers. They sat around the dinner table late into the night, laughing, high-fiving when they agreed on something and raising their voices when they didn't. They were voluble. They believed in both small talk and big talk. They were gracious and charming and diplomatic with guests in that upper-class way; their manners were impeccable and they knew how to make anyone feel at home. Including me.

Do you have to talk much, though, to know one another? Is that a given? My mother was not a talker. She was a woman of economical physical movement. See her in our house, the house that used to be ours, back in Sterns. See her at the table, watching the birds at her bird feeder. See her hanging clothes out on the clothesline that she herself strung between two two-by-fours that she herself dug the holes for and then cemented into the ground. See her tossing firewood into those big, messy piles on the porch, and see me lecturing her on how it needed to be stacked in neat rows instead.

My mother was a no-nonsense type. A woman who worked and worked and worked and wouldn't answer most of the questions I kept asking her, then made me go far away to college. Threw me out of the house and out of the state, was how it felt at the time, unlike most of my high school friends. The mothers of those friends had always been with them. These friends married one another. They lived now in Sterns and their children went to Sterns Elementary. Some of those children were already in Sterns Middle School. Sterns High, even. All of this I knew from reading the Sterns alumni newsletter.

"Do you have any kids, Clara?"

This was a question I heard a lot at the mixer before the one Sterns High School reunion I had gone to, our tenth.

"I don't, no."

Later in the evening, after a few drinks and a few hours: "Do you *want* any kids?"

No, I don't? Maybe, if I meet the right guy? I haven't thought much about it, to be honest? Minefields, all of them. Either *You don't know what you're missing,* or *Have you tried online dating because my cousin met her husband that way,* or *There's not much time left, is there? Don't miss your chance, now.* Tick-tock tick-tock. Gene mutation, were you in there? Were you listening? Maybe there was no chance at all.

Me to Tamar, late at night after I drove back from that reunion: "Why does it matter if I want kids or not? Why does anyone care?"

"It's not whether or not you want kids," she said. "It's that children are the ultimate defense weapon."

"What does that even mean, Ma?"

"You know what it means."

End of subject. The Fearsome had spoken. But I did know what she meant. From the outside looking in, which was where I was then and now, it took all your energy to raise a child, and all your money and all your time. So you couldn't for a minute think about whether the toll was too great. You walked around wearing the fact of your children like a shield, like armor, like a permanent excuse. You had no choice but to believe it was worth it.

My mother was not a woman of small talk. She was also not a woman of big talk, if big talk was defined as the kind that Sunshine's and Brown's parents were so good at, long evenings of expansive conversation with others who wanted to talk about string theory, maybe, or the California school of plein air painters, or whether a socialist female governor could ever win a presidential election.

Say it once and mean it. Provide no explanation or context.

Those were the rules according to Tamar, not that she would ever have put them into words that way. Putting my mother into words was the job of the one she called the word girl. My mother didn't hide behind me, then or now. She made no excuses for herself, then or now. She called things as she saw them, then and now.

Like my heart.

You have to get that fixed. You have to get that fixed. You have to get that fixed.

Words she had said to me multiple times ran along the bottom of my brain, peaking and valleying, like the readout on an EKG.

"Did she believe it was worth it, do you think?" I said to Sunshine and Brown. "Having a kid? A kid like me?"

They didn't look surprised at the change of subject. They were used to it. And they didn't say, Yes. They didn't say, Of course. They didn't say, How can you even ask that question.

"Don't ask us," Sunshine said. "Ask your mother."

....

"I made a grid for you," Brown said.

It was the next morning and we were at Walt's Diner, waiting for pancakes. Blueberry for me and Sunshine, plain buttermilk for Brown. Brown, the man of logic. Brown, the writer of code so precise it almost never needed revision. Brown, who would never need the services of Words by Winter, had constructed a *Jeopardy!* grid, with my mother the focus of every category.

CANS AND JARS	BASEBALL	BREAKUP WITH ASA	CHOIR BUT NO CHURCH	OUT-OF-STATE COLLEGE	SELF-EVICTION
$2000	$2000	$2000	$2000	$2000	$2000

"From the ridiculous to the sublime," he said. "I put the baseball one in there for me, but the others are all yours. Talk to Tamar. Talk to anyone who knows Tamar."

Just like that, she had gone from being The Fearsome to Tamar. It felt like a demotion. No! Keep calling her The Fearsome! The exclamation marks boldfaced themselves and marched along the bottom of my brain. !!!!!! But the change had happened without conscious thought. It was clear from the way Brown said the word. In the face of new information about The Fearsome, a spontaneous natural event had happened, and The Fearsome was now Tamar. It was like cell division. Once begun, it could not be stopped.

"Also, Brown and I want to help," Sunshine said. "We want to go with you when you visit her."

"You can't. She made me promise not to tell anyone. I owe her that. I *owed* her that, and I broke the promise."

"And for good reason. What does it matter at this point if anyone else knows? We want to see Tamar. We love Tamar."

The pancakes came, plate-size, and then the server with the special coffee-pouring technique came by and transfixed us by refilling our coffee cups. That was good, because the effort of talking about my mother this way, almost clinically, was too much. The pain of it sat there with us at the table, crowded in among the plates and mugs and maple syrup and the white bowl filled with tiny plastic tubs of butter.

"Also, when are we going to your boyfriend's bar?" Brown said.

"He's not my boyfriend."

"Boyfriend," he said again, ignoring me. "I love saying the word *boy-friend* in conjunction with you. All these years you've lived like a nun, and finally, a boyfriend. *Boyfriend.*"

"Also, free drinks," Sunshine said. "Don't forget the free drinks, Brown."

"He's not my boyfriend."

"He probably has nice hands," Sunshine said. "You know how she is about hands."

"Piano players," Brown said. "They're all about the hands."

"He's not my boyfriend. And I only played piano in college."

"But does he? Have nice hands?"

The bartender's hands appeared in my mind, fingers grazing the table where I sat. Prelude hands. That light touch. I watched my own fingers open three butter packets. Steam from the blueberries on the under-neath pancake curled out when I lifted the top pancake to spread the butter.

"He does," Sunshine said. "You can tell by the faraway nice-hands look in her eyes."

"Do you think he'd like Walt's?" Brown said.

"Who doesn't like Walt's?"

My pancakes were buttered. Time for the pouring of the syrup, which was a two-step process: first the underneath pancake, then the top pan-cake. Most people neglected the underneath pancake. Not me.

"The syruping of the bottom pancake has commenced," Sunshine said.

The syruping of the bottom pancake was a crucial step that required concentration, what with the size of Walt's pancakes—dinner plates—but I looked up halfway through. One of those times when you look up for no reason, except that there must be a reason, an animal kind of below-the-surface reason, and there he was.

"Winter, heads up," Brown said. "You're about to spill."

I looked back at my plate but too late. Sunshine and Brown had fol-lowed my gaze and were looking at him, leaning against the doorjamb, waiting his turn for a seat at the counter.

"Who's that?" Sunshine said. "Wait. That's not him, is it?"

It was. The bartender, descended from his dark bar north of Inlet and come down to earth here in Old Forge, waiting with the other mortals for a spot at Walt's. I said nothing. I dug into my pancakes. I did not look up again, either at the doorjamb or at Sunshine and Brown.

....

You might think that making your living writing three to five Words by Winter a day would be easy. You might think, How hard could it be for a word girl to churn out a few hundred words at a hundred bucks a hundred? You might think, Aren't words what she does, who she is, what matters to her?

You would be right, and you would be wrong.

You would be right when it came to someone like John Stein, a self-published poet who paid me to write blurbs for the back of each of his books, five or six of them a year. All the titles were variations on *Real Poems for Real People*. The latest was *More Real Poems About Real People with Real Problems*. Words for John Stein were easy.

> *In his latest volume, the cannot-be-stopped poet John Stein explores territory familiar to all those over fifty or with a family history of colon cancer. "Up There" takes the reader to literally dark places, places most of us care not to venture. And yet by journey's end, Stein's devoted followers may find themselves even more grateful for their polyp-free status. Suitable for all adult readers, those who have had their first colonoscopy and those who are contemplating one. Real poems about real people with real problems indeed!*

One hundred dollars, please.

But you would be wrong about other parts of it. That words were what mattered to me was true. That words were what I did was true. That words were easy was not.

What matters most is also what hurts most. If you were a person to whom words were living, breathing animals, animals that you loved and whose lives were in your keeping, then you couldn't take them for granted or treat them flippantly. Instead, you bent your brain into pretzels of strain, trying to find just the right words. You stood up and paced around the room, opened the porch door and stepped out into the cold morning air, roamed your eyes around the stalwart trunks of the white pines as if they held answers.

Easy? No.

Words for me were best sought early in the morning or late at night. In the morning they were just-born babies new to the world, depthless eyes fastened on yours. As the hours floated past they lost that newness, that innocence. They turned guarded and wary. They put up walls. They stood at the parapets with buckets of burning oil, ready to vanquish those who would steal the kingdom. At night, though, they rose again from the weary remains of the day, cool, dark air beckoning them back to the bower. A tiny light began to glow in their bellies. Firefly words floated up and glimmered among the white pines. If you were lucky you could catch some of them, keep them for a while and then let them go.

There was wonderment out there in the Words by Winter world, and sorrow, and regret, so much regret. There was wishing and hoping and more wishing and more hoping. Craft a note from a gay son to his born-again parents who believe that homosexuals will burn in hell. Craft a note from a girl to her lifelong crush, asking him to prom in a way that he won't be able to refuse. Craft a note from a middle-aged woman to her elderly stepmother, an apology for making her life hell when she was an adolescent. Craft a note like that, do it right, and do it in under a hundred words with a one-day turnaround.

See? Hard. So much harder than you'd think.

Speed and precision were essential. But the hardest part about words-making wasn't the words themselves but the invisible scaffolding that lifted their black-and-white stick-figure-ness from the page and turned it into heart and soul. *Dear Mister or Miss Winter, please help me. Dear Winter, I wonder if . . . Dear Words by Winter, I need your help.*

The only way out was through, and what through meant was that you had to transfuse the words you wrote with your own heart and soul. As Jacob wrestled with the angel, as Teresa of Avila contemplated silence, as Jonathan Livingston Seagull tried and tried again to lift his heavy body from the earth, so I wrestled, and contemplated, and tried. And tried again.

Jonathan Livingston Seagull, *the seventies book about the teleporting seagull? Did she really just stick a seagull in there with Saint Teresa and the angel-wrestling Jacob? Did I read that right?*

Yes, yes and yes. I put him in there because of Tamar. Jonathan Livingston Seagull, you squawking heavy bird, my mother read you over and over and over again. There must have been something in you that had thus far escaped me. As words were my witness, I would seek it out.

....

Can't we? No. *Why not?* No. *Come on.* No.

That was Sunshine and Brown, asking to go with me to the place where my mother lived now. They kept asking, and they wouldn't stop, and after a while it was harder to say no than to give in, so we all drove down together. Brown held the book of the week, *My Side of the Mountain.* Sunshine had a notebook and pen.

"Tell us what we should know," she said. "What to do, what not to do."

"Don't tell her she's wrong," I said.

"Like anyone would do that?" Brown said. "She wasn't called The Fearsome for nothing."

It was more than that, though. Different from arguing with an ordinary person about a point of fact, the way Sunshine and Brown and I might do when playing Jeopardy!

"It's more like training yourself not to correct," I said. "It's figuring out how to listen. To whatever she's saying, even if it doesn't seem to make any sense."

"Follow her," Sunshine said, and I nodded. Yes. *Follow your mother wheresoever she goeth.*

"And don't ask her to remember things. Don't even use the word *remember.*"

Vigorous nods. That was a no-brainer, was what the look on their faces said. But it was a far harder task than you might think, to train yourself out of saying, "Do you remember?" In the course of my failures, which by now were many, I had learned just how often that word wanted to be said. It lurked, a danger word, ready at any time to fall into the air between my mother and me and rend the fragile peace that not-trying-to-remember meant for her.

Remember when . . . ? A phrase that links one human being to other human beings. It is a phrase of heft and permanence, the verbal equivalent of Sunshine and Brown's old garage-sale telephones. It puts you into another world, a world that used to be and no longer is, a world that you and the person you're talking with both remember. Unless one of you doesn't.

"Remember when" was something that Sunshine and Brown and I said all the time to each other. We went back many years, to that first week of college. But before age eighteen, I had no one left. My high school friends and I had lost touch. Annabelle Lee was my mother's friend, not mine, and we exchanged no confidences. I might once have had Asa Chamberlain, but he let me go, and then he left the earth in a fury of blasted metal and flesh. Regrets for $2000.

We walked in together, me leading the way. Hello to the nurses, hello to the aides, hello to the woman who sat by the miniature rock fountain with its endless trickle of water, hello to the old man by the piano, one finger stroking its closed lid. Hello to the Jokes and Jingles Workshop attendants, sitting around the table in the conference room, today playing a game involving cards and cookies and laughter. You had to be in the early stages to attend Jokes and Jingles, and Tamar didn't qualify. Not that she would have joined anyway. Never a joiner, my mother. Always a loner. Like now, in the Green Room — it was no longer the Plant Room — the television remote in her lap.

"Tamar," Brown said. "Remem—"

"Brown!" Sunshine said. "Shhh."

She held the notebook up in the air — she was still clutching it — "Remem" — then she too stopped herself. See? It was harder than you'd think, not to use the word. *Tamar, remember me?* That was what Brown had been about to say. My mother looked from Brown to Sunshine and then to me, accusation in her eyes. She knew something was not right, but what?

"Ma, I'm sorry," I said.

"We pried it out of her, Tamar," Sunshine said. "It's not her fault."

"You pried what out?" she said. "What's not her fault?"

They didn't know what to do with those questions. Welcome to the club, best friends. Welcome to Jokes and Jingles. Brown handed her *My Side of the Mountain.*

"This book is for you, Tamar," he said. She placed it in the exact middle of her lap, the way she always did, but she repeated the question.

"You pried what out?"

"The keys to the kingdom," Brown said, which made no sense. But somehow it did the trick, because she nodded.

"Is it time?" she said.

"It is, Ma. It's seven-thirty. Time for *Jeopardy!*"

"Time for *Jeopardy!*" she echoed.

. . . .

The four of us sat together on the couch, waiting for the show to begin. Sunshine and Brown urged me on with their eyes, their *Talk to her* eyes, their *Time is running out* eyes.

"So, Ma," I said. "I've been wondering about some things."

"You have? Like what?"

"Like, um, like what baseball team you like."

Sunshine and Brown tensed. The air in the room changed. That was what tension did—it made the air still and solid, something you had to slice through to make progress. *Baseball?* was what their tension said. *Really? That's what you want to know about? You don't even care about baseball.*

"Baseball?" Tamar said. "The Egyptian Whalebacks."

"What? Who?"

That was Brown, swiveling on the couch to stare at her. She looked at him calmly.

"Did you say the Egyptian Whalebacks?"

She nodded.

"I've never heard of them," Brown said.

"You have now," Sunshine said, warning in her voice. Stay with her, Brown, was what the warning said. Don't correct. Follow her.

"Huh," Brown said. "Where do the Whalebacks play?"

"Egypt."

She frowned and gave him a poke in the ribs with her elbow, a where-else-would-they-play sort of poke, and I fought the urge to laugh. Brown was about to ask another question, but she poked him again.

"Shut up now," she said. "It's time for the heinous adventures."

"Ma! *Interviews*. The heinous interviews."

Don't correct. Don't criticize. Sunshine next to me tensed again, because I had told her, hadn't I, and hadn't she written it down in her notebook, that "Don't correct" was one of the cardinal rules? Tamar flapped her hand in my face: *Go away! Shoo!*

But she was laughing. My mother, Tamar, a woman so serious all her life that her own daughter barely remembered her laughing, was laughing like a little girl. She flapped her free hand at the television and Brown started laughing too. *Meet her where she is, Clara.*

"Here we go," I said. "God help us all."

Trebek, wearing a navy suit, strode across the stage toward his victims. Philip, who according to Sunshine looked like he could be a marine, appeared to be visibly shrinking from the camera. Sunshine reached for my mother's hand, a gesture she accepted, and from the corner of my eye I saw Brown, on her other side, pick up her other hand. Let the heinous adventures begin.

Philip turned out to be a martial arts expert and teacher. An image of him in a white suit tied with a belt, brandishing traditional Asian weapons in front of a mirrored wall while little kids bowed and called him Sensei, appeared in my mind.

"Did I call that one or what?" Sunshine said. "It's all in the posture. You can always tell."

"You did not call that one at all," Brown said. "You said he was a marine."

"Close enough. I still win."

"Shhh," Tamar said, and they instantly obeyed.

Philip had just received his Braiding Dad certificate from a three-hour hair-braiding workshop he had attended with his seven-year-old daughter. Philip had found the Braiding Dad class a more difficult endeavor than earning his second-degree belt.

"Really?" Trebek said, which made the entire moment fall flat.

"What a dipshit," Tamar said.

"Who, Ma?"

"The dipshit."

She jabbed *My Side of the Mountain* in the direction of Trebek, the all-powerful Trebek, who would not try to make contestants look good. He would correct their pronunciation and their spelling, and when it came to the heinous interviews, they would all end up looking like fools.

"You're right," I said, and she rolled her eyes. Of course she was right.

Martina from Brooklyn often found herself eating fast-food cheeseburgers and high-fructose-corn-syrup snacks in front of her neighbors because "I've had it with organic, locally sourced food, Alex. Had it." She fell into a certain category of contestant who tried to get chummy with Trebek. He cut her off midsentence and moved on to the lovely Julie from Delaware, who was the current high scorer and who, according to rumor, had once escaped a flood by using a child's sledding saucer as a flotation device.

"Is this true, Julie?"

"It's true. I pushed the saucer out a second-story window and then I, uh, I kept holding on to it until they rescued me."

"Isn't that interesting!"

"Dipshit," Tamar said.

....

"She doesn't actually seem that far gone to me," Brown said.

"'Far gone,' Brown?" Sunshine said. "Rude. But I kind of agree."

We were sitting in the Subaru in their driveway. Martina the Brooklyn cheeseburger-eater had come from behind in the final round and crushed pretty Julie the flood survivor, who had bet every penny on a wrong answer wrongly spelled. The three of us had walked Tamar back to her room and then poured ourselves Dixie cups of lemonade from the 24/7 juice station, drank them down and headed north.

"It was a good night," I said. "She was right there with us. Mostly, anyway."

"Does that change?" Sunshine said. "Visit to visit?"

If they kept coming, even once in a while, they would see for themselves. The fog still came and went, but the day would come when it would be there permanently. If they kept coming, they would see that. The words *if they kept coming* scrolled across the bottom of my brain like subtitles and I wouldn't let them out of my mouth, because then Sunshine and Brown might hear how much I wanted them to keep coming.

But Brown leaned forward from the backseat and rested his chin on the headrest of my seat, the driver's seat. "Can we come with you next time?" he said, and I nodded. Then the doors opened and they got out of the car, Sunshine pressing her hand against the windshield like a benediction, and into their house they disappeared.

When I left them I passed the turnoff to the cabin and kept on going, hoping to calm my mind. Miles and miles in the dark, heading north, deeper into the Adirondacks. Two-lane road, high beams lighting the night, shiny animal eyes waiting in the ditch. A deer. A fox. A coyote.

The only station was the oldies one, drifting in and out. All the songs of Tamar's era, the songs I had grown up with. Every song that came on the radio, I knew, along with almost all the words, because Tamar used to put her albums on and sing along to them every weekend. Those songs burned themselves into my brain. What Asa had said about songs being everywhere, and everyone knowing them, was true.

Clara, open the window. It's late. You're tired. Don't get drowsy.

My own voice inside my own head, telling me to be careful. I opened the driver's side window and cold air rushed in. Trees rose up on either side of the road and the road stretched before me like a parted sea. "Peace Train" came drifting in on the airwaves and I was fifteen and Tamar was singing in the kitchen as she put her new electric can opener to work. Cat Stevens, long gone into his world of religion, something Tamar would never forgive him for.

"What the hell's wrong with that man?" she used to say. "A voice like that and songs like that and, *poof,* he just disappears?"

"Cracklin' Rosie" came drifting in along with an image of Tamar watering the zinnias, the giant ones she always planted on either side of the front steps. She held her thumb over the hose so that the water sparkled out on the red and pink and orange double-headed blossoms and they swayed on their thick stems. She swayed with them, belting it out. "Sweet Caroline" next, and I remembered coming down the stairs late one night—I couldn't sleep—to see her lying on the floor, singing along to that song, the album cover, with Neil Diamond's face looming up from it, propped against her bent knees.

"Ma?"

Even back then I could hear the scorn in my voice, and here in the car I heard it again. Tight and hard-edged and abrupt. The judgment of my seventeen-year-old self traveling through the decades, back to haunt me here in the dark night, dark mountains rising around the car and me.

I remembered that she startled. The album fell out of her hands onto the floor next to her.

"What?"

"Um. What exactly is it that you're doing?"

I already knew what she was doing. She was singing, late at night in a quiet house, singing along to the songs she most loved. And what I was doing was trying to embarrass her into stopping. Send her into retreat, or come roaring out to do battle with me in the ongoing match. Angry Daughters for $400. But she did neither, did she? What she did, what my mother did, my young, young mother lying on the floor singing to the music she loved, was crumble into a ball right there on the floor and cry. More than cry. Wail. A cry so full of desolation that my heart leaped into overdrive then and there, pounding so fast that my eyes blurred and stars swam before them.

Did I say I was sorry?

Did I drop to my knees and start crying with her, out of shame?

Did I bring her a washcloth and wipe away her tears, cover her with a blanket, comfort her?

Did I talk to her about what was really going on inside me, the bewilderment and hurt after Asa broke up with me, the feeling that something had been lost, would stay lost forever, the panic and shame that had poisoned me from the night I had screamed those awful *You're a nothing* words at her?

Or, when she called my name in that choked voice of tears, did I turn and walk back upstairs and leave her there crying and then next morning in the kitchen not mention one word of what had transpired the night before? Mother, daughter. Tree, apple.

Thirty miles were gone now between Sunshine and Brown's house and the point at which the car and I were mindlessly driving north. I pulled over and did an about-face. *If a deer leaps into the road ahead of you, don't swerve. Keep going straight.* That was a Tamar caution, repeated over and over when she was teaching me to drive. But I knew, and I had always known, that if a deer did leap into the road ahead of me, I wouldn't keep going straight. I'd swerve.

In the darkness I drove and drove. Closing in now on the bar, the bar that would be dark by now, the bartender and the tattooed server gone to the homes they lived in, wherever those homes might be. On this night, I was the one who was awake. A word girl, making her way through the parted seas.

But the bar was still lit up. I slowed to a crawl. Through the big front window I saw the bartender behind the bar, washing it down with a rag. Both arms moved in unison, a practiced swirl of up and down. I inched past, barely moving, only my fog lights on. He couldn't see me in the dark. I was safe. But he looked up anyway and stopped washing the bar, stood there without moving, as if he could see into the car, as if he knew a woman out there was watching him and wondering about him. I pressed my foot down on the gas and sped away.

It was late, so late by the time I got back to the cabin, but I propped the little speaker on the window ledge and Jack and I sat on the front porch together listening to music. Emmylou sang about an orphan girl while the fairy lights twinkled from the sun they had stored up all day while I was gone. My mother's voice sounded in my head: *I always listened to you, Clara.* My own voice sounded in my head: *You know what kind of mother does that kind of thing?* Your *kind of mother. A nothing kind of mother. You're a nothing.* Dear Words by Winter, I am looking for words to write my mother. Dear Words by Winter, I am looking for words to resolve difficult issues with my mother, who is disappearing ahead of me down a road I can't travel. Dear Words by Winter, I am searching for words to tell my mother how sorry I am.

....

One Wednesday night the Subaru and I turned left at the village green. The Twin Churches were lit up. They were always lit up on Wednesday night, because that was choir practice night. Annabelle Lee would be in the rehearsal room at this very moment, her arms spread wide, the baton in her hand. I knew this because I used to spy on the choristers—which is the word for choir members, plural—when I was a child. Down the hall from the church house I would sneak in the dark, past the Sunday-school rooms I had never entered, down the steps to the closed door of the rehearsal room, where I would press my head and listen.

If you listen long enough, with your eyes closed, the voices of a choir become distinct. Not just when someone is singing a solo, but in general. What sounds like one voice from far away becomes many voices close up. I used to listen for my mother's voice, pick it out of the crowd.

It was 9:21 on the car dashboard. Choir practice was over. I watched as first the far-end hallway light went dark, then the near-end hallway light, then the church itself, with its stained-glass windows, and finally the light that illuminated the front steps. The church and its adjoining building transformed in an instant into dark hulks on this November night. Then the front door opened and the dark hulk of Annabelle Lee herself emerged. I got out of the car.

"Who's there," she said. Her voice was a sharp command. Not a question.

"Sorry, Annabelle. It's just me."

"Clara? Is your mother—?"

"She's fine. I mean she's not fine, but she's not why I'm here."

Annabelle Lee was silent. The mass of her moved down the steps in the darkness and came toward me.

"Can I ask you some things?"

"Such as?"

"Why did my mother always eat out of cans and jars?"

Her sigh gusted out white in the dark air. She bent her head forward and rolled it back and forth, one hand massaging the back of her neck.

"Follow me back to the trailer," she said. She always called it "the trailer," never "home" or "my trailer" or "my place." "It's too cold out here to be answering questions."

I parked behind the giant Impala. She held the door open and we went inside. I had Brown's grid with me, the way I used to have a written-out list on a piece of scrap paper next to the phone when I was a reporter. It was comforting. It was a thing, a tangible thing in the midst of intangible talk. The kitchen seemed to be the only place Annabelle Lee occupied in her immaculate double-wide. It was full of light and music —the soundtrack to *Hairspray,* with the "You Can't Stop the Beat" song having been set to repeat, apparently, the whole time Annabelle was at choir practice—and the smell of food, spaghetti and meatballs, so far as I could tell. Beyond the kitchen the living room and bedroom hallway stretched out dark and quiet.

There was a pile of clean laundry on the kitchen table and Annabelle began folding it. She wasn't someone who could sit still. She was like Sunshine that way; her hands had to be in motion, either conducting the choir or playing the piano or chopping vegetables or folding laundry. She was a precise folder: towels in thirds lengthwise, then thirds horizontally, so that no seams showed. Washcloths the same.

"So," I said, looking at the neat little grid in my hand. "Do you know why she always ate out of cans and jars?"

"She didn't. That only started after her mother passed. Her mother was an incredible cook. And when she died, Tamar gave up food. Real food, anyway."

"Why?"

"God knows, Clara. Penance, maybe. She was angry at herself when her mother got cancer. Angry that she hadn't pushed her harder to go to the doctor when she had symptoms. Or maybe it hurt, being in that kitchen without her mother. I don't know. She wouldn't talk about it."

I kept my eyes on the grid. *You are gathering information, Clara,* I told myself. *That is all you are doing. You will think about the information later. Right now, you are a gatherer of knowledge.*

"Okay. Thank you. Do you know why my mother always went to choir practice but never sang in choir?"

"Because your mother is not a churchwoman. She doesn't believe in religion. She thinks it's anti-women."

Anti-women, I jotted next to the question.

"Why choir, then?"

"Because she loves music. And me. Your mother is my best friend, in case you haven't noticed."

"Thank you. Next question. Was my mother a baseball fan?"

"Not to my knowledge."

I jotted **no** next to baseball.

"Next question. Did my mother tell Asa to break up with me?"

I was trying to ambush her, but she just looked at the list in my hand and frowned, as if the list had asked the question instead of me.

"Did your mother tell Asa to break up with you? What the hell is wrong with you, Clara? Your mother loved Asa."

"Then what happened between them?"

"Again, I don't know what you're talking about."

"The night before he broke up with me, they had a fight."

"I don't know what you're talking about."

I waited, but she wouldn't look at me and she didn't say anything else. I sighed.

"One last question, then. Why did she sell the house to the Amish and pack everything up and move herself into that place without telling me?"

She looked at me in surprise, her hands smoothing one gathered corner of a fitted sheet into the opposite corner. "So that you wouldn't have to," she said, as if it were obvious.

"But I told her I'd be back in a week. One week. Seven days. She couldn't wait that long?"

"It wasn't a question of waiting that long, Clara. You told her seven days? Then that meant she had to be out in six."

"But why?" The sound of my voice was more exclamation mark than question mark. Annabelle Lee was more than a match for it, though. An Annabelle Lee exclamation mark was the Final Jeopardy! of exclamation marks, compared with the wimpy Daily Double of mine.

"To save you the pain of it!" she thundered. "Jesus, Mary and Joseph, Clara! She's your mother! You're her daughter!"

As if that were all she needed to say, and then I would understand. But I didn't. Her hands smoothed the pile of folded sheets. She had folded the pillowcases in thirds and then thirds again too. No seams would show when it came to laundry at the trailer of Annabelle Lee. I imagined a closed cupboard door down that dark bedroom hallway and, behind it, stacks of perfectly folded towels and sheets.

"We do what we can, Clara," Annabelle said, as if she had read my mind. "When you're someone like Tamar, and you don't, you don't"— she groped for the right words and an image of my mother rose up in my mind, my mother pushing her walker down endless halls in search of me—"you're not a person who opens up easily, you're someone who maybe doesn't know how to talk to her daughter easily—"

She shook her head and turned around and walked the three steps from the table to the stove. Lifted the pot lid and stirred whatever was inside. Spaghetti sauce? Marinara? Something that involved tomatoes.

"You do what you can," she said, with her back turned to me. "And that's what she did."

There was a tone in her voice as if she were trying to figure out why I was so upset.

"She thought it would be easier on you, Clara," she added, enunciating each word as if she were talking to a preschooler. "She didn't want you to suffer the way she did."

"Suffer?"

"With her mother. It was long and hard, the way her mother died. And then when it was over, it was Tamar and all her mother's things, all the things Tamar had to figure out what to do with, her clothes and her dishes and her canceled checks and the Christmas presents she'd already bought ahead of time. Tamar had to handle it all herself. Her father was no help, believe me."

I had never heard Annabelle Lee say so much at one time. Nor had I heard her use my mother's name in that way, as if my mother were not my mother. As if she were a girl, a friend, someone I didn't know. Someone who had suffered.

"She did the best she could, Clara. She did what she thought would save you pain."

"It didn't," I said.

Annabelle Lee turned to me, wooden spoon dripping red, and nodded, her eyes shadowed.

"Welcome to the world," she said. She was a middle-aged woman now, lines around her mouth and eyes. Even heavier now than when she was young, if such a thing were possible, and I remembered when she was young.

....

It took me hours and hours to get through three Words by Winters next day:

1. A wedding toast from the best man to his brother, the groom, and the brother's fiancée, who was deeply disliked by the best man, which meant that "my secret hope is that the marriage doesn't last very long but you can't really say that in a wedding toast, can you, so barring that, I just want to keep it light and positive but generic, you know? Super generic. And I don't trust myself to keep it that way because I seriously dislike her, which is why I'm writing to you"; and

2. An invitation to the fiftieth-anniversary party of parents who had been married and divorced and married and divorced and married, so "maybe it should really be sixtieth anniversary but we're only counting the years they were actually married, and they're actually really funny together, but we, their children, are not very funny, so could you help us out? Please make it really, really funny. Funny is key. Here are photos of them from each of their weddings"; and

3. An obituary for a ninety-three-year-old mother by her seventy-year-old daughter, who was "not good with words, but my mother was, and she especially loved long, complicated words, and I would like this obituary to live up to her wonderfulness with that kind of words. Words

that very few people would even have heard of before, let alone understand. Maybe some long foreign words too? Words that you think she
would've loved."

See? Not easy. Exhausting, in fact. But: #1, done; #2, done; #3, done.
Three hundred dollars, please.

Afterward I went to DiOrio's and ordered a Tree Hugger sandwich
and walked back to the rotisserie chickens to wait for it and there was
the bartender, coming around the bread display.

"One McCauley Mountain for Chris," the deli girl called, holding a
wax-paper-wrapped sandwich in his direction.

Chris. Chris, not Christopher, was his name. Chris-not-Christopher
didn't know I was there, standing over by the rotisserie with its revolving chickens, waiting for my Tree Hugger. He walked up and the deli
girl pulled the sandwich back and laughed as he reached for it. He held
his arm steady in the air until she handed it over. "Thanks, Jaynie," he
said, and she smiled.

Why did I see her name as Jaynie instead of Janie? Or Janey. Jaynee,
even. Chris-not-Christopher turned, sandwich in hand, and there I was,
the many permutations of Jaynie scrolling through my mind.

"One Tree Hugger for Clara," the deli girl said. She didn't dangle my
sandwich in the air, though. She just set it on top of the deli case and
picked up her order pad for the next customer in line. Chris-not-Christopher retrieved the Tree Hugger and brought it to me and the rack of
revolving chickens.

"Here you go, tree hugger," he said. "Do you want to do something
sometime?"

"Sure."

"Good. Give me your phone."

I pulled it up out of my pocket, the tiny silver hammer almost falling
out but not. He tapped something into it. From the back pocket of his
jeans came a *ding-dong* sound.

"That's you," he said. "You're calling me."

He held my phone out to me and I took it. The chickens revolved on
their spits, and somewhere behind me a cash register kept beeping, and

the deli girl, whose name was Jaynie or more likely Janie, watched from across the way and winked at me.

....

2:47 a.m., the familiar waking time. Monkey mind. Was this how it began? Was this a sign that the plaque was forming deep inside my head, beginning to break off and clot the pathways, blocking memory, spinning me sideways and backward, setting me off down that road my mother was already far down?

"Stop it, Clara."

Talk out loud to yourself. Say your own name. Be your own doctor, your own nurse, your own statistician. Keep records, but keep them only in your own mind. That way you could deny that you thought about it as much as you did. If you were found to have compiled notebooks, slips of paper, columns and headings and dates and jotted notes, that might be seen as evidence in the court of Alzheimer's that the early was already onsetting.

2:52 a.m. and the minutes were passing by, the minutes of a dark night that was like the dark night last night, when you also woke at 2:47. Unless you didn't. Unless this was the only night that you had woken up at 2:47 a.m. thinking thoughts like this. Worrying. Because how would you know for sure if it was beginning?

We strongly advise genetic counseling if you are concerned. If you are thinking of someday having children. If you think you might be falling in love with a bartender that you never, ever want to put through this kind of pain.

3:07 a.m.

It was cold in the cabin. The electric flames of the electric fireplace glowed faintly in the darkness. The fairy lights still glimmered from the trunks of the white pines. Somewhere in the woods a fisher cat screamed and the hairs on the back of my neck prickled at the sound, the sound of a girl screaming, a girl in fear for her life.

Get up, Clara. Get dressed. Feel your way down the ladder with the car keys in your hand and open your door. Find your car in the darkness.

The Subaru roared in response. Down the curves and twists and slopes of Turnip Hill we went, and then through the darkened streets of Old Forge to the darkened parking lot of DiOrio's. I pulled in next to the handicapped spot by the front door. Kept the car running. Kept telling myself it was already morning, which sounded better than the middle of the night, better than the wee hours. The teeny-tiny wee-hour numbers: *one* and *two* and *three* and *four*. I stayed in my car, there in the parking lot of the store that would come to light in a few hours. Told myself again that it was already morning. The fisher cat was elusive and solitary and small and because of this tended to hunt only prey smaller than itself. My mother and I were the same exact height. A trapped fisher cat had taken over her brain and its wild twin screamed in the dark woods beyond where I could see. I had a fifty-fifty chance of the eFAD gene mutation. Genetic testing was recommended if. If. If. If.

Stop, Clara. Stop the monkey-minding. Practice detachment. Detach, detach, detach.

I would if I could.

....

The next time Sunshine and Brown and I visited my mother, she gazed amiably at Brown.

"How do I know you again?" she said.

"You met Sunshine and me back when your daughter was in college," he said. "It was a sunny day in the White Mountains. Parents' Weekend. You were driving a pickup truck."

Tamar listened intently, her head tilted toward Brown. *Follow where she goes,* I had told them, but it worked the other way too. We were scooted together on the couch in the Green Room, the four of us, waiting for our show to begin. The order on the couch was like this: Brown, Tamar, Sunshine, me. We were pressed together like the tiny Vienna sausages that, when I was a child, Tamar used to fish out of the Vienna sausage jar with her cocktail fork.

"It's good to see you, Tamar," Brown said.

"Good to see you too," she said, in that new echoey way, in that affable, un-fearsome voice.

"I brought you a gift." He tapped on her closed fist and she opened it. Obedient, the way she had never been. He placed a tiny jar of maple syrup in her palm and her fingers, again obedient, closed around it. "We made it ourselves," he said, "Sunshine and I."

"Maple syrup."

"Yup. We boiled and boiled and boiled it and then we burnt the shit out of the entire batch. All we got out of the whole mess was this one tiny jar. What do you think?"

"I think you're not very good at making syrup," Tamar said.

Now that was her. That was a Tamar remark. Surprise and happiness, electric, passed through Brown into Sunshine and from Sunshine into me.

"My daughter loved maple syrup," Tamar said.

"I bet she did," Sunshine said. She was already good at the not-criticizing and not-correcting, the not-pointing-out that Tamar's daughter was, in fact, sitting right here at the end of the couch.

"How do I know you again?" Tamar said.

"You met Sunshine and me back when we were in college," Brown said. "It was a sunny day in the White Mountains. Parents' Weekend. You were driving a pickup truck."

She listened as intently as the first time. *Keep going,* I said to Brown in my mind.

"We went to college with your daughter, Clara. She was pretty secretive about you."

"*Pretty* secretive?" Sunshine said. "She didn't tell us anything about you. Zip. Zilch. *Nada.*"

"Zilch," Tamar said, and then again: "zilch." It was like a new word, a word that she was testing on her tongue.

"So Clara hadn't told us a thing about you," Sunshine said, "and we thought you must be this creepy witch-mother, like a mother in a Hitchcock movie."

"Hitchcock." Tamar brought her fingertips together with care, one by one, and studied them. "Hitch. Hitch. Hitchcock."

"But then you turned out to be you!" Brown said. "The coolest mother in the crowd!"

"Not just the crowd," Sunshine said. "The world."

"The world," Tamar said, and she laughed that new chiming laugh of hers. Sunshine and Brown laughed too. It was a club of three, there on the couch next to me. They laughed and kept saying *World! World!* and pressed their fingertips together like a row of monkeys imitating an invisible lecturer. *Follow them wheresoever they goeth, Clara.* I pressed my own fingertips together and leaned my head on Sunshine's shoulder and listened to them laugh and talk. They were recounting the day they met Tamar, in all its to-them weirdness.

"You were wearing your lumber jacket," Brown said. "The oldest lumber jacket in the world."

"Lived-in," Sunshine said. "That's what that jacket was."

"It had seen a lot of living."

"A lot of wood chopping."

"It was a lumber jacket that had been used for actual lumber."

Actual lumber chopped by actual Tamar, who chopped wood for our woodstove my entire life long, something that as a child I accepted without thinking, like most children accept their lives without thinking. The woodstove was in the kitchen, and the rest of the house was freezing, so we spent most of our time in the kitchen, and that was the way it was. There was an oil furnace but we didn't use it. Too expensive.

They talked on, the three of them. Which was good, because the feeling of our kitchen and our woodstove was taking up all the space inside me. The table where we ate our can and jar dinners, the blue chair inches from the stove that we took turns sitting on, the wall behind the woodstove that I leaned against when sitting on the floor with a quilt around me, flashing through whatever homework I hadn't gotten done during study hall. So what if the rest of the house was freezing? So what if the broken zipper on her lumber jacket was held together with duct tape, and so what if there was always a faint, pervasive scent of mothballs coming from its lining? It was warm in the kitchen, and we were fed, and my homework was getting done, and the porch and the barn were filled with stacks and stacks and stacks of split wood, which meant that no matter how endless the winter to come, we would survive, because we had enough wood.

"How do I know you again?" Tamar said.

"We went to college with your daughter, Clara," Sunshine said.

"It was a sunny day in the White Mountains," Brown said. "Parents' Weekend. You were driving a pickup truck."

....

Back at the cabin, post-visit to Tamar, I sat down on the floor next to my books-as-coffee-table and put my arms around them, around the books of my childhood, my life buoys, my escapes, my worlds without end. The books-as-coffee-table was already reduced by more than half. Soon the table would be entirely disappeared.

How do I know you again? Did I ever know you? Will I ever know you?

Two of the stacks were lopsided, one because it held an especially fat novel and the other because it contained *The Velveteen Rabbit,* slender and long. A gift from Asa for my sixteenth birthday. The book I had tried for his sake to love, because he loved it so, because he had told me how his father, big rough Eli, used to read it to him when he was tiny, and how he would look up to see his father crying. How he, Asa, had every year drawn a picture of the rabbit, large and gentle and floppy and brown and white, and given it to his father on his birthday. But the story of the forsaken rabbit and sorrowful child had only made me sad. It still made me sad. I pulled it out of its stack and the coffee table shrank another half-inch. The smell of dust, that closed-up smell, wafted out when I opened it. Maybe I would bring it to Tamar. She could throw it in her pile of books-as-firewood.

I glanced up at the mystery photo, my mother with that soft look on her face, propped on the kitchen shelf. *Talk to me, Ma. Say something. Tell me something I don't know, will you, like why did you stop wearing that one pretty shirt?*

Silence. It was me and the disappearing coffee table, Dog in his urn and Jack in his bottle, watching. Beyond the cabin the fairy lights glimmered in the trees. And beyond that, far beyond, the bar with its little lights glimmered by the side of Route 28. What did I have to lose?

"Nothing," I said out loud. "You have nothing to lose."

Do we, as human beings, say that because it feels as if we do have something to lose? The smallest act, the fewest words, the tiniest of movements: they can feel enormous. Once set in motion, so many things don't stop. They gather and gather and gather momentum. They keep on going.

It works backward too. Had I picked up the phone more to call my mother, said things that were real, that were true, even if it felt agonizing to do so, back then, maybe it would not feel so hard now. Had I ever, even once, spoken to Eli Chamberlain in the wake of his son's leaving first me and then the earth, maybe things would be easier now.

Who's to say? Who's to know?

I pulled my tiny hammer earring out of my pocket and slid it into my ear, the first time in a long time. Then I picked up my keys from where they sat on the shelf next to Jack, and I got into the Subaru, and I drove north on 28. Old Forge was quiet. Most of the stores were closed, except for Adirondack Hardware, which was lit up like a steamship, and DiOrio's, where an employee stood on a ladder stringing up Christmas lights even though it wasn't even Thanksgiving yet.

The place was nearly empty when I got there. Chris-not-Christopher was washing down the bar in those same long, sweeping movements of his arms. You know how some people's entire bodies, their entire beings, open up when they smile? That was the way the bartender was. He looked up when the door scraped open, and there it was, that smile. Pure Prairie League was playing softly in the background. Pure Prairie League had been one of my mother's favorite groups. Not as high up as Neil Diamond or The Band, not as high up as Crosby, Stills, Nash & Young. Not even close to Leonard Cohen. But still. Up there. Top ten.

"My mother used to love this band," I said.

"She has good taste in music then. Tell me something else she loves."

"*Jeopardy!* The TV game show."

"No kidding?" He was still smiling. "My grandmother and I used to watch that every night when I was a kid. It came on at seven-thirty."

"It still does. And my mother still watches it, when I'm visiting her."

"Where does she live?"

"Utica."

An image of my mother was forming itself in his head; I could tell by the way he was nodding. What did she look like to him? *Shhh, Clara.*

I willed myself to stop talking, so that the shadowy, Utica-dwelling, *Jeopardy!*-watching woman he was picturing, whoever she looked like, would never be replaced by a woman with air-dancing fingers, struggling for words. *Shhh, Clara.*

"You have any brothers or sisters?"

I shook my head. But that was a lie, and it felt like a betrayal. "I had a twin sister but she died when I was born. Her name was Daphne. My mother was young when she had me. Us. Really young."

"How young is really young?"

"Eighteen."

It was happening already. A few words, and the image of my mother was building itself inside his head second by second, gathering power. *You have nothing to lose, Clara.*

"She raised me by herself. North of Sterns, which is a tiny town. Where I grew up is woods. The foothills, half an hour south of here."

"I know where Sterns is," he said. "Did she get tired of country life? Is that why she moved to Utica?"

No. Tamar had not gotten tired of the country life.

"Early-onset Alzheimer's," I said. "Stage Six already. She lives in a nursing home with a memory-care wing."

Shut the hell up, Clara. But I was a robot now and the robot part of me, unlike the real me, had no trouble saying the word *Alzheimer's.* The bartender stood on the other side of the bar, the wash rag in his hands, but his hands weren't moving. The words spilling out of me had made their way into his head, and he was preoccupied with my mother, that shadow woman forming and reforming herself in his brain.

"It's progressing pretty fast," I said. "She's cold all the time. Which is a sign."

I had told him too much, way too much. And too little, way too little.

It was impossible now for Tamar to materialize in his mind the way she should. From this moment on, when the bartender thought of my mother, what sort of woman would he picture? Not the fierce queen of the north woods. Not the level-eyed tough-as-nails Tamar. I willed his hands to start moving again.

You gave her away, I thought, *You just gave your mother away.* She was in the hands of the bartender now, and she would be there forever, a partially formed woman who would live in his head as Alzheimer's first and Tamar, the silent and fearsome woman who had lived so firmly in this world, a distant, distant, distant second. This was why my mother had not wanted anyone to know her situation.

My eyes blurred, and then the bartender came around the curved end of the bar and bent beside me. He was saying something but I didn't know what. What I knew was that his hands were warm and his fingers smelled like soap and lime and he kept them tight on my shoulders.

....

"When's the dipshit?" Tamar said. *Dipshit* now stood for the entirety of *Jeopardy!*: Alex Trebek, the contestants, the game itself. She waved her hands at the *knothole,* which was her new term for the television.

"Ma? Can I tell you something?"

"Yes."

I leaned in. She was frowning, but at the television, not me. Her fingers began sketching birds, or flowers, or words, or patterns without meaning, in the air between us.

"Sometimes I wish I had a baby."

"Yes."

"Asa's baby. Then he would still be in the world, somehow. He would still be here with me. With us."

"Yes."

Was she with me? Was she understanding me? *Tell her. Ask her.* Sunshine's and Brown's voices, egging me on. I kept going.

"Sometimes I imagine a baby. I make him up, what he would look like, how old he would be. If I had him when I was eighteen he'd be fourteen now. I wonder what he would be like. What he would be doing now if he were alive. If he had ever lived."

Words spilling out of my mouth. Things I had told no one, not Sunshine or Brown or anyone, about the un-baby I sometimes dreamed up, the baby who had never been and never would be.

"Yes," she said. "Okay."

"It's like he's living somewhere nearby. A parallel world."

"Yes. Okay. The parallel world." She pronounced *parallel* with slowness and precision. Pa. Ra. Llel. The parallel world, where the lost ones lived.

"Ma?"

She looked at me with her eyebrows up. Translation: "What? Spit it out."

"Did you ever think about not having me and Daphne?"

She wrinkled up her face. She made a brushing motion with her hand, a you-and-your-endless-questions kind of motion. She was abruptly with me, the fog mostly clear and the entire bay stretched out in front of us, glittering and bright. I had the urge to scoop her up and make a run for it, belt her into the front seat of the Subaru and take her somewhere far away, as if somehow a complete change of place would keep her mind right where it was in that moment. The Grand Canyon, the Tetons, the endless beaches of the Florida Panhandle.

"No," she said. "I didn't."

"But abortion was legal by then. You didn't even consider doing something?"

"I didn't know."

————

————

————

My mind, skipping beats, circling around what she had just said. I hadn't ever thought of that possibility.

"Wait. You didn't know you were pregnant? But how could you not know?"

She gave me one of her looks. A Tamar look. My hands bore down on the couch cushion, gripping its edges so hard that my fingers hurt. She was there. She was right there with me in that moment. But for how long? Long enough to answer?

"I was eighteen."

She lifted her shoulders. A tiny movement, bird bones against invisible air, but it was enough. Because with that movement an image of an eighteen-year-old girl came floating into my head, a feather of an image that landed there and would be there forever. A motherless girl wearing a lumber jacket, standing in the chill of an upstate New York fall, two babies growing inside her.

"You were too far along by the time you realized?"

She nodded. My question, asked and answered. Except not really.

"But if you *had* known? Would you—"

She clamped her hands on the cushion and pushed herself up from the couch. Away from the dipshit and back to walking. Back to the strolling of the hallway, the endless journey to choir practice. Maybe it was a moot point to her. She was a girl who had lost her mother the year before, she had only her nontalking dad. The beginning of me was the end of all her plans: Florida, adventure, a new life. I picked up the book of the week, *Harriet the Spy*, and followed her down the hall and added it to the pile by her bed.

....

Tamar got Dog for me when I was twelve years old. The school counselor had called her to express his concern.

"He said you didn't seem to be yourself," she told me. "He said you were hardly talking in class anymore and you were always sneaking off to the library. He said it was a 'marked change' from sixth grade."

She only told me this years after the fact, when I was eighteen and heading to the college in New Hampshire into which she and Annabelle Lee had strong-armed me, the college where they didn't allow dogs in dorms. Where I would be without Dog, my constant companion, for the first time in six years, a fact that tormented me. *Be sure to take him on a walk every day, one hour minimum,* I kept instructing my mother. *Be sure to give him a pig ear every other day. Be sure not to let him jump on anyone when they come to court. Be sure to rub his belly every night when he jumps up on your bed. IF he jumps up on your bed. Do you think he'll jump up on your bed when I'm gone?* Because he never had. It had always been my bed he jumped up on.

This conversation happened as she was driving and I was riding shotgun. We were past Hogback Mountain and closing in on Brattleboro, where we would head north, the backseat of the pickup crammed full with us and Dog and my belongings, but what I was really doing was asking her if Dog would be sad without me, if it would be too hard on him.

"Clara."

That was her *Calm down* voice.

Life changed when I was eleven and twelve. First when the old man, the one I used to visit every Wednesday night when my mother was at choir practice, died. And then when I entered seventh grade, the first year that Sterns Middle School included not just seventh and eighth grade but also ninth. A whole new territory of clanging lockers and stern teachers and a group of ninth grade boys who lined up on either side of the bus entrance and rated the girls as we walked into school on a scale of 1 to 10. A few girls were 10's. A few were 1's. Most were 4 or 5. The boys sometimes called out bonus points or demerits for certain physical attributes. One girl, who grew up north of Sterns and was the first one on the bus in the morning and the last one off in the afternoon and lived in a trailer with a rusted door that hung partway off its hinges, was a −3. Day in and day out: −3, until eventually her nickname was Minus.

Me? I was a nothing, because after the first two weeks I got off the bus and headed straight to the loading dock at the back of the school, where the custodian always had the big double doors propped open, and I threaded my way through the bowels of the furnace room into the back hallway and from there to my locker.

"And the counselor was right," Tamar said, on that long drive from Sterns to New Hampshire. "You weren't yourself."

"But what does that even mean?" I said. By then I had trained myself to make everything a reason to argue. "When you think about it, no one's ever really herself. In an existential sense, I mean." I listened to my own words and tried to convince myself that in some existential way they made sense.

"Bullshit," Tamar said. "Decide you're going to be your real self and then be your real self."

I remembered looking at her from my vantage point in the passenger seat, observing her unblinking eyes on the road, the set of her mouth. She did not know what the word *existential* meant, nor did she pretend to. She must not have cared what it meant either, because if she did, she would have asked me. And she would not have felt bad or dumb or ignorant when she asked, because that was the kind of person she was: always and only her real self.

Dog was present for that conversation, sandwiched between a sleeping bag—which Tamar thought might come in handy for extra warmth at college—and the heavy-duty black plastic garbage bags filled with clothes and towels and my winter jacket and a lamp and books and notebooks and laundry detergent and shampoo. The drive to the White Mountains was nearly six hours. He occasionally muscled his head up from between the overflowing garbage bags, which acted as a kind of restraining device, and pushed his nose into my shoulder. I kept reaching back to stroke his head and scratch him under the chin. I worried about Dog on that drive. What if a bigger truck came barreling up behind us and rear-ended us? Tamar and I were belted in, but all Dog had for protection were the garbage bags. Would he go catapulting through the windshield? He wasn't a huge dog. He was lean and long-legged, lacking bulk and mass.

"What are you thinking about?" Tamar said at one point. We were halfway to campus, halfway to the place where I would spend the next four years.

"Dog. What if we get rear-ended by a semi and he goes flying through the windshield?"

She shook her head. Her strange daughter. We stopped for gas, we stopped to let Dog pee, and then we were there, at a gray stone building, with all the other freshmen and parents and crammed cars.

Tamar hauled bags up to the third floor alongside me. She first cranked the truck windows down a few inches so Dog wouldn't overheat—no animals allowed in the dorms—and I glanced through the first-floor- and second-floor-landing windows each time I labored up and then ran down the stairs, to make sure that he was okay in there while we moved me in.

Then I was moved in. Then Tamar and Dog were in the truck, backing up, doing a slow five-point turn, inching their way back out the road we'd come in on, past all the other parents and their sons and daughters. She turned once and waved, a tiny wave. Dog's eyes were on me the whole way until the truck turned around a curve and disappeared.

And that was it.

I didn't remember much else of freshman orientation. I remembered meeting my roommate, Sunshine, and how she crossed out "Samantha" on her ID card and wrote in "Sunshine" in permanent marker, and I remembered meeting Brown, who lived in the room directly below ours. I remembered getting my own ID card, figuring out class times and buildings and how to fall asleep surrounded by hundreds of breathing and talking and laughing and drinking and vomiting and smoking and dancing and crying and singing people instead of by two: my mother and Dog.

Did I think about my mother and Dog much?

If I said no, that once I got there it was a blur, making my way through those first few weeks, meeting people and professors and figuring everything out, that would be true. But it would also be a lie.

I pictured them, Tamar chopping wood and taking Dog on his walk, the two of them sleeping in the silent house under the silent stars in silent Sterns. But I couldn't think about that for more than the second it took the scene to flash itself up into my head before I had to shut it down. *Calm down, Clara. Breathe.*

It was just the two of them, was why. The two of them in the one house and each of their days was exactly like the one that came before and the one that would come after. Unlike the way it was for me. Me and a thousand others my age around me and my life, my life that was blowing open, the ceilings and doors and windows of that life I had known in Sterns, the life my mother was so insistent I leave, now disappearing.

....

The next time I saw Dog in real life, after I left for my first year of college, was on Parents' Weekend. It had been only two months. Two months since I watched them disappear around the bend, Tamar driving and Dog with his head hanging out the half-open window, staring at me, unblinking.

Everything was different by then. I talked different I ate different I dressed different I studied different, focused and deep-down scared because everyone around me was smart. They all raised their hands right away during class discussions while I was still trying to understand the question being asked. They were all uppercase Confident College Students to my lowercase clara winter. It was a different world I lived in now, and I was a different girl in it.

That Friday I waited outside Mulberry Hall with everyone else who was waiting for their parents. There would be a Parents' Tea and a President's Dinner and a football game and a Campus Walkabout and a Sunday Brunch and I had the schedule in my hand as I waited. I was wearing the new boots I had bought at the boot store downtown, the real leather boots that took every penny of the money I had made over the last two months serving up breakfast in the cafeteria, my work-study job. Scrambled fried hardboiled poached. I had never heard of poached eggs before and if I had landed on Eggs for $400 and it turned out to be the Daily Double, I would've bet it all that Tamar had never heard of them either.

Then she and Dog were there and I forgot everything.

"Ma!"

She had parked somewhere—where, I didn't know; I hadn't seen the truck pull up even though I was outside watching for it—and Dog was on his rarely used leash. They were making their halting way through the crowds of parents and children.

"Ma!"

Sunshine was next to me, waiting for her family, and she looked at me with curiosity, but I didn't look back. I cupped my hands around my mouth and shouted again: "Ma! Ma!" but it was Dog who heard me first, or smelled me, because suddenly there he was. A bounding blur of fur leaping into the air and shoving himself against the unfamiliar leash, trying to get to me. Then he was on me and we were both on the ground, me with my arms around him, both of us pushing our noses into each other's necks because there he was. There he was, and there I was, and a lump rose up in my throat. Dog.

Tamar was there too, then, her hand white-knuckled around his leash. Jeans and white Keds that she had re-whitened for the occasion with roll-on polish. The roll-on marks were evident. She was wearing her lumber jacket. It was a cold day but I wore only a sweater because that was what we did back then in college: we pretended we weren't cold, we pretended that a crewneck sweater was all we needed even on a day of bitter wind. Her hand touched my shoulder.

"You're cold."

That was the first thing she said. I looked up from the ground at her Tamar face looking down at me. This was the longest I had ever been away from my mother. Her hair looked shorter. Dog had climbed up onto my lap with his paws on my shoulders. He was still pushing his nose into my neck, my hair, my collarbones.

"No I'm not."

"You are, though." Her palm was on my cheek. "Your cheek is like ice."

"I'm not cold at all," I lied.

I took her and Dog around to all the classroom buildings, to the dorm where Sunshine and I had hung India batik prints on the walls to "warm them up." A phrase that belonged to Sunshine, along with the batiks, a phrase and a thing I'd never seen before that fall. I told Tamar that my classes were lots of work but great, that I studied lots but it was nothing I couldn't handle, that I had made lots of friends — the word *lots* kept coming out of my mouth — that the sleeping bag was coming in handy, that on Friday nights we all walked into town with our fake IDs for pitchers of happy-hour beer and 2/$5 Cape Codders and screwdrivers, followed by dancing at The Excuse, that the cafeteria food was really not bad at all, even poached eggs, once you got used to them.

What was really happening was that I was pushing it all at her, all this information, all this breeziness and chatter, because what was done was done. She had forced me out of Sterns and out of upstate New York and out of everything I had known until now. She had banished me from my own life, and even though I had raged and fought against her grim decision, I had gone along with it, hadn't I? I could have run away, couldn't I? I could have flat-out said no. But I hadn't.

I had always assumed I would live in Sterns, where my childhood friends grew up and would continue to live, solid black arrows of parents and children and grandchildren within a few miles of one another. In leaving, I had thought my mother was forcing me out, but the truth was this: she had seen a bigger life for me than I had imagined. And she had been right.

But right didn't mean easy. I couldn't take the presence of her, the literal Tamar presence of her, her in her re-whitened sneakers and her jeans and her lumber jacket held together with duct tape patches on the inside, her hand still gripping Dog's leash.

I wanted her so much.

I wanted to be in her kitchen, my kitchen, our kitchen, sitting next to her by the woodstove. I wanted Dog, Dog with the old stuffed monkey that Asa had given him dangling from his jaws, turning three times in a circle before thumping down onto the rug beside us and tucking himself into a fur comma. I missed her so terribly, now that she was there, right beside me, and I had to shut down that terrible missing so that it wouldn't crush me with its power.

My mother walked beside me, Dog on his leash. She listened to all my surface chatter. She followed my arm with her eyes as I flung it right and flung it left, describing the wonder of the days I was living now. She went to the dinner and the brunch and the tea and the campus walkabout with me, she and Dog, and both nights of the weekend they left me on campus after dinner and drove out to the pets-allowed cheap motel half an hour away.

Sunday morning they left. She put her arms around me and squeezed my shoulders. She said nothing and neither did I. Then she and Dog got back into the truck and drove down from the White Mountains and over the Green Mountains, crossed Lake Champlain and made their way into the Adirondacks, to the house where I used to live but didn't anymore and never would again.

....

I got a ride to the Utica thruway exit for winter break my senior year in college. Tamar was there to pick me up, but Dog wasn't in the backseat waiting the way he usually was.

"Where's Dog?"

"He didn't want to come."

"Since when? Did you tell him you were coming to pick me up?"

She said nothing. Gave me a look. Tamar was not a believer in explaining to animals what was going on, the way I was. If Dog didn't feel like a ride, then she wouldn't press the issue. By the woodstove he would remain, his head resting on that old stuffed monkey.

But when I walked in the door, he struggled up from the rug and the monkey and wobbled toward me. Those were the words: *struggled* and *wobbled.* Tamar was turned away from me, shaking the snow off her jacket and scarf.

"Ma," I said, tried to say, but nothing came out.

Dog had made his way to me but his head was tilted and stayed that way, as if he couldn't lift it all the way up.

"MA." That time it came out.

She turned then, and saw me crouched down next to him. Confusion and surprise and then something else flitted over her face and I knew she was suddenly seeing him the way I was, with eyes new to the scene, eyes that hadn't beheld my dog in four months. She crouched down then too, and we both put our arms around him. The memory of a night the spring of my senior year in high school flooded into my head. I had been out at a party, one of the constant parties that seniors seem to have, the same franticness to all of them, as if time were running out. I came up the dirt driveway late, in my flip-flops. The house was dark. The door was unlocked. No sound from upstairs, where Tamar was either asleep or lying awake silently.

Dog, though. Dog was waiting for me at the door. He wasn't a barker, just a low *rrff* once in a while, if an unfamiliar car pulled into the driveway. He pushed his head into my leg, there in the dark kitchen, and I fell onto the floor next to him. I lay down and clutched him as if I were drowning and he was my life preserver. I had missed Asa all night long, missed his presence next to me at the party, and in that moment I missed him with my whole body, aching for him, for the life we had shared, the one he had abandoned for the army, the life I too was about to leave behind.

Once I returned to college after that winter break, Dog took himself out in the woods to die. He had taken to standing by the door, nosing at it, and Tamar would let him out, but when she went to let him back in a few minutes later he wouldn't be there. He wouldn't come when she called either. She went searching for him, in the old storage barn, down the dirt road, in the woods. Each time she found him he would be nearly invisible, a shadow by a dark tree. Each time, she led him back to the house with one hand on his head to encourage him along.

That was the way I imagined it. My mother didn't use any of those words. Her words were more like *He kept wandering away down the dirt road* and *He wouldn't come when I called.*

"Remember when Tamar called to tell me that Dog had died?" I said to Sunshine and Brown in the car. We were on our way back from DiOrio's. "He'd died the night before, but she didn't tell me. You were with me when she finally called the next morning. The next morning!"

Neither of them said anything. I could feel them talking, though, without words, in that way they had. Brown cleared his throat. He was riding shotgun. "Maybe she wasn't sure how to tell you," he said.

"Give me a break. 'Dog died.' That's all she had to say. She should have told me right away."

Sunshine leaned forward from the backseat and put her hand on my shoulder. "Listen, Clara," she said. "Remember we told you she used to call us sometimes? That was one of those times."

"What? Why?"

"She was worried. She didn't want you to be alone when you found out. She wanted to make sure we were with you when she called. She knew what Dog meant to you."

But Tamar was *my* mother. Dog was *my* dog. Italics scrolled along the bottom of my brain.

"How often did she used to call you guys, anyway?"

"Once in a while. When she was worried about you."

My mind, with the influx of new information, was adding and subtracting, shaking everything up and redistributing it. Shuffling a deck of memory cards. A Jacob's ladder, each tile clapping down upon the next.

Dominoes. Games of chance and skill barreled their way through my mind, each of them built around the image of my mother on the phone, the heavy old phone in the kitchen at our old house, talking to Sunshine and Brown over the years that I had known them. I pictured the *Jeopardy!* grid that Brown had printed out for me, back in the cabin, pinned under a shot glass on the kitchen table.

CANS AND JARS	BASEBALL	BREAKUP WITH ASA	CHOIR BUT NO CHURCH	OUT-OF-STATE COLLEGE	SELF-EVICTION
$2000	$2000	$2000	$2000	$2000	$2000

"But I'm her *daughter*," I said, as if somehow this would bring insight that had thus far escaped me.

. . . .

"Do you know anything about her dreams?" Sunshine said.

"She sleeps okay," I said. "As far as I know, anyway. Sylvia or whoever's on duty that night calls me if she gets too agitated."

"No, the other kind of dreams. Things she wanted to do, places she wanted to go. Is it too late or could we take her somewhere?"

"She told me once she wanted to go to San Francisco."

My mother had told me this late one night. She always went to bed early, before me, but on this night I went to the kitchen to make some popcorn, and she was sitting at the kitchen table reading something. Number one, she was not a reader, and number two, when she looked up at me her eyes were wet. She was wearing the same pretty white shirt as in the mysterious photo. The shirt I didn't remember her wearing in later years. The sight of her crying twisted something up in me.

"Ma? What are you reading?"

I pretended I didn't notice she was crying. Stop crying, Ma. Stop it. She slid the paper, stapled sheets of notebook paper, across the table to me. It was an essay I had written for Great Books. *Compare and contrast*

Virginia Woolf's dream of a room of her own to a personal dream of your own. Stupid topic. Why was she crying? Stop crying, Ma.

"I didn't know you wanted to go to Hong Kong," she said.

MA. STOP CRYING.

Who wouldn't want to go to Hong Kong? Sampans and red lanterns and the Star Ferry and that famous harbor. Chinese food. Why *not* go to Hong Kong? But I had chosen it at random, because it was far away and easy to write about and sounded like a place that a person who wasn't me would dream about. A dream that sounded like a dream but wasn't my real dream, which was to one day, some far-off day, live inside a world of words. Words to bring back the old man, words to wall off the memory of Asa, words to build barriers, words to take them down, words to soothe the savage breast. Stop crying, Ma.

"Me, I always wanted to go to San Francisco," she said.

"San Francisco?"

I laughed. San Francisco was the most doable dream in the world. Get in the car and head west. Eventually you'd hit the Pacific Ocean. Hong Kong, now Hong Kong, even though I was only pretending I wanted to go there, was a different matter entirely. I stood there in the yellow light from the lamp she'd dragged over to the table—Tamar hated overhead light—and laughed. At her. Instantly, she stopped crying. She looked away. She got up from the table and turned herself sideways to slip past me in her Tamar way. Her two-dimensional way, which was how thin my mother was. She didn't say another word about San Francisco, then or ever.

Back then, if you had asked me why I was laughing, I would've told you that compared to Hong Kong, San Francisco was such a tiny dream. Tiny, small, a laughable nothing kind of dream.

If you asked me now why I was laughing, I would tell you that I was an angry, sad girl who hated to see her mother cry. Whose world went black when her mother cried. Who would've done anything, who *did* do anything, like laugh at her right in her face, to make her stop.

Now, fifteen years later, I pictured Hong Kong in my mind. Did the lanterns still hang from sampans in that famous harbor? Or were sampans a thing of the past? I wouldn't know, because I hadn't been to Hong

Kong. The dream I dashed out on notebook paper when I was seventeen and a senior at Sterns High School was a false dream, one I made up to finish a paper as fast as I could, a paper I got an A on.

Tamar's dream, though? That was a true dream. A real dream.

"She wanted to go to San Francisco," I said again. "But I think it's too late."

....

"Maybe we could bust her out," Brown said. "Not to San Francisco but for the weekend. Or a day, even?"

It was the next morning and we had just finished breakfast at Walt's. No wait, no lines, because the foliage—the ridgelines on fire, folding one over the other on their curving march to the far horizon—was done for the year.

"I mean, it's too late for San Francisco," Brown said. "I get that. But what about Old Forge? Is it too late for Old Forge?"

"Music, maybe?" Sunshine said. "She always liked music."

"Yes! A concert!"

"Or a drive," I said. "She likes drives. Or she used to."

"Yes!" Brown said again. His exclamation-mark voice. "A drive up to Lake Placid, maybe, and then some food, and some music."

Outings for $200. An afternoon with Tamar. Okay. Next day we piled into the Subaru, hours earlier than usual so as to have her back in the early evening. But it was a day of confusion and brain fog. The walls were coming up, or going down, and she was wary.

"Ma?"

She sat on the couch in the Green Room and shook her head at me. Here I was again, the strange woman who kept calling her Ma.

"Excuse me," I said. "Tamar?"

"Yes?"

"We were wondering if you'd like to go for a drive."

Her eyes went from me to Brown and back again. Suspicious. Maybe it was Brown's excitement, radiating out from him into the air of the room. She looked him up and down, carefully, then back to me. Wary.

It was only when she noticed Sunshine, still standing in the doorway, that she relaxed.

"It's you," she said, and Sunshine smiled.

"It's me," she agreed. Tamar patted the spot next to her on the couch and Sunshine sat down.

"Pretty girl," Tamar said. Sunshine's sitting down seemed to settle her, and she gestured at Brown and me to sit in the rocking chairs. Which we did.

"Do you want to go on a drive with us, Tamar?" Brown said. Still hoping. His whole plan for the afternoon was almost visible there in the air: the drive, the food, the music. But she shook her head.

"I miss my daughter," she said. "I can't find her."

Brown and Sunshine looked at me and opened their mouths, their hands already lifting off their laps to point to me, the daughter, the daughter! Right there! Right here in the room with you, Tamar! But I frowned at them. *Don't argue. Don't correct. Remain calm. Remain detached.*

"It must be hard, missing your daughter," I said.

"Oh, yes. It's very hard." She pinched her thumb and fingers together and scribbled them in the air as if she were holding a pen. "Those things, you know—pinpricks. Clouds."

"Pinpricks and clouds."

"She was good at them. Clouds."

"She was good at making things up, maybe."

"Yes. That's what clouds are."

She frowned at me. Her daughter the word girl wouldn't have said something dumb like that.

"You miss your daughter," I said. "And I miss my mother."

She looked out the window then, past Brown and Sunshine, past me, focused on something out there or maybe nothing out there. I wanted to say something, something that would pull her back with us, but she started to hum. She motioned us to sing—her fingers waving as if she were a choir director—but I couldn't. That was all right, though, because Brown took over and began singing with her. That same baffled king, still composing his hallelujah, the king my mother never tired of singing about. Her alto, Brown's tenor, Sunshine's arm around my shoulders. And the inked wire holding me together.

....

Next night I went back to the bar. It was not a busy night and I sat on a barstool and helped the bartender polish wineglasses. Around and around each rim with a clean cotton dish towel, hold it up to the light and examine it for any remaining marks, then stand up and slide it into its slot on the overhead hanging rack.

"So you were a piano major?" the bartender said. Not a college man, he was curious about college, about majors and minors, semesters and schedules.

"I was."

"But you never tried to get a job using your piano?"

I shook my head and waited for him to tilt his head in that typical quizzical way and ask, *Why not?* But he didn't do that. What he did instead was wait. The bartender was good enough at waiting to beat me at my own waiting game.

"I studied piano because I loved it."

"And the loving it was enough?"

I nodded. Unlike most people, the bartender didn't pursue the topic, didn't ask why I had studied something I hadn't used since. Didn't ask why I had put all those vast late-night solo soundproof practice room stretches of time into getting better and better and better at something that I had then abandoned.

Even though I hadn't abandoned it.

I never said that, though. It wouldn't make sense. How could I explain that all those hours, fingers crawling or flying or stumbling over the keys, up and down and up and down, thousands of miles of black and white notes floating up out of the massive stringed throat of that instrument, had embedded themselves in me, in my blood and flesh and bone, in my heart, so that wherever I went in this world, music went with me? As hymns were to Asa, so my piano was to me.

"It was a refuge. Somewhere I could go and sit and work and work and work and when I was done it was like I had worked myself into another world."

He smiled. "Another world where everything was beautiful and nothing hurt, like Gayle's tattoo?" He nodded in the direction of the server.

"Where beautiful was inconsequential. Where beautiful and ugly and in between had disappeared, because your fingers had played themselves out and there wasn't anything left to think about."

Just then my phone buzzed, vibrating against my thigh deep in my pocket, in its home next to the hammer earring. "Ma," read the screen, which meant not Ma but someone who looked after Ma. Sylvia, usually. The phone twinkled and shook in my hand.

"This is Clara."

"Hi, Clara. It's Sylvia."

"What's going on?"

"She's having a hard time tonight. She keeps looking for you. She says she needs to go outside and find you. I'm sorry for calling so late. I thought we could calm her but—"

"I'm on my way."

The phone went dark and I pushed it back into my pocket. The bartender's hands folded the dish towel into half, then quarters.

"Your mother?"

"The nurse."

"What's going on?"

I shook my head. I pictured her searching for me, pushing her walker up and down hallway after hallway, stopping at the Green Room, stopping at the reception desk, at the juice station, at the cleaning closets. Picking her walker up and throwing it at the wall. Yelling at Sylvia.

"I have to go."

"Do you want company?"

"No thanks." Already I was mentally in the Subaru. But as I got up from the stool—goodbye, quiet bar, goodbye, quiet conversation, goodbye, upside-down wineglasses shining in your quiet rows overhead —my heart flared.

I sat back down and breathed. Breathed in, breathed out. Long and slow. But my chest shook with frantic fluttering. I closed my eyes and put my fingers on my carotid artery and pressed.

"You okay?"

He came around the end of the bar and took my other hand in his.

"What's happening?"

"Nothing."

The fluttering intensified. I had to lie down. Where? The floor was a bar floor, and the chairs and stools were high and small. The long black booth in the back was empty and I made my way toward it, my eyesight fuzzy, and lay down and drew my knees up and closed my eyes. There was the sound of a chair scraping across the floor. He was sitting next to me, his knees touching my hip.

"Clara, what's going on?"

"It's just a glitch in my heart. It races sometimes and I have to lie down until it goes back to normal. It's nothing."

If you say things with authority and calm, if you project a do-not-touch aura around yourself, people listen to you. They back off. You can remain pristine, an island unto yourself. No one will try to take charge of you.

Not so with the bartender. His hand was on my heart now, right below my breast—two fingers, I could feel them—measuring the pulsing flutter. I opened my eyes to see his narrowed, looking at my chest, which was shaking with the effort of my heart. I closed my eyes again.

"You're touching my boob."

"I'm touching your heart."

"It's a boob-heart continuum."

My breaths were short. I tried to lengthen them out but they stayed quick and shallow.

"Don't call 911," I said. "It's nothing."

But my heart was working as hard as it could, shuddering and jolting with effort. It should have stopped by now, the way it always used to. My heart was a different animal these days. *You have to get that fixed. You have to get that fixed. You have to get that fixed.* Was it possible to pass out when you were lying down? Stars materialized in the air above me and swirled in patterns like the ones Tamar's fingers made when she was searching for the right word. Tamar. Tamar trolling the hallways, looking for her daughter.

"Can you do me a favor? Can you call that last number back for me?"

I took my fingers off my pulse and pulled the phone out and handed it to him. A tiny sound chimed on the floor. My earring. My hammer earring was down there. "And can you" — but he had already picked it up, and he was putting it in my held-out palm and closing my fingers over it.

"There you go," he said, and then, "Hello? I'm calling on behalf of Clara Winter. She's having car trouble, and —"

———

———

"Okay, great. I'm glad. Who knew that seagulls were so calming?"

He slid the phone back into my pocket. "Crisis averted," he said.

"How so?"

"They started reading to her," he said. "A book about a seagull named Jonathan, they said."

....

Two hours. That was how long it took my heart to stop the crazy.

Two hours, hours in which all the remaining noise of the bar gradually drained away. In which the front door, with its scraping sound of wood on wood, opened and shut, letting out the last few customers and letting in a blast of cold air each time. In which the sounds of rubber on asphalt and the humming engines of passing cars and trucks faded as they curved away from the curve of the road where the bar was perched. In which Gayle the server came over to check on us, saying, "You guys okay back here?" with genuine concern in her voice, and when the bartender said, "Yeah. Just waiting for her heart to slow down," she said, "Got it," as if it were a normal thing to happen in the bar, as if it happened all the time, and then her footsteps retreated across the wooden floor.

Then came the scrape, scrape, scrape of barstools and chairs being upturned on tables, and the swish, swish, swish of broom on floor, followed by the softer swish of wet mop, and finally the swift jingle of keys being swiped from a hook or from inside a pocketbook. Gayle's footsteps, the sound of which was now familiar, came closer again.

"Bye, guys." And she was gone.

It was me and the bartender then, waiting on my heart. The overhead hanging lamps, like Gayle's footsteps, had become familiar, and so had the shadows in the big-beamed ceiling they illuminated. A small constellation of frilled toothpicks clustered in a pool of soft light near an overhang, almost directly above my head. Someone — someones — must have taken straws, stuck the frilled ends inside, tilted their heads back and filled their lungs. Toothpicks, rocketing ceilingward.

The bartender was whittling, there on the chair next to the bench where I lay flat, heart still hammering. A slender limb, drawn from a bucket of them, lay across his lap and he shaved off slivers. The clean smell of new wood filled the air around us.

"What're you making?" I said.

He turned the limb over, examining it. "Nothing that I know of. Yet anyway."

"What kind of wood is that?" Woods of the North for $200, even though I, as the daughter of a woodswoman, already knew the answer.

"Red pine."

Correct. I pointed at the bucket. "And the rest of them?"

"That one's scrub oak, that one's maple, that one's white birch, that one's white pine."

He barely looked as he rattled them off.

"Do you have a favorite?"

"Plywood." He looked up at me, gauging to see if I was dumb enough to think plywood was a kind of tree.

"What a coincidence," I said. "Me too."

"Liar. Plywood is no one's favorite wood."

"I beg to differ. Plywood's what my kitchen table's made from. Partly, anyhow."

I pictured the stacks of books underneath my table, and the books-as-coffee-table, and the books-as-bed in the tiny cabin. The guys at Foley Lumber had sliced a sheet of plywood in half for me and I had lugged it home in the Subaru and muscled it up on top of the books to make the table. One of the bartender's hands braced the piece of red pine in his lap and the other held his pocketknife as he shaved off paper-thin shims. He was good with his jackknife the way my mother was good with an ax. I watched and I didn't say anything.

The bar was quiet around us, and the sound of a single cricket who had made his way inside from the cold drifted through the room. My heart trembled and shook inside me, a rebel, unwilling or unable to stop its frantic beating. I pulled my phone out to look at my favorite photo of Sunshine and Brown, to call up their presence beside me. There they were, their arms spread wide against a backdrop of the Rockies, a cross of snow on the side of a mountain in the distance. Brown's hair and the scarf Sunshine was wearing to cover her chemo-bald skull blowing wild in the wind. Both of them laughing. I sent them a telepathic message: *Hello, my darlings. It's happening again. Yes, I know I have to get it fixed.*

I held the phone straight up in the air above my head. "Want to see my friends? That's Sunshine. And that's Brown."

The bartender leaned forward and craned his neck so that he could see. Then he put down his whittling, pulled three chairs together in a row and lay down on them. Me on the cushioned bench, him next to me on hard wooden chairs. Now we could both look up at the phone above our heads without straining.

"And where was this photo taken?"

"In Colorado. They hiked up and took the gondola down."

I scrolled past to the next. I had a whole album of Sunshine and Brown photos.

"And where's this one?"

"Here. At my place. In the living room slash kitchen slash dining room slash everything room of my house slash one-room cabin."

He pointed. "Am I looking at a coffee table slash pile of books?"

"Nay, sir, you are looking at a books-as-coffee-table. That photo was taken months ago, though. The books-as-coffee-table has mostly disappeared now."

He took the phone and brought it close to his face, enlarging the photo to study the disappearing table. Then he swiped to the next photo.

"Who's this?" he said. "She's pretty."

It was the mystery photo of Tamar, propped up next to Jack on the little kitchen shelf. Why I had taken it—a photo of a photo of a mystery—I did not know. It wasn't as if I couldn't look at it every night when I got home. But here she was, with me in my phone.

"That's my mother."

"I figured. There's a resemblance."

Was there? I took a long breath and *beat*, my heart was back to normal. I counted to thirty-two, randomly and because it was my age, then sat up. Blood spun away south, down through my body.

"Back to normal?" the bartender said, and I nodded.

The bar was dark except for the lights in the back, where we had been waiting so long. It was past midnight. The bartender put his arm around me outside, by my car. He smelled like soap and leather and lime and denim and wood shavings. Then we went our separate ways, whittled-down piece of red pine in his hand, tiny silver earring in mine.

....

Asa died when I was living on the Florida Panhandle, during a stretch of time right after I quit being a small-town reporter. If you went to college and majored in piano but didn't intend to make your life about music, and if you had always loved words, it would be logical to accept a job as a reporter, wouldn't it?

Wrong. The job of reporting, like most jobs that used words, was about not the love of words themselves but the usefulness of words. The everydayness of words. Ways to convey information via the alphabet. When I chose reporting, I didn't know yet that it had nothing to do with loving words. It took me a long time to figure that out.

Thursday nights back then were when I used to call my mother. Thursdays with Tamar, a routine that began when I was living in Lake Placid and working for the *Adirondack Times* and continued on to the Panhandle years. She would pick up on the third ring, the way I watched her do all my life. *Ring, ring, ring,* then snatch it up halfway through. Even if she was standing right next to it when it rang, even though it was a Thursday night at eight o'clock and it could be no one but me, she would wait until it had rung exactly two and a half times.

"Tamar Winter speaking. How may I direct your call?"

"Ma. It's me."

"You're looking for Ma? One moment, please. **MAAAAAAA!**"

Right in my ear. Full-blast.

"Jesus, Ma! Stop it."

"Certainly, caller. Ma will be right with you." Pause. Then, in her normal voice, "Hello? Clara?"

"Can you please stop doing that."

"Doing what?"

"MA."

"I have no idea what you're talking about. How was your week?"

"It was okay," I would say, already tired of the phone call. Of the ritual. Of the way it never changed. "My week was okay."

"Anything interesting happen?"

Her use of that word used to infuriate me. "Everything's interesting, Ma, if you look at it the right way."

Sometimes now I thought back on those calls. *Listen to yourself, Clara. Listen to how you used to talk to your mother. You knew so much more than she did, didn't you? You were so much more sophisticated, so much more world-weary, so much more advanced.*

Had I been a child and still living with her, my mother would never have put up with the way I spoke to her in those phone calls. And I would never have spoken to her that way. That changed when I was seventeen, though, after Asa and I broke up. Words and scorn and distance became my weapons, and did I use them? I did. The young boxer danced around her middle-aged opponent, throwing words and phrases with precision. Lightning blows rained down upon the older woman and she retreated, thin and silent, to her corner.

....

The Life Care people and the AD and eFAD forum people were united in their advice on nearly all fronts. If you decided to get the genetic testing done, you had to confer with a genetic counselor pre-test. If you were the primary caregiver for someone with eFAD or AD, you had to take care of yourself as well as your loved one. It was called "self-care" and it was critical to the stability and health of all parties.

And they were right about everything, I supposed, the way that Sylvia was right when she warned me not to use the word *remember*. None of the advice went far enough, though. The word *remember* was a two-edged sword. There were things I wished I didn't remember. Like the way I felt when I saw that look in my mother's eyes, the night I machine-gunned those words at her in the darkness and she turned the lamp on. Like the feeling in me when Eli Chamberlain guided his son into his truck the day we broke up and then drove him away from me. Like the way my mother had spoken to me one winter break when I was home from college and she came upon me looking through Asa's high school yearbook, turning by heart to all the pages where there was a photo of him.

"Clara, it's over."

We were sitting at the kitchen table. She must have seen a look on my face.

"But—"

"No buts," she said, and something in her voice made me shut up. "It's been over for years now. Once a decision is made, you can move only forward. That's what Asa did. You should too."

She was done. She was a say-it-once sort of person. And she was right, which was something I now knew. But I began moving sideways instead, and I kept moving sideways for a long time. From New Hampshire to Boston to Florida, I moved sideways. If I started living in a different country the fall that Asa Chamberlain and I broke up, then I started living in a different universe the day that Tamar called to tell me he was dead. I could still hear her voice, the way she said my name when she called. I had quit reporting and was living in that house on stilts, working on what would become *The Old Man* and teaching GED classes to prisoners—you would not believe how many prisons there were on the Florida Panhandle—and eating a lot of shrimp.

I was sitting on a folding chair watching a pot of shrimp when the phone rang. You had to remove them from the boiling water as soon as they turned pink. Otherwise they were tough and flavorless. I didn't want to answer the phone at all but it kept ringing. *What's the goddamn urgency?* I thought, but then something in me shifted, something told me to pick up, and I did.

"Clara."

"Ma?"

"Clara, Asa died this morning. He died in an explosion in Afghanistan. He was in a Humvee and it blew up."

The shrimp, the folding chair, the ringing phone, my mother's voice. All the hours after it, the days, the fact that Tamar arrived the next evening, having driven all night and all the next day too, to get to me, to haul me back north with her to Sterns, to watch over me until I could talk again, until I could breathe, I didn't remember.

He died. I kept coming back to that, even now. Asa was in my heart and my body. I still woke from dreams in which he was walking toward me down a road made of sand, shifting sand, with his hands held out toward me, smiling.

....

You have to get that fixed.

But what if something happens to me?

Every time someone told me I should get my heart fixed—Sunshine, Brown, the cardiologist, my mother—that thought stole into my head. What if something happened to me? Who would take care of my mother? Who would visit her, go to the Life Care meetings, discuss her medication, follow her wheresoever she goeth?

Her index finger brushed my forearm, tracing the beginning of the inked wire.

"What's that?" she said.

"A tattoo."

She had seen it before, many times, unlike most people. My ink was a slender line that started high on one inner forearm, wound around my upper arm and then across my shoulder blades and down the other arm, ending just below the elbow. Invisible most of the time. But the thermostat was always set high in the place where she lived now, and I had pushed my sweater up above my elbows.

My mother turned my arm this way and that, her hand steady, examining again what she could see of the inked wire, and a night when I was four years old came washing over me. She had woken me up to bring me downstairs onto the cold porch because the aurora borealis was pulsing in the night sky. *Look, Clara. It's the northern lights.* I was so tired. I leaned against a porch post. She held my hand to keep me upright.

"Why?" she said now, her head tilted, studying the thin line of wire.

"It holds me together," I said. "If I go like this"—and I pushed my sleeves up and twined my arms around each other—"then I can't come apart."

She nodded, as if she understood. Did she, somehow? Brown's voice came into my head: *Ask her.*

"Did you have anything like this, Ma? Anything to hold you together?"

"Yes."

"What was it?"

"Work. Wood. Len."

She said "Len" conversationally, as if he were someone she knew well, a husband or boyfriend or dog or cat—Len, who kept her steady. There had been no Lens in her life though, none that I knew. She was gone again. Gone into a parallel world where someone named Len was holding her hand on a freezing porch, pointing at the heavens alive with color. Sadness washed through me. *Follow your mother wheresoever she goeth, Clara. Meet her where she is, not where you want her to be.*

"What do you most like about Len, Ma?" Careful phrasing. No *remember*s, no corrections.

"His music," she snapped. "You know that."

We were sitting on the edge of her bed. She picked up her pillow and placed it on my lap with a firm push. A dunce cushion for a dunce. Which I was, because by Len, she must have meant Leonard Cohen. The man whose music she had loved as long as I could remember. Len, her good friend the musician. Len, her old buddy the singer-songwriter. Len, the baffled king composer. She was with me, my mother, right then and there. *Ask her,* came Brown's voice again. *There is no time,* came Sunshine's voice. What could I ask her about? I cast my eyes about the room. A copy of *The Old Man* was splayed open on her nightstand.

"Are you reading that book, Ma?"

It was a used library copy that had not come from me. Who had given it to her?

"Sylvia reads it to me."

"Do you like it?"

"Like what?"

"The book."

"It's strange. It's a strange book." She frowned. "The girl, she" — she searched for the word then suddenly curved her body forward with her arms over her head, as if she were about to dive into a deep lake, and the motion somehow panicked me, as if we were standing on the actual edge of an actual cliff — "jumps."

"Maybe she likes to jump."

"No! No! Not jump!"

Distract. Redirect.

"Who gave you that book, Ma?"

She leaned back and regarded me, as if I were a stranger, as if we hadn't just been talking.

"She was a strange child," she said. "A tree. A houseboat. A cabin. A covered wagon. All of them. She was a" — she fumbled for the right word and began to whisper words in succession, shaking her head after each one, a *No, no, that's not right either* kind of motion — "plains. Snow. Oxen. Blizzard. She was a blizzard. A blizzard girl."

"Pioneer," I whispered back. "She was a pioneer girl."

She nodded. That was the word she was looking for. She could rest now. She looked at me patiently. "What's your name?"

"Clara."

"That was her name too!"

Her eyes lit up. It was a miraculous coincidence. These dark searching nights of following your mother meant that you had to follow her into a world that used to exist, one in which she called you her word girl and rolled her eyes at your dreams of being a pioneer girl who braved the winter blizzards, a world in which you used to make up fake books about winter so that you could write real book reports about them. A world that if you could, you'd do over. Do differently. Because this time around you'd know that it would end. That there would come a time when you and your mother would sit on a couch together, and she would lean toward you politely, asking your name.

"Ma, can I ask you about some things?"

"Yes."

"Why did you tear up my MVCC application? Was it because you were angry at me?"

She picked the pillow up again and placed it on her own lap, then back on mine. The pillow of dunceship. The pillow of distraction. Try again. Rephrase.

"You must have been so angry with me."

"Why?"

"Because of the night I screamed at you. The awful things I said."

"You were a, a . . ." Frustration wrinkled her face and her fingers came off the pillow and into the air, searching. "You were a, a . . ." She scribbled in the air. Letters? The alphabet? Words? Then it came to me.

"Word girl?" I said and she nodded in relief. Her fingers closed and made a fist and she pounded the pillow on her lap. Yes. I was a word girl and I had to go away. She sank back against the headboard, gone again into that parallel world. The word girl was gone too, spiraled away into the coiled shell of my mother's mind, if that was where memory lived. Unless there was somewhere else that memory went, an invisible place where everything that ever happened to everyone on the planet was held safe, untouched and untouchable.

I wrapped my arms around themselves and against my body, wire holding me tight together.

....

How did they do it? How did Tamar Winter and Annabelle Lee, women unfamiliar with the ways of the elite, women who had not studied past high school, women well-schooled in the ways of the rural world, its byways and dirt roads and woods and hymns and milkshakes but schooled not at all in the ways of college and how to get into one early-decision with a full package of scholarships and grants and work study, manage to apply in my name and come up such massive winners?

When you hear about first-generation college students, how hard it is for them to navigate their way in a world so unfamiliar, maybe you inwardly roll your eyes, thinking, *Oh, please, it's not that hard.* It is, though. It was only now, when I looked back, when I pictured myself in those New Hampshire mountains wearing my fake leather boots from Payless and the mittens that Crystal from the diner knitted me as a going-away present, that I saw just how hard it was.

So hard.

People like Sunshine and Brown and my other friends from college, they didn't know what it was like for someone like me, someone from Sterns, who grew up surrounded by plenty of people who never considered college, who didn't graduate high school and didn't care, because life wasn't about school and jobs didn't need degrees and you learned how to work at the side of your mother and father: on the farm, in the trades, cleaning houses, waiting tables. But so few at my college were from lives like that. Most were from cities, or the rich suburbs just outside them. They had gone to prep schools, country day schools, which was a term, like poached eggs, I had never heard before I got to college.

It was bewildering. Overwhelming. Like learning a new language, one that used English words and English names and English terms but was a language parallel to the one I grew up in.

So how had my mother and Annabelle Lee learned that language?

"We faked it," was all Annabelle would say. "And by we, I mean your mother. She was determined."

"Why, though?"

"Because she knows you, Clara."

She and Annabelle must have huddled over the college applications when I was out of the house. She let me go on for a long time, didn't she, with my MVCC plan, until she knew for sure I had gotten into the college of her choice early-decision, the admissions committee particularly impressed with the power of my essay about someday traveling to Hong

Kong, that the full aid package had come through. Then came the January day that she ripped up my MVCC application.

She drove me to New Hampshire and she came back alone.

....

"Time speeds up in a situation like this," Sunshine said. "You just have to keep trying, Clara."

How would you know, I wanted to say, but didn't. Because they did know. Sunshine's cancer had sped everything up for the two of them, just as early-onset was speeding everything up for me. Sunshine had had to figure everything out with her parents, get everything said, everything settled, in case there was no time.

"Keep talking to her."

That was their advice to me about everything these days. Keep talking. Keep asking. Keep at it. Do it anyway, all of it, no matter if it scared you. Whatever you could find out, find out. When I was younger I believed that the stories I didn't want to remember could be pushed so far down inside me that they would stay there forever. But I knew now that I had been wrong.

The memory of Asa kept coming back to me, the day we broke up. The way he stood there, the way he kept shaking his head. It was the day after the night that something had happened between my mother and Asa. Had she told him to break up with me? No, that wouldn't be possible. He was a grown man, nineteen years old, with a full-time job driving truck. Sometimes I tried to convince myself that they hadn't argued at all. That they had just been sitting at the table chatting, waiting for me to return home. But that wasn't the case. The way Asa brushed past me when I got home, the way my mother wouldn't meet my eyes, the way the next day everything fell apart. Something had happened. But no one would talk to me about it.

It was after that day that my mother must have set the college plan in motion.

Reckon your losses.

That was what the bartender told me to do, when I told him about Asa. How he had helped me find my earring, how he loved *The Velveteen*

Rabbit, how his father, Eli, used to read it to him. How Eli had come driving through the woods to retrieve his son on the day that he broke up with me, the day that Asa's car wouldn't start, how he had put his hand on Asa's shoulder and guided him into the truck and how the curtain that Tamar was watching behind had dropped back down over the window. How I had not spoken to Asa again, much as I wanted to, and not to his father either, even after Asa died in Afghanistan.

The bartender listened in silence.

"It comes back to me," I said. "I keep seeing the two of them. That day. I keep hearing my voice."

"You haven't talked to his father since?"

"No. At this point it's too late. Nothing can be done."

My voice wanted to speak in exclamation marks—!!!—but I would not let it. *Nothing can be done! Nothing can be done!* scrolled across the bottom of my brain.

"Something can always be done," the bartender said.

Around and around and around the wineglass went the towel. He had been polishing that wineglass for ten minutes. Twenty minutes. A lifetime. Who was the bartender to tell me what to do? He had never known Asa and he didn't know Eli and he could give me no advice because this was not his situation to deal with. Protests rose up inside me but behind them was Eli, guiding his son into the truck on that awful day. Behind them was that old velveteen rabbit, loved and abandoned. Behind them was my mother, looking up from her Neil Diamond album and crying. Behind them was Blue Mountain at the museum, cross-legged on the floor with the other children, their faces turned up like cups. The skinless walked among us.

"What would *you* do?" I said.

"I'm not a word person like you. I'd carve something out of wood, probably. A talisman of some kind."

"Like what?"

He shrugged. "Something that felt right." He reached up and put the wineglass in its overhead rack, sliding it into place with both hands. It gleamed and sparkled and shone. Bright and clear, unlike the fairy lights at the cabin, glimmering in their shadowy ways.

"I used to make stories," I said. "Stories were my talismans. But I can't do that right now. If I wrote about everything that's happening right now, with my mother, with the past and the present, she would be trapped forever in those words. A bug in amber. And then I'd have to live forever with her like that."

He put his hands on mine. They were warm. They were always warm.

"We all have to live forever with the things we've done," he said. "We all have to reckon with our losses."

....

"Adirondack Mountains That Could Also Be Children's Names for twelve hundred, please," Brown said, and I slammed my hand down on the table. We were playing Jeopardy! and I was far in the lead.

"What is Blue Mountain?" I said.

"What is a terrible answer?" Brown said. "You're slipping, Winter. If you and your boyfriend ever choose to name your future child after an Adirondack mountain, promise us you'll do far better than Blue."

"I agree," Sunshine said. "Choose your mountain carefully. Not Bald. Not Haystack. Not Whiteface. Geez, especially not Whiteface."

"Or Dix," Brown said. "That would ruin your kid's life. Think about it."

"I've got a worse one," Sunshine said. "Nippletop. Who in God's name would name a mountain Nippletop, let alone a child?"

"Remember your nippletops?" Brown said. "They were the nipple-tops of the century."

"They were pretty awesome, weren't they?"

We all made prayer hands and bowed our heads in the direction of Sunshine's sinewed chest. She had decided to go flat in the wake of her surgery.

"There are some good names in the high peaks," I said. "Like Marshall. Or Phelps. Or Cliff. Esther. McKenzie."

"What about Grace?" Sunshine said. "I like Grace."

"Grace is a good name," Brown said. "Can't go wrong with Grace."

"It's settled then. Grace can come for sleepovers when Winter and the boyfriend get sick of being parents. We'll make her cinnamon rolls for breakfast."

"With extra frosting because Winter won't be around to stop us."

"We'll play Candy Land and Chutes and Ladders with her. You know damn well Winter and the boyfriend won't."

They were off and running, configuring out loud how they could put a toddler bed into the corner of the study, next to the window. How they would have to move the cleaning supplies to a high shelf during the toddler years. How Winter and the boyfriend could list them on school emergency forms so they could pick her up if she had a fever. How they would be Grace's cool aunt and uncle, which meant that Grace would, in a way, love them more than she would love Winter and the boyfriend. Maybe they should start collecting stuffed animals and picture books for Gracie now. What about a college fund? You were supposed to start those things early, right? Even fifty dollars a month would be a help to Gracie eighteen years from now.

"She's already gone from Grace to Gracie?" I said, and they looked at me patiently.

"Of course she's Gracie," Brown said, and Sunshine nodded. "You can't call a little baby Grace."

There was a time, with Sunshine and Brown, a year after the second diagnosis and the second surgery, when they were hell-bent on adoption. The same conversations, about where the baby would sleep and what if there were more than one baby, sibling adoption maybe, or twins, two for one, and was Old Forge Elementary a good school, and what if their kiddo or kiddos — they had already progressed to "kiddo or kiddos" — were bullied on the school bus. Should they go straight to the principal or should they begin with the bus driver? Or maybe go straight to the bully, circumvent the authorities entirely? All that talk stopped after Sunshine's third diagnosis, when they were told that people with certain recurrent health conditions were not adoption-eligible.

"Have a baby, Clara," Sunshine said. "Have a baby so we can baby-proof the house and sing her lullabies and read her picture books."

"And stop the bullies," Brown said. "And make her great Halloween costumes."

They were joking, except they weren't.

"Just do it?" I said. "Like the Nike ad?"

"Yeah," Sunshine said, and Brown said, "Yeah. Do it for us."

A tall boy appeared in the doorway, dark hair obscuring his eyes, one arm around skinny little Blue Mountain. An imaginary visitor from the parallel world, not allowed over the doorsill. A look passed over Sunshine's face, as if she saw something too. Maybe her own parallel-world children, growing up there without her.

....

The bartender was telling me about his early days in Rochester, about his grandmother and his too-young, too-drugged parents.

"So your grandmother raised you?" I said.

"She did. From three on, anyway. After the DSS stepped in."

It was a freak-cold day in late fall, colder than cold, the kind of cold that sweeps in upon the Adirondacks on gale-force winds from the Arctic north or the stormy Atlantic, precursor to the months of winter that will follow. The bartender and I had met at Walt's for breakfast and now we were wandering the streets of Old Forge, if *wander* was a word used to describe two people hunched deep into their collars, gloved hands shoved into their coat pockets, hatted heads bent low against the gale, winter-booted feet trudging forward, ever forward. My hat was one of Sunshine's, her very first scallion, an experimental hat far too big for a baby's head. Or even my own head.

"Are you cold?" the bartender said. I could barely hear his words against the wind, the scarf, the hunched-collarness of the conversation.

"Oh, no," I said. "Not at all. Who could possibly be cold in this balmy weather."

If you take the question mark off the end of the question, it transforms itself into a sarcastic statement. You can do this with your voice or on paper. Either way, it works.

"Sweet baby Jesus," the bartender said, "can we please go inside."

The bartender knew the power of an un-question-marked question too, apparently.

"Apparently we will have to," I said. "It's either that or face the certainty of death by Adirondacks-in-winter-ness."

I was consciously using the word *apparently* inside and outside my head as much as possible in an attempt at the reverse of aversion therapy. The more the Life Care people said *apparently,* the more I too said *apparently.* In that way I would grow accustomed to it and stop wincing internally every time I heard it. In that way I would stop associating the word *apparently* with everything that my mother had lost and everything that she would keep losing. That was my hope.

Into Adirondack Hardware we went. My feet, even in fake-fur-lined boots, were numb with cold. I stepped on my left toes with my right foot and then my right toes with my left foot, but nary a toe could be felt.

"Now would be an excellent time to amputate one of my toes," I said to the bartender. We were standing in one of the far back rooms, by a display of Swiss Army knives.

"And why would I want to do that," he said.

He was still un-question-marking his questions. The un-question came out slightly muffled, as if he had once had a speech impediment but long ago overcame it. I knew why he was talking that way, though. I was talking the same way. It was a form of winter speech impediment known to northerners the world over, the *My lips are too cold to form words properly* speech impediment.

"Because"—I was going to say, *Because five toes are excessive, and who really needs that tiny one on the far end anyway, have you ever taken a serious look at a pinky toe*—but instead I put my hands on his shoulders and leaned up, way up because the bartender was taller than me, and kissed him. It was a shadow kiss, a whisper of a kiss, a kiss that neither of us could feel because our lips were so cold from the cold Adirondack pre-winter. But maybe we could feel it, maybe we did feel it, maybe the bartender felt it the same way I felt it. As if an unseen someone had been collecting invisible tinder and invisible twigs and invisible small, perfect fireplace logs for years and years and years, and had built them into a perfect, invisible pre-fire. And our cold whisper of a kiss was a struck match, and now the fire was burning between us.

The bartender took off his mittens and put his hands on either side of my face. I could barely feel them because my cheeks were so cold and so were his hands, but I did feel them. I felt the bartender's hands, holding my face steady.

"Don't cry," he said, because that was what his hands were doing to me, making me cry. "Or do cry. Do whatever the hell you want, Clara."

I could have said, *Apparently I am,* or something else like it, and in that way be a smart-ass and also keep working on my reverse aversion therapy, but I didn't. I didn't want to be a smart-ass. What I wanted had nothing to do with words at all. What I wanted was for the bartender to keep his hands on my face, for me to feel the slow burn of his palms, warming from within. What I wanted was the sound of his voice behind the words he was whispering to me, softly and slowly and over and over: *I got you.*

....

Genetic counseling was recommended if you had a family history and you were considering getting the test. Genetic counseling was strongly, strongly advised if you had a family history and you were a) considering getting the test, and b) considering having children, or c) falling in love with a bartender and projecting into the future by imagining him getting in his car and driving an hour south to visit you in the place you would end up living in sooner than you wanted, sooner than you ever could have imagined, unless a cure was found and found soon.

I made that last one up. It was fake.

But it was the one on my mind.

Because how could I put him through that? Over and over I imagined it: a winter night in January and the phone rang and he recognized the number and his shoulders sagged and before he even answered the call he was mentally preparing for the drive and for what awaited him once he got there. *Clara's agitated,* the voice said. *We're having trouble calming her down. The usual tricks aren't working.* And he hung up and put on

his winter coat and zipped it up and pulled on his boots and headed out
to the frozen car and backed it down the frozen driveway and drove the
dark, frozen roads all the way to Utica. Or Rome. Or Syracuse. Wherever I was living, in that faraway far-too-soon imaginary future.

He and Sunshine and Brown would come up with tricks for me. I
could hear them now, brainstorming:

"Read to her," Sunshine would say. "For sure read to her."

"Read her what, though?" Brown would say. "The word 'read' is a
very broad category when it comes to Winter."

"Anything."

"Not anything! For God's sake, Sunshine, she is not a 'read anything'
kind of person."

"She is now, Brown. Unless you haven't noticed."

That was where I stopped with that particular fantasy. So far down
the road that any words would do? No. That was a world where I wasn't.
Where I didn't want to be, because I could see it all too clearly. The
bartender would walk beside me wheresoever I went in the hallways of
wheresoever I had ended up, and he would talk me out onto that sugar-
sand beach, or onto that Vermont peak, or down that desert trail, and
then he would talk me back in. At some point he would probably take
my hand, and I would probably let him. But I wouldn't be me at that
point, and he wouldn't be the man he had been with the me I was now.

I needed to know if I carried the mutation, and I needed not to know.
It was too hard to contemplate the knowing, and the not knowing, and
the not knowing what I would do if I had it.

"Talk to him," Sunshine said. "He's your boyfriend."

"He's not my boyfriend."

"Why not? For that reason? Because you're scared of the future?"

I said nothing.

"What would your mother say to that?" Brown said. "What would
your mother think of you, being a chickenshit?"

I'm not a chickenshit. But I kept the words inside me, where they
burned and turned sour in my gut.

"Don't you want to know, though?" Brown said. "It's, what, a twenty-
five-percent chance or something?"

"Fifty," I said. "Fifty percent. Five-oh. And I don't know if I want to know. They don't let anyone young into the trials, so what's the point?"

He looked at me with what in his eyes? Surprise, maybe, because it was clear that I was ahead of him, that I had thought about it already.

"And if there's no cure yet and no trials they'd let me into, then how would knowing change anything?"

"It would give you the chance to make plans."

"Plans for what?"

"The future."

"How so?"

He looked to Sunshine, silent next to him, for help. She was most of the way through another scallion hat. She had been making a lot of scallions lately. The fade of dark green to pale green to near white was her favorite color combination of all the hats she made, which was too bad, because parents loved the strawberries. There was always a sizable backlog of scallion hats.

"What if we had known?" he said to her.

"Known what? That I would get cancer when we were so young?"

"Yes. Would it have changed things? Have you ever thought about that, like, gone back in the past and thought about what, if anything, you would have done differently? Thought about what *we* would have done differently?"

Her fingers didn't stop. "Yes."

"And?"

"I would have said to you, 'Fuck it, Brown, let's have a kid. Let's have a kid now.'"

Her fingers didn't stop crocheting and she didn't look up from the scallion and her words hung there, each one a punch at a punching bag hanging in the cinder blocked windowless gym of the past. *Fuck it, Brown, let's have a kid. Let's. Have. A. Kid. Now.* Each one a realization to me, that of all the variables that genetic testing would mean, this was the one that mattered most to me. My possible, future, undreamt-of, unknowable, maybe-not-possible child. Where was the bartender right at this minute? I pictured him bent over a table whittling, a bucket of wood next to him on the floor, shavings spiraling out from his knife.

"Do you guys think things can sometimes be, like" — they waited for me patiently while I waited for the words, the words that wouldn't come — "not complicated?"

"Things like what?" Sunshine said. "Bartenders?"

"Maybe."

"So you *have* been seeing him?"

"Kind of. At his bar a couple times. And in town."

They sat across the table, studying me. They were talking to each other in that way they did, with no words. I felt the conversation taking place and I closed my hand around my silver earring. If the old man and Asa had once been in the world, weren't they still? In some way, something of them must still be here.

"Can it be just . . . simple, sometimes?"

They nodded. Brown cleared his throat. "Yeah," he said. No exclamation marks in his voice. "It can."

"Do you guys want to come to the bar?" I said.

They were still nodding. They weren't laughing at me. They weren't making remarks about my boyfriend, or about free drinks, or about the nunlike existence they had witnessed over the years. Yes, we'll come to the bar, was what their nods were saying.

....

"Listen to me," I said. It was the next night and we were driving up to the bar. They were going to meet the bartender. Free drinks! Free drinks! That had been their rallying cry the first couple miles, but the closer we got, the quieter they were. "If I someday get that heart procedure, and if something happens to me during that heart procedure —"

"Which it won't," Brown said, but "Brown," Sunshine said. "Stop."

"Will you promise me that you'll keep visiting Ma? That you'll take care of her?"

"Nothing's going to happen," Brown began again. "Didn't that one guy describe it as the slam dunk of the —"

But Sunshine stepped in again. "Yes," she said. "We promise. And if something happens to me —"

Brown began to protest again, his voice beginning its climb into exclamation marks.

"Brown."

That single word, one syllable, and the exclamation marks disappeared. "If something happens to me," Sunshine said, "promise me that you two will take care of each other. Promise me that you won't let Brown sell the house or do anything major for a year, Clara."

"I promise," I said.

"And Brown, promise me that you will go over to Clara's cabin and sit on the porch with her whenever the monkeys start scrambling. Take the place of that goddamn bottle of whiskey and that dead dog."

"I promise," Brown said.

"Then it's settled," Sunshine said. "We're all taken care of."

"You're forgetting yourself," Brown said. "What if something happens to *me?* What about you?"

"I'll have Clara," Sunshine said. There was a *duh* sound in her voice. "She'll take care of me."

I put that away in the back of my mind, Sunshine's surprise at Brown's question, as if he should know that of course Clara would take care of her, and my own surprise at her confidence in me. We were at the bar then, the bar where lights were strung up around the roofline and windows twinkled in the dark November night. Then we were pushing open the door, and a couple sitting next to it gasped and shivered from the freezing air, and then the bartender was looking at us and smiling from behind the bar, and he turned to Gayle, who was ringing something up on the cash register next to him, and said something, and she nodded and turned around and flashed me a smile.

The bartender came around the end of the bar and pointed toward the back booth where we had waited hours for my heart to stop racing. He held out his hand to Sunshine, then Brown, and "Chris," he said, and "Sunshine" and "Brown" and "Heard a lot about you," Brown said, "a lot for Winter anyway," and he nodded in my direction as if the bartender knew exactly what he was talking about — that Winter was chary with information in general, and surely he, the bartender, would already have learned that about her—which wasn't true, because I wasn't that way around the bartender. Did he look surprised? Did he look puzzled? Did he look as if he were about to debate Brown's words? He did not. What the bartender did was take my hand in his and hold it.

"Gimlets for the table?" he said. "Clara likes them."

Behind the bar Gayle lifted the bottle with a flourish and upended it so that the gin streamed steadily into first one shaker and then another. She lifted them high too and shook them back and forth, pirouetting them in an air ballet that she made up as she went. The words on her inner arm were dark and indecipherable from across the room, but I knew what they said. Sunshine and Brown and the bartender were talking about crocheting and whittling and code-writing.

Gayle brought us another round of gimlets without asking and slid a bowl of popcorn between us, popcorn that must have been made by someone back in the kitchen, because it was too fresh and hot and salty and buttery to come from a machine. She handled the bar alone, even after it got busy, so that we could keep talking.

And we kept talking. About Dog, and how he watched over me from his blue urn in the cabin. About fireflies, which might or might not live on air alone. About one-person cabins. About furniture, including furniture made entirely of books. About Sunshine and Brown's heavy wooden slab of a table found curbside in Boston. About Sunshine's former breasts. About the pros and cons of working from home, the way Sunshine and Brown and I did, as opposed to working in a bar, the way the bartender did. About the bartender's grandmother, the one who had raised him, the one laughing, with her arms around him, at his high school graduation in the photo taped to the cash register. About the blankets and stuffed animals we had carried with us as toddlers. Brown still had the blanket he had been found in, a white flannel blanket printed with stars that had been swaddled around him on the steps of the courthouse in Jefferson City, Missouri, which was something I had never known until just then. We talked about my heart and about John Stein's latest book of poems, *More Real Poems About Real People with Real Problems*. We, meaning Brown and Sunshine, talked about my tattoo. Sunshine wrapped her arms around her chest and rocked back and forth, mimicking me.

"She holds herself together with wire," Brown said. "Wire and words."

"That was how we knew something was up when she first moved back," Sunshine said, "even if we didn't know it was about Tamar. She kept doing the hold-herself-together thing. Like, all the time."

"Did you freak out when you saw the entire tattoo?" Brown said. "The way it winds around her?"

He looked to the bartender for confirmation, but the bartender was shaking his head and smiling, as if he didn't know what Brown meant, because he didn't. He had never seen me without clothes. We had kissed only the once, on that frigid day in Adirondack Hardware. I watched as comprehension dawned on first Brown's and then Sunshine's face. They didn't look at each other but I could feel them communicating in their silent way. *They haven't slept together?* they were saying to each other. *Whoa.*

....

"Has he met Tamar?" Brown said to me, as if the bartender weren't right there. We were all standing outside the bar. My Subaru and the bartender's big white boat of a car were the only ones left, and it was freezing, and our breath puffed out in clouds. Soon the snow would begin to fall, and the mountains would be blanketed in white, or blue, or pink, or dark green, depending on the light and the time of day.

"I have not," the bartender said. "But I'd like to."

"Come with us, then," Brown said.

Hello, hello, I'm standing right here. Hello, is she not my mother? Is this not an invitation that I should be the one to make, Brown, not you? Who says I want to have the bartender meet my mother, anyway? Those were all the thoughts that on another day would have run through my head, and which I would have turned from thoughts into sentences. But that day must have been past, must already have been in the rearview mirror, because I didn't even think them, let alone say them.

"What should I expect?" the bartender said, but he wasn't asking

Brown or Sunshine. He had turned to me and he was asking me, not them. "What should I know?"

"Nothing," I said. "*Nada*. Zip. Zilch."

"It's better to have no expectations," Sunshine said.

Maybe it would be an evening when Tamar was there. Maybe it would be an evening when she was gone, walking the endless hallways in search of her daughter. Maybe she would recognize Sunshine and Brown and not me, or me and not them. Maybe she would recognize the bartender even though she had never met him.

"Nothing it is, then," the bartender said.

He shook hands again with Sunshine and Brown, put his arm around my shoulders and squeezed, then got in his car and drove off north.

"Okay," Brown said, and "Okay," Sunshine said, when we were in the car.

"Okay," I said too. Because we all knew what we were saying. The conversation that was happening among us, the miles back to their house, was happening below the surface. Wordless Conversations for $400. *He's a good guy, Clara, he's a good, good guy.* That feeling went around and around the car, from me in the driver's seat to Brown riding shotgun, his arm stretched back to hold hands with Sunshine in the backseat. And this, too, the feeling that *Sometimes it's simple. Sometimes it's not complicated at all.*

....

It was the bartender's first visit. We walked in to find her at the juice station, turned sideways, her walker leaning against the wall. She held a Dixie cup beneath the apple juice spigot, then moved it mid-splash to the cranberry juice spigot. Drops of juice splashed onto the tray beneath.

"Hey, Ma," I said.

She turned, again mid-splash, and examined me. Brown-red juice sloshed in the tiny cup in her hand.

"Orange juice," she said.

"You want some?"

She nodded. I moved to help her but the bartender was quicker. He slid another paper cup off the upside-down stack and then moved around her to the orange juice dispenser, which was separate and next to the ice chest.

"Here you go," he said.

She took the cup and drank it down in one go and held it out to him again.

"More?"

She nodded. He filled it, she drank it, while Sunshine and Brown and I watched.

"It's like community theater," Brown whispered.

"More like improv," Sunshine said.

My mother handed the empty cup back to the bartender and shook her head when he held it up inquiringly.

"How do I know you?" she said.

"I'm a friend of your daughter's."

"He's my bartender," I said.

She nodded and flapped her arm in the direction of the Green Room. "The knothole?"

"Sure," he said. "Let's go."

He held out his arm and she took it as if he were her square-dance partner and they were about to do-si-do. Down the hall we went, with them leading the way.

"How do I know you?"

"I'm your daughter's bartender."

No answer. Maybe it was one of the nights she didn't remember she had a daughter. Then she spoke.

"My daughter hates beer."

"She does!" Brown said, exclamation marks in his voice because she was there, she was tracking the conversation. "Who in their right mind hates beer?"

"She's always hated it," Sunshine said. "Remember when we used to make her drink it, freshman year?"

"It was good for her. She needed loosening up."

"We used to make her play pool too."

"Also good for her. Even if she could never remember the rules. Who forgets how to play pool one week to the next?"

"The same kind of person who plays piano every single night of her life for four years and then leaves it behind," Brown said. "That's who."

The bartender turned around. Tamar still had hold of his arm and they were inching toward the Green Room. "She didn't leave it behind," he said.

Brown opened his mouth as if he were about to argue, then closed it. Sunshine, pushing the walker down the hall so that Tamar would have it nearby when she needed it, smiled. Maybe they said nothing because the bartender was still new-ish and they wanted to be polite. Maybe they said nothing because it would be too confusing for Tamar. Maybe they said nothing because they heard something true in the bartender's words and thought, *He's right.*

....

Lumber Days had come upon Old Forge, and Sunshine and Brown and the bartender and I were wandering the streets. Early December, pre-Christmas in the northland, and all the shops and bars and restaurants were lumber-themed. Birdhouses that looked like Lincoln Log cabins, bird feeders carved out of a single length of birch, Christmas tree ornaments in the shape of pine trees, rough-hewn bears chainsawed out of oak for two hundred dollars, extra if you wanted your name burned onto their bellies.

"Look, Winter," Brown said. "A chainsaw bear for only two Words by Winters. Doesn't every porch deserve a chainsaw bear?"

"Too gifty," I said. "Just like everything else about Lumber Days. I like the Woodsmen's Field Days better."

"Of course you do," Sunshine said. "You've always been a sucker for a handsome lumberjack."

"Don't make the bartender feel bad, Sunshine," Brown said.

"Oh, I'm sure the bartender knows his way around a piece of wood," Sunshine said, and then blushed. "Oops. Sorry, bartender."

Adirondack Hardware had set up a Lumber Days photo booth inside their store, next to a display of decorated fake Christmas trees, before which Brown stood shaking his head, muttering about plastic trees made in China, for sale right here in the Adirondacks, what was the world coming to, it was like a silent insurgency, a dagger in the heart of the tree farm industry, and here on Lumber Days weekend, for God's sake.

"Let's dress up in period lumberjack costume and get our photos taken in the photo booth," Sunshine said. She was a sucker for period costume, British, especially — Merchant-Ivory films, movie adaptations of Jane Austen novels — but she would settle for Americana if she had to. Pioneers, Old Sturbridge Village, covered wagons, the hallowed days of Adirondack guides and the estates they served. A trunk next to the booth spilled over with homespun long dresses, breeches and vests and waistcoats and fake mustaches and large lace-trimmed hats. A mishmash of generalized pioneer-ish finery. I pulled on a linsey-woolsey apron.

"Check out my linsey-woolsey," I said.

"You only put that on because you wanted to say the words 'linsey-woolsey,'" Brown said. "Admit it."

It was true. Linsey-woolsey. Said often enough, it blended together into the exact sound and feel of the material it was named for. Coarse and strong. Built to last. Linsey-woolsey, linsey-woolsey, linsey-woolsey. Linsey-woolsey could be a girl's name, a proper name that appeared on a birth certificate but from which the *woolsey* was left off in real life, leaving Linsey to stand alone. Linsey. A pretty name. A name that reminded me of the gauzy white embroidered shirt my mother used to be so fond of, the shirt she was wearing in the photo we had christened The Mystery.

The bartender put on a fringed buckskin vest, jammed a Stetson on his head and held his arm out to me. There was only one stool in the photo booth, so I sat on it and he stood behind me and placed his hands on my shoulders. The photo countdown began to flash.

"Look straight into the mirror and look stern," I said. "Like an old-school lumberjack thug."

We simultaneously frowned at the mirror. My hands suddenly looked un-lumberjack-like, too smooth, too unworn. I looked for linsey-woolsey pockets to jam them into, but then the flash went off and I had missed the first photo. I stuck my unworn hands behind my back but the bartender was standing there. The next flash went off. I sat on my hands for the third, which wasn't right either, and finally the bartender pulled me up off the stool and wrapped his arms around me. "Think thug," he said, and the fourth flash went off.

We took off our period costumes and waited for the photo strip to emerge into the metal cage. Sunshine and Brown were arguing over who should get to wear the buckskin vest next. Brown claimed it was an outer garment suitable for males only.

"I don't disagree," Sunshine said, "but the fact is, I would look cute in that vest. Plus, I'm a cancer survivor."

"Let's do survivor smiles in our photos," Brown said.

"Only if I get to wear the vest."

The photo booth plunked out our photos and the bartender and I studied them.

"These are terrible," I said. "Look at me."

"These are great," the bartender said. "Look at you."

Every photo of me was disarray: me frowning at my hands, me hiding my hands, me blurry mid-turn, me swallowed up by the bartender's arms.

"Good God, Winter," Brown said, peering at the photo strip. "What are you, two years old? Can you not sit still?"

But I had quit looking at myself in the photos and was looking instead at the bartender. Unlike me, he was not fidgeting or trying to hide his hands. He was not looking straight into the mirror, nor did he look stern. In each photo he was looking down at me, and his face had a certain look on it. Not of laughter, or impatience, or forbearance in a let's-get-this-over-with kind of way. None of those words applied. I looked from the photo to him, the real him, and that look was still on his face. Though Brown was standing next to us, the sound of his voice and the laughter in it receded. The feel of the buckskin vest brushing my arm as Sunshine put it on was barely there. The bartender looked at me and I looked at the bartender.

"Chris?"

That was the sound of my voice, almost inaudible even though it was me talking. Me saying his real name for the first time. He nodded.

"Yeah," he said. "That's me."

And it was. It was him. Him with that look on his face, nodding and now the beginnings of a smile, because was I looking at him the way he was looking at me? As if I loved him?

Not *as if.*

The world rose around us again: Sunshine and Brown standing next to Chris and me, both of them silent and watching, knowing that something had just happened. A group of teenagers bent over the trunk of dress-up clothes, waiting their turn for the photo booth. Johnny Cash sang about a ring of fire on the store PA system. My mother's words floated into my head: *Bullshit. Decide you're going to be your real self and then be your real self.*

The car heater blasted on the way home, drowning out conversation, not that any of us were talking. Much had already been said, and most of it silent. I held Chris's hand in the backseat of Sunshine and Brown's station wagon but I didn't look at him because my mind was filled with *fifty-fifty* and everything it meant in that moment: I had found him, I didn't want to let him go, and I didn't want him to live through what I was living through, either. Flip sides, same coin.

We were halfway up Turnip Hill Road, me studying the photos again, when something else came to me. The look on Chris's face was familiar. *You have seen that look before,* I thought. But where? I kept looking at the narrow strip of photos, chemical-smelling and still a little tacky to the touch. Me in motion, the bartender straight and still, that soft look on his face. Then I knew.

That thin wisp of worn photocopied paper propped up on the kitchen shelf in the cabin. My mother, younger and smiling. The look on her face was the same look on the bartender's face in the photos in my palm, shimmering up from the frayed paper on the shelf next to Jack. She had saved that photo all these years, ever since she stopped wearing that pretty shirt. In it, she was looking beyond me, at whoever was taking her photo.

My mother had loved someone. And someone had loved her back.

Final Jeopardy

It was not possible.

That was my first thought. Because had she ever been on a date? Had she ever kissed anyone? Had she ever asked someone to a Sadie Hawkins dance, or been to a prom? Had she ever gone to a bar with someone and put quarters in a jukebox and played pool and ordered a second cocktail because she was having fun? Had she ever sat across from a man who had put on a clean shirt for the occasion, at a small table with a tablecloth and a candle and not one but two menus, one for wine and one for food? Questions shoved up against each other in my head.

No and no and no and no and no.

The interviewer, her legs crossed, her fingers hovering over her keyboard—"Miss Winter, to your knowledge, did your mother, Tamar Winter, ever go on a date?"—*No*, before the quotation mark was fully slotted next to the question mark. "Did your mother, Tamar Winter, ever go on a date*No*." A broken sentence. Part question but mostly *No*.

Why so quick with the No, though, Miss Winter? Wouldn't you want her to have gone on a date? Wouldn't you want your mother to have had some happiness in her life that way, a few hours where she was not just your mother, but a young woman out with a young man who thought she was lovely?

Lovely? *Lovely?* Stop it.

It was not possible to think of her as anyone other than exactly who she was, who she had been: a woman of the north woods, a lumber-woman in a lumber jacket, a splitter of wood, a remover of decals, a non-Sunday singer in a choir, a manless woman, a boyfriendless woman, a husbandless woman, a dateless woman, who was, who had been, my mother. The word *lovely* did not apply, but for the fact that it did.

After I waved goodbye from the porch, I went straight to the shelf in the kitchen. My mother's faded face smiled up from her perch next to Jack. My heart skipped a beat and then began rocketing around its prison of sinew and bone, looking for a way out. *Et tu, heart? Heart, quiet thyself.* But the wayward heart did not listen, and down I lay on the floor, photo flat against my shaking chest, the diminished stacks of books-as-coffee-table rising around me.

New images of my mother scrolled by, leaping and dancing across the spines of the remaining books of my childhood. Tamar with her hair French-braided, wearing that pretty white shirt, standing on the porch and smiling as a car drove into our driveway just beyond the frame of the picture. Tamar at the Boonville County Fair holding the hand of a faceless, bodiless, voiceless man just beyond the frame of the picture. Tamar at Hemstrought's Bakery in Utica, pointing at a half-moon cookie and smiling at a man just beyond the frame of the picture.

Just beyond the frame of the picture. He, whoever he was, was there. Had he been there all along?

"You are way overreacting here, Clara," I said out loud as the photo and I lay on the floor by the books. "Calm the hell down. It's a photo."

But there are times when you know a thing, immediately and of a piece, and you can't un-know it. You can't convince yourself that you are overreacting. I held the photo above my head and looked at it this way and that way, sideways and upside down. Nothing made the look in my mother's eyes go away. Nothing from here on out would make the softness, that softness I had never seen, go away.

Who? When? How? Where?

. . . .

Out the door and into the Subaru the minute my heart reverted to a normal rhythm. Down the half hour to Sterns, then onto Fox Road. When Annabelle opened the door I held the photo up in front of her, pincered between my thumb and forefinger. She leaned back instead of forward—middle-aged eyes, reversing course—and squinted. When she didn't say anything, I waved it back and forth, dancing it through the air between us. I didn't trust the steps I was standing on. They were made of plastic and flimsy metals. They could give way at any time. I waited for her to say something.

"Nice to see you too, Clara," was what she said, after a minute or so. She stood aside so that I could come in, but I didn't move. From what I could see and smell there was nothing baking in her kitchen, nothing bubbling on the stove under a pot lid. "How can I help you?"

I said nothing. I stood there and kept holding the photo. If my instinct was right, then Annabelle would crumple before my silence and tell me what she knew about this unfamiliar Tamar Winter dancing in the air before her. She would tell me about the look on my mother's face. She would tell me who had taken the photo.

I stood silently, and so did Annabelle. She tilted her head as if she were trying to figure out why I was holding the photo before her like a piece of evidence. She frowned. She looked at me, except not really, because her eyes didn't meet mine. And when someone's eyes won't meet yours, even though you can tell they're trying to make their eyes meet yours, when their face turns even a fraction of an inch away from yours, when you can feel the unease flowing through their body even though they are forcing themselves to stand elaborately, casually still, that's your answer.

Cultivate silence. Silence, and patience, and determination.

Now that I had my answer—she knew who had taken that photo—I stepped inside. The trailer felt warm. Not thermostat warm, not oil or gas or baseboard or electric-space-heater warm but warm by nature, as if Annabelle herself, the great furnace of her body and her heart, were all that was necessary. I pulled out a chair from the kitchen table and sat down. Annabelle stood across the table from me. She was trying to intimidate me by not sitting down, not joining me, as if that would make me stop whatever it was I was doing. Too late, Annabelle. You've already given yourself away and there's no going back.

I laid the photo in the precise middle of the table. "Who took this?"

"No clue." She was trying not to look at the photo but her eyes kept dragging back to it, as though there were something fascinating about it.

"Where was it taken?"

"No idea."

"When was it taken?"

"You got me."

The kitchen was the detaining room and Annabelle was the suspect, trying her best not to cave until the public defender arrived.

"Annabelle, tell me what you know."

She shrugged. "It's a nice photo of your mother. Something else to add to the pile."

"The pile? The pile of what?"

"Things you have of her. Memorabilia."

"She's still around, Annabelle. She's not dead."

"You know what I mean."

The sentences sounded like Annabelle sentences but the Annabelle-ness of her voice was gone. She sounded quiet. She sounded tired. The photo lay on the table between us, a jigsaw piece missing its puzzle. She pressed down on one slightly ripped corner with the tip of her finger, as if she were trying to make it whole again.

"You know more than you're telling me," I said. "Please, Annabelle. I'm trying to figure out my mother."

I meant to sound like a detective, insistent on the piece of evidence on the table between us, but I didn't. I sounded like myself.

"Did she . . . have a boyfriend?"

It didn't come out right when I said it. There was a squeak at the end of *boy*, and *friend* trailed off. I tried again. "Or, like, a girlfriend?" That didn't sound right either.

She shook her head. Immediate and clear. No. Not a girlfriend.

"Some guy? After I went away, maybe?"

Shake. No one in my mother's life after I went away. But she kept shaking her head, too long to make a point, and suddenly another possibility came to me.

"Are you saying there was a man in my mother's life when I was around? Before I went to college?"

She kept shaking her head, or trying to, but her eyes slid away. The giveaway.

"Before I went away?" I said. Repeating myself, as if there were a chance she didn't understand. "While I was still here? I mean here as in Sterns, living with her in our house? Back then?"

She wouldn't look at me.

"Who?" I said.

Silence.

"WHO."

Silence.

"I *will* find out, Annabelle." My voice was on the edge of breaking. My most-hated voice, the tremble. "If not from you, then from someone."

She put her hands on the back of the chair in front of her and sighed. "Clara. Leave it be now."

"I can't leave it be when I don't know what it was. Who it was. My mother had a *boyfriend?* And I never *knew?*" The italics went squiggling by at the bottom of my mind.

"Honey," which was something that Annabelle had not once, ever, called me or anyone else I knew, "it was long ago and far away. Leave it be."

And that was it. She was done talking.

....

"Who was it, Dog?" I said to his ashes.

Dog must have known. If there was someone in my mother's life, before I left or after I left or in the middle of my leaving, Dog would have smelled him. The nose of a dog could smell 400,000 times better than a human's nose, although how any scientist knew that for sure, with that level of precision, was beyond me. But the fact was, Dog would have been able to smell the scent of anyone who came within touching distance of my mother. One deep snuff, the way he used to do when we came home from anywhere we'd been, no matter how close or how far, was all he needed.

Dog had known. Annabelle had known. The someone my mother loved had known. Who else had known?

Had she kissed this person, whoever he was? Had she taken her clothes off with him? Slept with him? I sounded like a child. I sounded like an idiot. I sounded the way a person stepping gingerly into an ice-cold lake looks.

"For God's sake, Clara," I said out loud. "Don't be a fool. Of course she did."

Who had he been, though? Someone up north, in Watertown, maybe—I seized on Watertown because my mother had spent many days there, scraping old decals off milk trucks and applying new ones —and maybe there was a man up there who she worked with. It couldn't have been anyone in Sterns. They whisked through my mind anyway, random neighbors and teachers and men, their faces as familiar to me as the urn that held Dog's ashes: Burl Evans, William T. Jones, young Joe Miller the mechanic, Mr. Silvester the custodian, every male teacher I'd ever had from Sterns Elementary and Sterns Middle and Sterns High School. No. None of them. It was not possible. Except that it was.

"How oblivious did I have to be, not to notice what was happening, Dog?"

Very.

"Was she that good an actress?"

No.

"So you're saying that I just didn't notice? That I had one vision of her and no room for anything else?"

Yes.

I sat there on the porch and pictured my high school years. All those afternoons and evenings with Asa, slipping out to meet him, roaming around the country roads, walking into the clamor of parties and out into the cool darkness filled with the songs of night birds and tree frogs, the squeak of boards on his porch, the silence of cement on mine, the long backseat of his car where we loved each other. Where was Tamar in those memories? She was home in Sterns, leaning against the counter eating supper by herself, out chopping wood, whistling for Dog and heading down Williams Road, driving down to choir practice, lying on the couch and reading that ridiculous seagull book yet again. Maybe, on rare occasions, meeting Annabelle Lee at Crystal's Diner for a milkshake.

Unless she wasn't.

"Your parents are divorced?"

That was a question Asa asked, back in the beginning of us, before I told him about the beginnings of me. It was a reasonable assumption, but I shook my head and spat out a laugh so hard that it startled us both.

"No," I said. "Ma was never married."

"Okay," he said. I could still hear the careful tone of his voice. "Does she have a boyfriend or anything?"

"Oh my God no. My mother is not the boyfriend type."

"Why not?"

"Why *not?* Look at her! She's just, she's not, she's, I mean, come on, can you even . . ."

Even what, Clara? I asked myself now. But I knew the answer already. Had I ever imagined my mother as a person someone would want to hold, to touch, to kiss? Imagined her causing a man to feel his heart open? Feel his blood quicken? Feel himself moving closer to her, his hands in his pockets because he wanted so much to touch her? No and no and no and no.

But someone had.

....

"How go the Words, Winter?"

I could hear the uppercase *W* of *Words* in Brown's voice. He did that whenever he was feeling snarky about my line of work. Sometimes he spoiled for a fight, and if he needled me long enough he knew he could get one. Sunshine shot him a warning glance.

"With difficulty," I said. "And stop uppercasing the word *Words,* and don't think I can't hear that you're doing it. Also, I don't need your scorn."

"Clara. Correction. I have scorn for those who pay you to write their words, not for the words that you provide."

"Well, today the words I provided included a eulogy for a father despised by all his kids, a retirement toast for a boss despised by all his employees, and a fiftieth-birthday card from a sister to the brother she's been estranged from for twenty-three years."

"Ouch."

Yes, ouch. It had been a tough day in the word business, a Tough Days for $2000 Daily Double bet-it-all kind of tough day, so tough that I had worked outside on the freezing porch so as not to fill the air of the cabin with the sadness and anger inside those assignments, and the shock and bewilderment inside me. Onward, ever onward. The tough assignments kept coming.

"You guys, I found something out," I said.

They looked at each other in their silent, telepathic way. *You guys* was what they were saying to each other. *She never says "you guys."*

"And what was it that you found out?" Brown said.

"That there was someone in her life. My mother was in love with someone."

"No way!" He spluttered out one of those surprise-laughs. "Not The Fearsome."

"Yes way."

"What makes you think so?"

"That photo."

"Whoa! You found a photo? Like, a *you know what I mean* kind of photo?"

"Stop it. No. That photo, The Mystery, the one you've already seen. The one with her wearing that white shirt. It's the look on her face. She was in love."

They were both instantly quiet, in the same way I had gone quiet when I looked at the strip of photo-booth photos of the bartender and me. They knew I was right. They didn't know how they knew, or how I knew, but we all knew I was right.

"Who would it have been, though?" Brown said after a minute. "Don't you know everyone in Sterns?"

"I thought I did. But whoever he was, I obviously didn't know him. And he's obviously not around anymore."

"What about Annabelle?" Sunshine said. "Did you ask her?"

"Yes."

"And?"

"She clammed up and wouldn't look me in the eye. Which just confirms it."

"The Secret Lives of the Sternsians," Brown intoned, in a PBS-announcer sort of voice. "We'd tell you about them if we could, but they're secret."

"Shut up, Brown," Sunshine said. "Not funny."

Brown shut up. Not funny. I looked down to make sure the wire was holding me tight together. What was happening inside me was that the past was expanding again, horizons pushing out to make room for new information. My mother, with a man. My mother, with someone who wasn't me and wasn't Annabelle. Who? For how long? Why were they not together? What had happened?

Sunshine put down the baby hat she was crocheting, a serious move for her, a woman whose hands always needed to be in motion. "Ask your mother, Clara."

"She doesn't know who I am half the time anymore."

"Ask anyway."

But I shook my head. I had already said too much. It felt as if I had betrayed her: Brown's splutter of a laugh and Sunshine's quieted hands and the soft look on my mother's face in that photo combined to make my heart swell with a feeling I couldn't at first name because in conjunction with my mother it was so unfamiliar. I waited for the word to come to me, and as I waited, with the two of them looking at me, I pictured my mother as she looked back when I was in high school, in her jeans and her Keds and her un-made-up face and her dark hair pulled back in a ponytail or a braid or a knot. Not so different from the way she was still, down there in the place where she lived now, where she deadheaded the orchids and trod the hallways back and forth and up and down. I waited for the word to name the feeling inside me, and then it came floating up out of the darkness:

wonder. Wonder was the feeling inside me, that my mother had been loved and loved back. That there were rooms within rooms within her, rooms filled with white and light and space, rooms I'd never known about.

....

If the place where my mother lived now called, I picked up instantly.

I had given the number its own special ring tone: Old Phone. Old Phone was the sound of the telephone we had when I was growing up, that heavy receiver attached to the long curly cord, the telephone that we never referred to as "phone."

"This is Clara."

"Hi Clara. This is Sylvia. I know you were here just last night but to-day's been a rough day. Your mom's been crying on and off all morning. She's agitated. She's been looking for her daughter. And a cookie."

Sylvia pronounced the words carefully, as if the words "daughter" and "cookie" might be foreign to me.

"She keeps trying to get out the French doors," she added. "She won't step onto the black paint, though. Which is good. I pulled the curtains so she can't see out, but still."

She waited. I knew what that wait meant.

"Okay. I'm on my way."

It was late afternoon and it had been only one day since I had seen my mother, one day since I had not asked her about the photograph that lived now in the back compartment of my wallet. But Sylvia wouldn't call unless she had tried everything she knew. I locked up the cabin and stepped onto the porch. Winter in the Adirondacks and chilly, the sun already falling.

As my mother tended the orchids in the Green Room, so did Sylvia and I tend my mother. Tamar, past and present, the fragments thereof. It was an hour from Turnip Hill to the place where she lived now.

Sylvia looked up at me from behind the desk and smiled. The sympa-thetic smile, was how I thought of that particular kind of smile, a smile I would hate from anyone but her.

"You made it."

She pointed to the Green Room. Much went unspoken, with Sylvia. She was a few-words woman.

"Ma?"

She didn't hear me. Maybe she didn't want to. She was pacing back and forth in front of the big picture window, leaning on her walker. An aide at her side, watchful for falls, looked up and nodded at the sight of me, then slipped past out the doorway. My mother's walker made its aluminum sound on the tiled floor as tears ran down her cheeks. She was crying. My mother was crying.

How many times, as a child, had I seen her cry? Only twice. That night with the Neil Diamond album, and that other time, when she sat at the table reading my paper about Hong Kong.

Maybe there had been times I didn't know about. Maybe there were times, say Wednesday nights, after she finished being justice of the peace, at our scrubbed kitchen table, after she was done meting out justice to the DWIs, the petty thieves, the property-line trespassers, the tax-valuation arguers, when the circumstances of life overwhelmed her and she put her head down on the tabletop and cried. Maybe there were other times too, after the love, whoever he was, left her, and she was alone. But what did I know?

"Clara," she said, and again: "Clara."

"Are you thinking about Clara, Ma?"

She nodded. I stepped toward her and took her hand. She let me.

"Clara," she whispered.

"Do you miss her?"

"I lost her," she said.

Then, in a single swift movement, she lifted the walker in both hands and flung it against the wall and began to wail. My heart was off and running then, speeding yet again, a high-speed chase of one beat after another. *Too thin, too dehydrated, too stressed.* Two out of three at any given time would bring on an episode, and now the episodes just kept coming.

Thumpthumpthumpthumpthumpthump, my insistent heart jackhammered away. I tugged my mother toward me. Sylvia and the aide were there swiftly and silently, but I shook my head at them. No. Let me.

"Shhh, Ma," I said. "Shhh. Sit down, Ma," and eventually she did. The green couch in the Green Room, orchids, heavy on their stems, bowed down on the opposite wall. Sitting was better. My heart could hammer away but there would be no fainting.

"My daughter," Tamar said. Her eyes were bewildered. "I can't find her."

Do not question. Follow.

"I'll help you find her."

I breathed in deeply and let it out slowly.

"Here's what we'll do," I said. "We'll check this room, and then we'll check the hallway, and then we'll check the dining room, and then we'll check your bedroom, and then—" She was nodding. I let my voice turn into a chant. A hum. A prayer. This is what we are going to do, Ma. We are going to find that lost girl. I turned my head and Sylvia was in the doorway, still watching. She gave me a good-job-Clara look and then retreated to the desk with the aide.

"I just have to lie down on this couch for a minute, Ma. Is that okay?"

"Your heart?"

Her voice, until that minute a voice unlike hers, was back. Her hand touched the side of my throat, a practiced, instinctive movement. She was checking my pulse. I closed my eyes and focused on breathing in deeply and letting it out slowly until the beat was a normal person's again.

"Fix," she said.

"I know. I know, Ma. Pretty soon."

"She flew away."

Follow her, Clara. Wherever she goes, follow her. I pictured a winter day, a lost daughter, wind spiraling her up above furious snow into brightness beyond

"Maybe she did, Ma."

"Where?"

"I don't know. We can look for her, though. We'll just keep looking for her."

Around the Green Room, one lap, two laps, three. A pause by the orchids each time. Then out into the hall, pause by the desk, down one hallway and then the next, past the silent dining room and the lemonade and juice stand. Pause for a Dixie cup of apple juice each. Into Tamar's room, where her bed was made and the table lamp was turned on and the curtains were drawn and all the books I had brought her were stacked crisscross beneath the window the way I had stacked them yesterday, as if they were logs for the woodstove and we were back in Sterns, readying our firewood for the winter. Tamar tossed the logs and I made orderly stacks. Logs and books — the ritual was the same.

Reckon your losses. Forgive us our trespasses, that we may forgive those who trespass against us. As she hurt you, so you must have hurt her. Apologize. Remember, Clara, that you don't know the whole story. No one ever knows the whole story.

"I'm sorry, Ma. You must have felt that you couldn't tell me things."

"Like what?"

"Important things."

"Like what?"

She was parroting.

"You loved someone, didn't you? But you never told me about him."

"You loved someone?" she said.

Another kind of parroting, another kind of non-answer. Yes, I did love someone, Ma. I loved Asa, and I love Sunshine and Brown, and I am on the verge — no, the verge has been verged — of loving Chris. And you. I love you, Ma.

"I'm sorry I was so hard on you, Ma."

"Hard on you?"

"Yes, hard on you. Always badgering you about Daphne back when I was a kid, for one thing."

She was leaning on her walker. We had made it to the doorway of the Green Room, where the television was on, sound muted. She looked up at me and frowned.

"Who's Daphne?"

Some things, you couldn't imagine they would ever disappear, like the memory of your own baby. But they did disappear, apparently, to use the Life Care Committee's favorite word. And the fact that they disappeared made other things that you wanted to do, like show your mother the photograph and ask her about it, impossible. My heart leaped off the tracks again, began again its jolt and shudder in my chest. Twice in the space of one hour? That had never happened before. Tamar was still looking at me with that frown, waiting for me to tell her who Daphne was, but I put my hand to my chest and her eyes followed.

She pushed herself up. That unsteady gait, no aluminum walker for balance, hands stretching toward me. She put her hand over mine, over the *beatbeatbeatbeatbeat* that made our fingers and palms quiver. Her hand stayed on mine and I lay down on the couch and looked at the ceiling, at the ugly acoustic tile, until my heart caught mid-sprint and again returned to a steady beat.

"There," she said, as if my heart had gone missing and was now returned. She was right. I sat up.

We stayed there on the couch for a while, my mother and me, her hand resting on my hand. Twenty years ago would have seen me asking her about my father, about my dead twin sister, about my grandparents, and her silent in the face of those questions. Now I was asking again, and again, and again, about all manner of things that I knew now must have felt to her back then the way rain felt when it was near freezing and driving horizontally into your skin. Cold needles pricking all the exposed places. Did my questions still hurt her? Or was she beyond them?

....

"It's an outpatient procedure," the electrocardiologist said. "What we do is thread catheters up your femoral veins into the heart, then we provoke an episode so as to get the lay of the land and see where exactly the misfire is happening."

"Episode?" I said. "Provoke?"

His office was in Utica, down the block from the doctor that Tamar and I had met with. It was just the two of us in the examining room, dusk falling over the Mohawk Valley outside the single window.

"Yep," he said. "In at seven, home by five. It's the slam dunk of the cardiology world."

Slam dunk. Just the way the other cardiologist had described it. Was that the way the cardiology textbook described it? He must have seen a look on my face. "What, you're not an NBA fan?"

My mother's voice sounded inside my head. *Bullshit. Decide you're going to be your real self and then be your real self.*

"Don't try to make this a small thing," I said. "Don't joke about this."

He was looking down at his desk, shuffling through the forms they had printed out for me, but at that he looked up sharply. The air between us was different. That was what happened when you cut away the banter underbrush to behold the sparkling river.

"This is my heart we're talking about here," I said. "My one and only heart. So give it to me straight. Once you see where the misfire is happening, then what?"

"Then we'll cauterize that spot."

"Burn my heart?"

"Cauterize it."

"You're going to burn my heart. Say it."

"Ms. Winter, in order to permanently cure your paroxysmal supraventricular tachycardia, yes, we will burn your heart in one tiny, precise place."

He pushed the stack of papers over to me and I signed on the lines he pointed to. "It's good you're doing this," he said. "You'll get your normal life back again."

After the appointment was scheduled and the nurse went over all the pre-op notes with me and the receptionist stamped my parking ticket and I kicked the automatic door opener with my boot because I could—I could walk and run and hike and kick things as much as I wanted—I drove to the place where my mother lived now, where once again she was pacing the halls with her walker looking for the little bird who flew away.

"My daughter," she said. "My daughter."

"I'm right here, Ma."

It was still hard not to use the word *remember*, as in "Remember me? I'm her. I'm your daughter." But it was no longer impossible. She had been roaming farther afield this past week, Sylvia had told me on the phone, trying to get outside. Now her daughter was here, walking up and down the halls with her, the two of them and the tennis-balled walker, but she was still searching.

"I can't find her," she said. "She's out there"—we were at the doorway of the Green Room and she jutted her chin at the wide black swatch of paint in front of the locked French doors—"but. But."

"But," I agreed, because it seemed right to agree. "You know, Ma, maybe she's right here."

She shook her head. No. No, she was not right here. We moved on down the hall to the juice station. Dixie cups only. Because of the re-membrance—*apple juice is good*—and because of the forgetting—*but I drank a cup of it just five minutes ago.*

"My daughter."

"Right here, Ma."

"My daughter."

Distract. Redirect. Put a stick in the spokes.

"Hey, Ma? I came to tell you that I'm going to get it fixed," I said. "My heart."

I expected her to frown and shake her head, to look down the hall and set the walker in motion again. But my mother surprised me. She reached up and touched my collarbone, traced it down to my heart.

"Good," she said.

....

Talk to Chris, Sunshine and Brown said. Stop trying to imagine your way into his head. Stop trying to predict the way he'll react. You're not him, are you? Your name is Clara, not Chris. Stop trying to think your way through all the scenarios, all the what-if-thises and what-if-thats. He's a grown-ass man; let him think and talk for himself. Stop putting off the conversation. Whether you have the gene or not, it's a conversation that has to happen.

Variations on sentences spoken by them on various days or nights when my fear of the PSEN1 gene spiderwebbed itself into my thoughts about Chris.

Did they urge me to get the test or not get the test? No. What they urged me to do was talk to him.

Get in the goddamn car and drive up to Inlet and get out of the goddamn car and walk into that bar and Talk. To. Him.

That last one was me. *Hell* and *damn* were as far as Sunshine and Brown would go. I breathed in and breathed out and breathed in and breathed out and then into the car I got and up to Inlet I went. It was early evening but the bar was nigh-on deserted. That was what happened in the land of winter, this north country land of dark-at-five-p.m. Chris was making his way around the room with a bucket and a sponge and a towel, scrubbing the tables and drying them. Gayle must have left early. He looked up and smiled when the door scraped open. He never seemed surprised to see me.

"Can I help?" I said, and he handed me the towel. I copycatted his movements, compensating for lack of arm length by leaning over farther. *Talk to him, Clara.*

"So here's the thing," I said. We were on the third table now, and in a rhythm. It was like a dance. "I don't just have a weird heart condition. It's more complicated than that. Because my mother was officially diagnosed with early-onset Alzheimer's, there is a fifty-percent chance that I carry one of the four genetic mutations that cause it, with PSEN1, which stands for presenilin-1, being by far the most common of the four."

I sounded like the audio version of a layperson's textbook on Alzheimer's. My voice was disembodied from my insides. I kept going.

"If I do carry one of the mutations, then there is a very strong probability that I too will develop early-onset Alzheimer's. And while a test that would determine whether or not I carry the gene exists, I am not sure that I want to find out."

My voice was steady and calm, imparting important information, information that I had learned long ago and that the bartender needed to know. Did he, though? Did he really need to know this information? Too late, Clara. Keep going.

"I'm telling you this, so, like, you know," I said, and he laughed.

"That sounded so unlike you," he said. "Like, you know, you don't usually use 'like' like that."

"But did you hear what I said?"

"Yes."

"Okay, but do you understand what it means?" My voice did not sound disembodied from me anymore. It was not steady or calm. He kept washing the table—we were on table six by now—but he glanced up at me.

"I do."

"Tell me, then. Tell me what it means."

"It means that there's a fifty-fifty chance that you will get Alzheimer's disease, and if you do, you will likely get it much earlier than most Alzheimer's patients, who get it in old age."

He stood up and stretched, the sponge dripping soapy water down his arm, and nodded at the towel I was holding. "Do you need a fresh towel?"

"Is that all you have to say?"

"About the towel?" He was smiling again. "Yeah."

"Chris."

"Clara."

Why had they told me to talk to him? Why had I gotten in the car and driven up here? Why was I standing here crushing a damp towel to death between my hands? None of this mattered to him. The bartender didn't lie awake at night doing the fifty-fifty gene mutation math the way I did. *You're an idiot, Clara. You're a fool.*

"I'm going to go," I said.

"No you're not. Sit down."

He dropped his sponge in the bucket, pulled the crushed towel from my hands and dropped that in the bucket too. He pulled out a chair and waited until I sat. Then he sat too.

"I'm sorry I laughed," he said. He wasn't smiling anymore. "But I already knew everything you just told me. I've already thought about it."

"About what, though? You've already thought about *what?*"

"About if you have the PSEN1 gene, or one of the others. Don't look so surprised. I'm as good at Google as you are. And I already know how I feel, which is that I could walk out of this bar and get hit by a bus and die instantly."

"Oh, for God's sake! Why does everyone always say that! Why is getting hit by a bus *always* the example!" I said. The exclamation marks emboldened themselves, growing larger with each sentence, along with the words themselves. **"Also! You are not going to walk out of this bar and get hit by a bus, Chris! There are no buses here!"**

"Point taken. Here's a better example. I could walk into Foley Lumber tomorrow and be wandering around the plywood display and a sheet of plywood could come tumbling off the stack and hit me on the head and break my neck so that I die instantly."

"*Plywood?* Please."

"Plywood's heavier than you think, Clara."

"You're willfully missing the point."

"I'm not missing any point." He reached across the table and put his hands over mine. "Clara. I'm signed on for the duration. Whatever the odds are."

"The odds are fifty-fifty, Chris."

"And I accept them."

"Well, that makes one of us."

I did not accept the bus odds, I did not accept the plywood odds, I did not accept the Sunshine cancer odds, I did not accept the PSEN1 odds. None of these were odds I accepted. But I was stuck with them anyway.

We all were.

....

A letter addressed to Tamar from a Frank Dutton at the Dairylea plant up in Plattsburgh came to the cabin on Turnip Hill. The yellow forwarding address label was affixed to it at an angle, the way they usually were, as if whoever slapped it on there did it in a hurry. Maybe it was a machine. A rebel machine. A machine constantly sent to detention. I slid my finger under the flap and opened it up.

Dear Tamar, We miss you up here and hope you're doing well these days. Things aren't the same without you. Wish you'd reconsider! Any chance lol? If not just wanted you to know that your sneakers and Dairylea jacket are in the locker—want me to send them to you? If so let me know. Hope you're well, oh I already said that didn't I? Well you know me, can't keep my head on straight. Your friend, Frank

I didn't remember a Frank Dutton or the mention of a Frank Dutton, but that was no surprise. Tamar never talked about work and I had never pictured her as having friends at Dairylea. Annabelle appeared in my head, rolling her eyes, her voice its usual impatient tone: *Of course your mother had friends at Dairylea, Clara. She worked there for almost thirty years, Utica, Watertown, Plattsburgh, all over for God's sake. Pick up the phone and call this Frank person, whoever the hell he is.*

I picked up my phone and called the number scribbled at the bottom of this Frank person's note, whoever the hell he was, politely not pointing out to Annabelle, even in my head, that Annabelle clearly didn't know who this Frank person was either, and wasn't she the one who called herself my mother's best friend?

"Frank Dutton."

"Hi, Frank. This is Clara Winter. I'm Tamar's daughter."

"You don't say!" His voice transformed from business to warmth and welcome, words full of exclamation marks. "Tamar's daughter! How is that mother of yours!"

"Doing okay," I said, which was what I said every time someone asked me that question. "Hanging in there."

"Where's she living now? With you? Or with the boyfriend?"

The boyfriend? The boyfriend. The boyfriend? I pulled the phone away from my ear, then pressed it close again. *The boyfriend. The boyfriend. The boyfriend the boyfriend the boyfriend the boyfriend the boyfriend,* scrolling along the bottom of my brain. Out the window the sky was turning itself to navy; the light was gone by four-thirty these days. The boyfriend.

"What's his name again?" Frank said. "I always called him Woodsman, for that Woodsmen's Field Days cap he always wore, but I'll be damned if I can remember his real name."

When you weren't looking for answers, not thinking about answers, answers appeared. Like now. There was only one man who wore a Woodsmen's Field Days cap, and to my knowledge he had never taken it off.

"Eli," I said. "Eli is his name."

I listened to my voice saying his name and I listened as Frank Dutton kept talking in exclamation marks—*Of course that was his name! How the hell is Eli, anyway! Is he coping with the whole thing okay? I'll admit to you I was worried about Tamar when she drove up with him because, you know, she's a hell of a woman, which of course YOU know because she's your mother! But hell if she didn't end up with a hell of a guy even if I only saw him just those few times all those years ago! Sorry for all these hells but you're Tamar's daughter, you can probably handle them!*—but my brain hadn't caught up to the information yet. Yes, it'd be great if you sent me the sneakers and her Dairylea jacket, and no, she isn't with me or Eli at this point, she's living in a care facility, actually, and yes, I sure will tell her, and yes, I will for sure stop by if I ever find myself up in that neck of the woods, and thank you so much. My voice kept speaking answers to his questions but my brain was on autopilot.

"She sure did talk about you, Clara," was the last thing Frank Dutton said before we hung up, the exclamation marks gone from his voice. "Talked about you all the time, all those years. That spelling bee you won, that fancy college you got into, that book you wrote. I never saw a woman so proud of her kid."

....

If the day ever came when I got the test and found out if I had or did not have the gene mutation, maybe it would feel the way this did, as if you were standing at the top of a peak that had been shrouded in clouds, and the clouds had broken suddenly. Behind you, all the way that you'd climbed, was your past. Ahead of you was your future. Here at the summit you held the jigsaw puzzle piece that placed pattern to chaos. The puzzle piece that gave you the information you needed to figure out certain things: A child or not. A spouse or not. A future that stretched out or didn't.

Eli Chamberlain and Tamar Winter.

I sat on my chair on the porch, wrapped up in the quilt, and held the puzzle piece in my hand and looked back. Not thinking so much as re-configuring. The times Eli had stopped by our house to bring Asa something he needed, the times the four of us had sat at the kitchen table and played blackjack or rummy. The times when, after Martha left, Tamar had given me a ride to Asa's house and stopped in for a while. The times we had run into Eli at the gas station or the post office or the bank or the grocery store. The times we had been sitting in a booth at Crystal's Diner and watched him push the door open and smile and wave.

All this time.

How long?

I did not know. There was no way to tell from the conversation with Frank Dutton.

I tried to imagine my way back into the way we were then. Asa and me. It had been a long time, and at first the same memories that conjured themselves up in my brain were the same ones that always did: Looking up from the pits below the bleacher to see Asa looking at me from the concession stand. Driving around the back roads late on summer nights, all the windows open and my hair blowing back in the breeze, him driving one-handed with the other hand holding mine. The notes that, before he graduated, he used to stick through the slats in my locker, each one a heart. A heart in crayon, a heart in pencil, a heart in pen, a heart made of tiny pieces of duct tape carefully angled together to form the necessary curving swoops.

All those images came to me the way they always did. They had long ago worn grooves into the pathways and circuitry of my brain. They would be with me forever, and even if I had the gene mutation they would be among the last to go, because the disease tended to rob your memories backward.

Knowing what I knew about Asa, what did he go through when he found out about his father and my mother? I tried to imagine my way into his mind and his heart. It was like a Words by Winter assignment x 1,000. Go back in time, to a time that was filled with so much confusion and hurt that you can't bear to think about it, and think about it. Put yourself in your own place and then put yourself in another's. This was when being the Winter of Words by Winter became unbearable.

I did it anyway. I sat on the porch and felt my way back into the darkness. High school. Asa had graduated. His mother had moved out. I conjured him in the rooms of the house he lived in with Eli, that house I knew so well, moving from kitchen to living room to bathroom to bedroom. I conjured up plates of food, the hiss of beer cans popped open, Eli watching over him, cooking for him, saying goodnight to him. How many days or weeks or months went by before Asa found out about his father and my mother? Feel your way back, Clara.

Someone looking at me on the porch might have seen a woman sitting still as wood in a chair in the night, but that would be only the chalk outline of the beaten body. Because when you go back, back, back down the back roads of your own time on earth, it takes all your energy. It takes all your focus. It takes almost more than you can bear, to feel your way into the heart of someone you loved and still love.

It was when I had made my way fully back into the heart of those conjured-up years that I knew when he had found out, and what he had done. The last of the missing puzzle pieces came to me on a lidded platter carried by a sorrowful servant, who set it silently down.

Asa would have blamed his father and Tamar for his bitter mother's departure. He would have been furious and bewildered and filled with desperation. He would have seen no way out—his girlfriend's mother? His own father? His mother? With me, his girlfriend, entirely in the dark?—and he would have cut himself out of the picture. What Asa would have done was exactly what he did: break up with me, enlist in the army, leave the next week for basic training and years as an army mechanic, and then, after the Twin Towers fell, go to Afghanistan.

....

And Tamar?

I went back in time with her too. I imagined my mother the way she had looked fifteen years ago. Not much different from now, if now had not traded so much balance and clarity for bewilderment. I imagined her in the kitchen of that house in the foothills, that house she had lived in all her life. Looking up from the work schedule she was trying to plot out for the week, her every-Sunday task, trying to keep to her normal routine even though earlier that night Asa had come by and told her he knew, he knew what was going on with her and his father, and how could she, what was she thinking, what about his mother, so what if she and his father had always had problems, and what about Clara, what about *Clara, what about Clara, what about me and Clara, did you ever stop to think about us?*

Asa.

Next day Asa was back, standing in the driveway with her daughter. Something was happening. I pictured my mother pulling the curtain aside with one finger, just enough to see out. A cool fall day, a hint of winter to come on the edges of the breeze. She had watched me stand in front of Asa, arms out, saying, "Why? Why, Asa, why?" She had watched Asa shake his head. Back and forth and back and forth. "Why, Asa?" Back and forth. "Why, Asa?" Back and forth.

My mother had watched Asa break up with me. Worlds were coming apart, and so was her child.

This was where it got harder. I had to be my mother, imagine myself into her with the knowledge that I now had, the knowledge that she and Eli Chamberlain had loved each other. What happened inside her, when she pulled that curtain aside and knew that Asa and I were no more?

Correction: This was where it *should* get harder. This was where I *should* go back and forth in my mind, trying to imagine exactly what went on inside my mother, the trying to figure out what to do now because Clara and Asa weren't but she and Eli were. Could she and Eli keep seeing each other? Martha had moved out by then, a divorce was in the offing or soon would be; would somehow the children be okay if she and Eli, at some point in the future, were in the open? Could it all work, somehow? That scenario was what I should be trying to conjure up, what I should by way of imagination and empathy be ferreting my way into, except that there was no such scenario.

I already knew what had happened that day. What happened was that my mother witnessed the breakup, watched Asa try but fail to start his car, called Eli to come get his boy, and then called it off with Eli.

At that moment my heart clawed at itself the way Eli's heart must have when my mother told him it was over. The sense of a man bent over his kitchen table, fingers clutching it for dear life, kept coming to me and I couldn't shake it. He lost so much. His son. My mother. And me, too, the girl who, he told me once after he and Asa and I took the brewery tour and he had drunk the two beers they give you for free in the old-time parlor afterward, was like a daughter to him.

I got up from the porch and loaded my quilt-wrapped self into the Subaru, the way Annabelle Lee loaded herself into her ancient Impala, and I drove to Annabelle's trailer. I told her what I thought I knew and I watched her eyes shift away from mine, up to the ceiling, then finally back to me.

"So?" I said. "Is that the way it went down?"

"Well," she said, "you know your mother."

"Is that a yes?"

"It's the way she told me it happened, yes."

"Why did she break up with him?"

"Because in the wake of what Asa had done she could not see any way to stay with Eli," Annabelle said. "'I can't hurt my daughter. I can't hurt her *more*.' Exact quote."

But the way she said it, the words *she could not see any way to stay with Eli* translated and retranslated themselves in my mind as *She did it for you* and then *It broke her heart* and then *It broke his heart too.*

"She thought it was the only way she could spare you yet more hurt," Annabelle said. "You know your mother, Clara."

"I don't know if I do."

"You're trying. I'll give you that. Late in the game or not, you're trying."

. . . .

Why the army? The Chamberlains weren't a military family and the military had never been part of Asa's plan. His plan was to drive truck for

Byrne Dairy and maybe buy his own big rig someday and be his own boss, be a long-haul trucker. That way he could see all fifty states. Hawaii he would have to fly to, but it was possible to drive to Alaska, if you had the time, and that way you could knock off a vast portion of the west. A big map of the United States hung on his wall, colored pins stuck in all the states he'd been to so far. Only eighteen. Barely over a third.

In a different life this would have been one of those questions I would ask him, in that imaginary future years and years hence, when everything that had gone wrong was long in the past, and we were sitting on a bench somewhere, setting things right between us. He would ask me about college and I would ask him about the army and what it had been like all the years up until his deployment, and from the filling-in of generalities we would narrow down and down and down until there was enough ease between us that we could tell each other that we had truly loved each other, that it had been real, and how sorry we were, sorry how things ended.

But there would be no conversation years hence, because there was no Asa. First enlistment and training and finally deployment and death. The quickness of it still startled me awake sometimes, my heart thudding in the dark, sweat rippling over me in waves.

There was no one to ask now. No one to fill in the blanks. When Asa broke it off with me, I broke it off with Eli, and we had not spoken since.

"Eli tried," Annabelle said. "He did try."

"How?"

"Called her. Drove up to Watertown once, when she was up there working on the trucks. Wrote her a letter."

"Wrote her a *letter?*"

She frowned. "Yes, he wrote to her. You're not the only person in the world who can write a letter, Clara. Most people do learn how to write, you know. Usually in first grade."

Of course they did. Everyone learned how to print and some still learned cursive, and everyone now used a keyboard and a computer and a smartphone and if you were blind you might still learn how to write

Braille but knowing how to write and writing a letter to the woman you loved, the woman who broke up with you, were two separate animals. Annabelle was watching me with her eyes narrowed, as if she were daring me to say something else about writing so that she could leap on it and remind me that I was not the only person in the world who could put words to feelings.

"Annabelle."

She lifted her eyebrows, still waiting, waiting for me to mess up so that she could pounce. It was exhausting. Could she not see that? Could she not see that I was no longer the woman I had been even a few months ago? No longer the girl I had been in high school, oblivious, unable to see my mother as anything but my mother? Could she not see just how hard I was trying?

"I know everyone learns to write," I said. "But it's hard to imagine Eli Chamberlain sitting down and writing a letter."

"Why is it hard?" she said, after a pause. Her voice lacked the *Ha, I've got you now* pounce it had earlier. Maybe she was trying too.

"I guess because in all the time I knew him I never saw him write anything. I never saw him read anything either. He wasn't a word person, is what I'm trying to say. At least the Eli that I knew."

"I would say that is accurate."

"So if he wrote my mother a letter, then he must have—"

"Loved her," Annabelle finished. "Yes. He did."

"What did the letter say?"

"I have no idea."

"She didn't show it to you? How do you know he wrote it, then?"

"Because I watched him write it." She pointed at the kitchen table where I was sitting. "He wrote it right there, on a piece of Twin Churches stationery that I gave him."

New information. My mind erased the image of Eli Chamberlain sitting at his own kitchen table, the table that he and Asa and I had sat around playing cards many a night, and conjured him up here, in Annabelle Lee's trailer kitchen, full of the scent of baking and cooking, loud with music.

"Why?"

"Why did he write the letter here? Because, Clara. Because you're right. Writing is hard for most people. For Eli, especially. Dyslexia, whatever"—she swiped the air with her hand, as if she were banishing the word from the world—"and he was afraid."

"Of what?"

"That she wouldn't respond. That she wouldn't write back, wouldn't call, wouldn't ever talk to him again."

"And did she?"

"What do you think?"

She stood by the table, the solid, unmoving bulk of her. Annabelle Lee, a fortress unto herself, a castle surrounded by a moat full of alligators, defender of all things Tamar Winter. For a long time now I had interpreted her simmering anger as anger at me, impatience with me, annoyance with me, but for what? For not being a good enough daughter? For caring too much about words? For leaving Sterns and never coming back? But now she set her hands on the posts of the chair before her and I saw her differently. As my mother was disappearing, so too was Annabelle's best friend, her one true friend. Keepers of each other's secrets.

A memory rose up in my mind: my mother and Annabelle, sitting in a booth at the back of Crystal's Diner, suspending straws full of milkshake above their mouths. Some kind of contest. Both of them laughing so hard that they dropped their straws and spilled milkshake everywhere.

"My mother hardly ever laughed except with you," I said. Annabelle nodded, even though she couldn't picture the scene in my head. She was willing to follow me. "She's a serious person."

"Yes," Annabelle said, as if everyone knew that. "So are you. You were a tough kid to raise. The way you were always words, words, words and smart, smart, smart? She didn't feel like she was a match for you. She didn't know how to help you. She said that to me once. 'My daughter is beyond me,' is what she said."

A lump swelled up in my throat. My mother, not a match for me? My mother, not knowing how to help me? I tried to picture a Buddha in my mind, one of those potbellied laughing ones that people like to put in their gardens. *Calm, Clara.*

"She sent you away for your sake," Annabelle said. "Do you know that now? 'There's too much hurt here for her, Annabelle. It's a big world out there.' She figured you were stronger than you knew at the time. And she was right, wasn't she?"

"She was. Which doesn't make it easier. Then or now."

"That's the way of the world, I guess," Annabelle said. The exclamation marks were gone from her voice.

"Annabelle?"

"What?"

"Can you—" But what? What could she do? "Can you tell me something I don't know about my mother?"

"Like what? That she loves Leonard Cohen?" she said, and rolled her eyes because Tamar's love of Leonard Cohen was something we both knew.

Had I ever seen her groan and roll her eyes like that, the way a teenager would, the way I used to do? *Annabelle Lee was once a teenager too, Clara,* I reminded myself. Of course she had been a teenager, and of course so had my mother been. But most of your life you knew that only in a factual way. You didn't feel it. Until you saw your mother's childhood friend roll her eyes at your mother's Leonard Cohen worship and suddenly she was young again, and so was your mother, if only in your mind. Memory, reconfiguring itself.

"She was addicted to that man," Annabelle said. "Neil Diamond and Jackson Browne and Joni Mitchell too. But Leonard Cohen? She used to refer to him as her future husband."

"She did not!"

"She did! She used to call him Len! *Len,* can you imagine?"

Yes. Yes, I could imagine. I shook my head.

"It's so unfair," I said. "She never had a chance! She never got to do anything she wanted to do!"

My voice was full of exclamation marks again, chasing one another around the table, angry points of black. But Annabelle shook her head

at me again and half laughed in an *Oh, you poor dumb girl* kind of way.
Then she opened a drawer next to the stove and pulled out an envelope.

"This is for you," she said. "Your mother left it with me, said to give
it to you when the time was right."

Clara. My name on the manila envelope in my mother's angular, el-
egant scrawl. Inside was a bank statement to a savings account in my
name, with a single cash deposit made a year earlier. A huge amount,
many tens of thousands of dollars. Sterns National Bank, Clara Winter,
for deposit only.

"The house," Annabelle said, when it was clear that I didn't understand.

"What do you mean, the house?"

"You know how the Amish are. It's cash only, with them. Where'd
you think that money went?"

"To the nursing home."

Annabelle snorted. "She got a long-term-care policy for that. Years
ago. I told her she was nuts—those things are way too expensive. But
she got it anyway. 'I don't want Clara to have to worry about money,'
she said. 'Ever.'"

I looked at the bank statement, at my mother's signature and back at
Annabelle.

"Am I an idiot?" I said. "My whole life, did I misread my mother?"

"Idiot? You?" Annabelle said. "Maybe in terms of financial forensics,
but you were the state spelling bee champ, for God's sake! No one in the
whole goddamn valley would call you an idiot. You're the farthest thing
from an idiot, Clara Winter."

She strained upward to the high cupboard above the stove and pulled
down a dusty bottle of Jim Beam, uncapped it and poured us each a
shot. Jim, not Jack. Cut from the same cloth, though.

"You're a daughter," Annabelle said, the teenager gone from her voice
and eyes now. "That's what you are."

....

The key to surviving the heinous interview, if and when I ever made it
to Los Angeles and onto the show in real life, would be advance prepa-

ration. Survival lay in the clues that you gave the producers beforehand. You had to give them only tiny tidbits of your life, impartable information that you didn't mind others knowing. Fragments chosen with care.

What would I not mind anyone knowing? That I was afraid of doing a headstand. That I was good at French-braiding hair. That I was a piano major in college.

TREBEK: So, Clara, rumor has it that you were a piano major
    in college?
ME: That's true, Alex.
TREBEK: And something of an obsessive piano practicer?
ME: That's true too.
TREBEK: But you never played the piano for your friends?
ME: Nope.
TREBEK: And you no longer own or play a piano?
ME: True and true.
TREBEK: Is that so! Well.

At that point, I would have survived the contestant interview portion of the show, having given away nothing of value, nothing of importance. The viewing public would have no clue that all those years of practicing the piano had ingrained it into me, so that there was a permanent piano in my heart and in my brain, and that sometimes when I woke up at night I closed my eyes and placed my fingers on the invisible keys and played and played and played, until the dark went away and I played myself back into sleep.

My mind and my heart would still be my own. No one watching me during the contestant interview would know how it hurt to drive by the house I grew up in, way out there in the foothills, the house my mother and I didn't live in anymore, but that I kept doing it anyway. They wouldn't know that sometimes I drove by Annabelle Lee's trailer too and sent my thoughts to her through the invisible air, thoughts of how sorry I was that this was happening to her too, how hard I knew it was for her as well as for me.

No one would know how my mother's brain — that sharp, sharp brain of hers—clicked on and off now. Like a half-broken light switch that you kept flipping even though most of the time it didn't work anymore.

I had come across my mother talking to a wall. Not a metaphorical wall either. A real wall, made of plasterboard, painted light green, a key strung on twine hanging from it on a hook. The key might be metaphorical—a key to a locked room? A song? Someone's heart?—but it was also real. It hung in my mother's room. Sometimes when I came to visit her now, I knocked, then turned the knob so softly that she didn't hear it. And there she was, talking to a lockless key as if it were her oldest friend. Once I found her singing to that key, a single line from her man Len, three words repeated over and over. *So long, Marianne, so long, Marianne, so long, Marianne.*

No one would know that on nights like that, playing my way back to sleep on the invisible piano sometimes took hours, from Hanon scales to Chopin to Shostakovich to Bach to the Beatles to Christmas carols. I played as loud as I wanted because who was there to hear what was happening inside my brain? The last song I played now was not the Chopin prelude. It was the one about the baffled king composing hallelujah, my mother's favorite song.

....

"Ma?"

She looked up from the walker. We were doing the circuit, the circuit of hallway and juice and Green Room and hallway and juice and Green Room, and around and around and around she went, where she stopped, nobody knew, except that she didn't stop. She only went.

"I'm sorry about Eli," I said. The expression on her face didn't change. I said his name again: "Eli." She pushed forward, heading toward the Green Room.

"Ma?"

On she went. *Talk to her, Clara. Tell her how you feel. Things that you want to say to her, say now.*

"Not sorry that it happened, Ma. That's not what I mean. I'm sorry that it ended."

And I was. They could have been together, I thought now. Time would have softened the edges, wouldn't it? Eased the strangeness of it, the new configuration of family and love and friendship. To me, at least, if not Asa.

I looked back on my childhood now and thought, *She had to shield herself from you, Clara.* Tamar was a woman of stillness, and her child was a blunt instrument who would throw and throw questions at her while she gathered silence around her like a cloak. And now?

The days were going by, each of them a ticking clock, and my mother's condition was worsening "significantly faster than we had anticipated." It was the "what we hoped wouldn't happen, Clara" scenario. She was "probably quite a bit farther along than we thought when she first came in, apparently," losing physical strength and balance, losing comprehension, gaining agitation and confusion. Was she with me yesterday, when I last saw her? Did she recognize me? Did she remember that I was her daughter, did she remember my name?

Yes, yes and no.

....

"She's going down fast," I said to Sunshine and Brown. It was like a mantra. A chant. Sometimes now I just showed up at their house. The demon child descendeth.

"It's a one-way street," I told them. "She's at the far end of the spectrum. They alarmed her chair and her walker and her bed. She's a human alarm now."

They let me babble. They didn't argue. They didn't point out the clichés and repetition, the unlike-Clara way the words came out. They offered food. Whiskey. Board games. They offered themselves, the constancy of their presence and their friendship, and it wasn't enough but it almost was.

"The coffee table is gone," I told them. "All the books are with her now."

They nodded. They had been to the cabin and they had been to the alarmed room where Tamar lived. They had seen the disappearance of the coffee table, the appearance of the books-as-firewood. Books to keep her warm. Books to burn. Books never to be read again.

"The only one she ever opens is *Jonathan Livingston Seagull*," I tell them. "So which is the book I read to her? *Jonathan Livingston Seafuckingull*. From Jonathan's mouth to God's ear. Those are the only words she wants, apparently."

Words had power. Bossy little Kandace saw Blue Mountain begin to shrink when she made fun of his name, and she kept making fun, so that he would keep shrinking. Sticks and stones might break your bones but words, words would break something inside the marrow of those bones, something that might not ever put itself back together.

The only way to fight the shrinking and the breaking was to fight. Fight with everything you had. However you could, fight. Fight with words, if you had them. Fight with poems. I did.

I have spread my dreams under your feet, I told Blue Mountain when he came back into the quilt room that day. *Tread softly, because you tread on my dreams.* You might be thinking he laughed. You might be thinking, *He's a dinky little kid, he doesn't know anything, he has no idea who Yeats is, he has no understanding of what those words mean.* You would be wrong. He stood and listened, those dark eyes on me, until his teacher came back to retrieve him. You can change the air of a room with your words. Even if you say them out loud only inside your head, the air around you will turn deeper, softer, stronger. Maybe Blue Mountain would remember, in some part of himself at some later point in his life, at a time when he most needed it, that someone in his childhood spread her dreams underneath his feet and blessed him with words he could no longer remember.

....

I found the letter when I was restacking the books beneath the windowsill, creating order from chaos. *Jonathan Livingston Seagull* was missing, and the room looked wrong without it.

"I read it to her too sometimes, when she's agitated," Sylvia told me when I went looking for it. "Sometimes in the middle of the night, when she's trying to find her daughter, I get it from her room and show it to her, and then we sit down and I start reading."

Neither of us mentioned the fact that I was the daughter my mother was looking for. We were used to that by now. It was accepted between the two of us that the daughter was an entity, a not-me named not Clara but "my daughter."

An aide brought it back as I was restacking the book pile for the third time. You had to get the proportions right. You had to make sure the ratio of fat book to thin book to tall book to short book was balanced; otherwise the woodpile would be unsteady and precarious. When you went to remove a piece of wood from one end, the entire pile might fall, and then where would you be? Standing in the middle of a mess of wood, trying not to cry.

"Here you go, Clara," the aide said. "Sorry. I started reading it and forgot to bring it back. Strange book."

I flipped it open and kept flipping, the way you did when you were nervous and you didn't know what to say. *Don't take it out of her room again,* were the words on my tongue, but they seemed so harsh, and why? *Who cares if they take it out of the room,* I said to myself, but I did. I cared. I nodded my thanks and the aide smiled and left.

The letter fell out. A plain small envelope, thin and white. On the back: a circle of yellowed tape that must have stuck it to one of the back pages and a sketch of the village green in front of the Twin Churches. On the front, in pencil gone over again with pen: *Tamar Winter, Route 274, Sterns, NY 13354.* No return address. Unopened.

The image of Eli Chamberlain, his head bent over Annabelle Lee's kitchen table and his hand moving laboriously on a sheet of stationery, reared up in my mind. The address, penciled and then penned over the pencil, the way someone unsure of himself would do it. The way we had been taught in elementary school to write our book reports. "Write it in pencil, then read it over and check the spelling and your word choices and your grammar," our teachers said. "Take your time. If you want extra credit, you can rewrite the whole thing in pen."

Eli Chamberlain had not rewritten, he had traced.

That big man, hunched over the table. That big man, writing in pencil. That big man, making his last stand for my mother. I did not slit the seal. I put the envelope back in the book. All these years, she had kept it.

....

Next day the Subaru and I pointed ourselves south on Route 28. We were nearly at the junction of 28 and 12 when, instead of going left, I went straight across. Gravel road, cornstalk stubble on the right, Christmas tree farm on the left. Deeper into the countryside north of Sterns we went, past the water tower with the red dragon painted on it, past the old stone schoolhouse, past the one-room church. Left onto a dirt road, rumbling in the frozen ruts left by tractors and pickups. The closer we got to Asa's house, the house where Eli lived alone, the more my heart hurt. The hurt was real, like a bruise inside my chest. I pressed my hand against it, the other gripped hard on the steering wheel. Tamar would not approve of one-handed driving.

"Nine and three," she used to say. "Both hands on the clock."

Her voice was quiet and even when she taught me to drive. I used to have a safety-belt system rigged up with the seat belt and bungees, a corsetlike system that kept me strapped in. It was a system I had come up with after the old man died, when everything seemed breakable, perishable, destroyable. All the bad *–able* words, and none of the good ones. Those were the days of Dog and the seat-belt safety system, of scrabbling monkey mind and scrolling words. Those were the days of fear.

"Put your foot on the gas and then on the brake. Smooth, now. Not jerky. Check the rearview mirror. Check the side mirrors."

She wanted me to be safe. To stay on my toes. To pay attention. I knew that now.

The Subaru and I pulled into Eli's driveway and parked. My heart thumped in its cage, strained against the ribs that held it tight. Fifteen years since I had been here, at this house and this barn, this place where I used to spend so much of my time. I took my hand off my heart and got out of the car.

Eli opened the door before I could knock. I started to say something but I couldn't, because his arms were around me and I was crying so hard that nothing came out but snot and tears. He tightened his arms and I cried into his coat. He smelled the same, like himself, and the like-himself smell brought the smell of his son over me, rolling in like waves. Asa, Asa.

"I loved him," I said. "And I loved you too."

The words came choking out, a strangled scream wrapped inside them. Eli nodded.

"I know you did, baby girl. I know you did."

Baby girl. He used to call me baby girl. The shock of hearing it again —no one in my life had ever called me baby girl but Eli Chamberlain, as if I were his beloved daughter, his girl who had never grown up— made me laugh and then cry harder. Because I had never talked to him. Never called him, never written anything, when Asa died over there.

"I'm sorry, Eli. I'm so sorry. I know all about it now."

His arms were still around me. He was so much older now, a man in solid middle age, but half my life ago, when I was seventeen, he had been a young man. I could see that now, could picture his face and his big shoulders and his big laugh, back when I was a girl and his son and I used to go riding around with him. He had barely been in his forties then, a decade younger than my young mother was now.

"IshouldhavecalledIshouldhavecomeseeyouIshouldhavewritten."

Words tumbled out of me, not enough space in between them to make any sense, but they must have made sense anyway, because he nodded, I felt him nodding. Then we were sitting on the old bench that was still on the little front porch. So many summer nights his son and I had snuck back late, sat on that same bench and held each other as dark smoothed into dawn.

"I feel so guilty," I said. "I was so angry at her when things must have been so hard for her."

"You couldn't have been as angry at her as Asa was angry at me."

"How did he find out?"

"Martha told him. She wanted him to know why she moved out. She blamed me. Which was justified."

Martha Chamberlain, the tough nut.

"He broke up with you because he saw no way out," Eli said. His hands were spread in front of him, as if he were trying to explain something puzzling, something almost incomprehensible. Theoretical physics. "He saw no way through Martha's anger, no way that your mother and I could be together, no way that the two of you could ever be happy in the middle of it all."

The sight of my mother and Asa across the kitchen table from each other, that night when the air was thick with words that had already been spoken, words that neither of them would ever recount to me, rose up in my mind. *No way out.* The words, little dark knives of hurt, severed by.

"And he knew how much you loved your mother, and he didn't want to hurt you any more than he felt he had to. He didn't want to say anything bad about her to you."

"He didn't have a lot of perspective," I said. "Neither did I. I know that now."

He turned his big hands palms up, then laced them together. They sat quietly on his lap, a giant lump of laced-up fingers.

"Perspective," he said. "The gift of growing up."

I hitched myself a little closer to him and laid my hands on top of his. A complicated Jenga tower rose up in my head. It began with four people who loved each other, me and Asa and Tamar and Eli, and it ended when Asa yanked the middle block from the stack and it all came tumbling down. We sat together in silence until Eli spoke.

"How's your mother?"

"She's okay."

"Is she?"

I shook my head. No. She wasn't. She was going away, faster and faster every week now, and he knew it as well as I did, because he didn't say anything else. There was so much I wanted to say to Eli, so much I wanted to apologize for, but everything I wanted to say was translating itself into another language, a wordless one that he already understood.

....

The next time I went to Annabelle Lee's house, dark had fallen. Early, the way it did in December. I drove up the driveway and parked next to the Impala. Her double-wide shone bright in the car headlights. It still looked brand-new and had looked that way for all the years I'd known her. It was lit up like a ship, and when the door opened, the smell of fresh bread wafted out. Annabelle Lee wore a Kiss My Blarney Stone apron and The Doors were belting out "Riders on the Storm" from the enormous speakers that doubled as a coffee table. I stood on the rickety stairs and breathed in the warmth.

"What?" she said, at what must have been a look on my face. "You think choir directors go home and listen to hymns all day? Let go of your preconceived notions, Clara. They'll be the death of you."

"I came to tell you I'm sorry," I said.

"What are you sorry about?"

"For a lot of things, starting with my mother thinking I was a lonely child. She told you I was a lonely child, right?"

She nodded.

"I wasn't," I said. "I wasn't lonely. I had the old man. I had some friends at school. Later I had Asa. And I had books."

"Books you did have," she said. "She always called you her word girl."

I pushed my hand down in my pocket and held onto the silver earring. Yes. I had been a word girl. Her strange child, her word girl.

"But mostly?" I said. "I had her. I had my mother. I had Tamar Winter."

Annabelle Lee nodded and I tipped my head back to keep from crying. An old white pine towered at the edge of her lawn, close to the road, just like the white pines at the cabin on Turnip Hill Road. Starlight filtered through the crown of the pine like lace against the navy December sky. Annabelle shut the door and leaned against the stair rail—it swayed—and looked up too. The two women who knew my mother best, standing together in the wintry air.

"I know you did," Annabelle said. "She was always there."

It was true. Tamar had been there, chopping wood outside the storage barn, anytime I looked out the kitchen window. She had been in the kitchen eating out of jars and cans with her cocktail fork. She had handed me book after hardcover book about a child facing the perils of the world and overcoming them on her own. Every step of the way, she had been there. None of those thoughts came out, though, because they were monkey-minded together in a clump in my brain. Messing up my words. Messing up my ability to talk.

"I wish I had told her how much I missed her when she made me go so far away," I said.

"You can still tell her."

I could hear Sylvia's voice telling me the same thing. That there was power in the voice. That hearing remained when the other senses had faded.

"I wish I had told her a long time ago."

"There are things I wish I'd told my mother," Annabelle said. "And things Tamar wishes she'd said to hers."

"How did my mother do, after I was gone?"

Annabelle shrugged. "You know your mother."

What that meant was that she had toughed it out, the way she toughed out everything that came her way. My heart quickened and the look on Annabelle's face softened.

"For what it's worth, I think she knew how much you missed her."

"You do?"

"You know how she always called you on Thursdays?" I nodded. "She used to be relieved when you'd get annoyed at that whole phone shtick she used to do. She took that as a good sign. 'She's making her own way in the world,' she used to say. 'That's good.'"

Orion, the archer, and Cassiopeia were visible now. The Big Dipper, its arm obscured by the red pine. Constellations of the Northern Sky for $800, please. Annabelle Lee and my mother and I were all three of us northerners, all three of us familiar with the northern sky.

"She woke me up once when I was four years old," I said, "and she brought me downstairs and onto the porch so I could see the northern lights."

"Did she?"

"She did."

"And? Were they beautiful?"

Yes. They were beautiful, in a strange and unearthly way.

....

The next time I went to visit Tamar I signed her copy of *The Old Man*. *To Tamar Winter, with admiration and love.*

My full name I wrote out in careful script, the way a name deserved to be written. No slashes or curls or undulating waves standing in for multiple letters, the lazy way out. The forces of evil had to be fought with all the means at our disposal, and if you were a word girl, then names were distilled words and had to be treated with respect.

On the windowsill, the hammered-metal bookends that she called the iron claw held the one book that still mattered to her: *Jonathan Livingston Seagull.* All her other books were stacked beneath the window, the worn hardcover edges of each perpendicular to the one above and below. A pile of book-logs to see her through the winter. *Jonathan Livingston Seagull* was the only book in the whole room that hadn't belonged to me first. It was the only book I ever saw my mother read, and she read it over and over, until the edges of her small blue paperback copy were worn nearly off.

"Ma! Why are you so obsessed with that stupid anthropomorphized-seagull book?"

Me as a high-schooler, badgering her. Embarrassed that she had chosen *Jonathan Livingston Seagull,* of all books. *Anthropomorphized* was one of my favorite new words and I used it frequently back then. I asked again — "What's with you and that seagull?" — but she remained silent. So I stole the book from her nightstand one Wednesday night, when she was at choir practice, and I read it myself to see what the fuss was about. At first I was looking for a hint — a friendship, a romance, a mystery, something funny, something sad, something, anything — to see what kept her so riveted.

Now I thought, *You were looking for her. You were trying to figure out your mother.*

All I knew back then was that the book made no sense. It was about a seagull who could travel anywhere he wanted, at any time he wanted, by the sheer force of his mind. A seagull who believed that if he just thought hard enough and long enough, if he focused all his powers, he would transform.

I read it all that one Wednesday night, and then again the next Wednesday night, and a final time a week later. Searching for a clue. A trail of bread crumbs to follow.

Now I thought, *She was looking for a way out.*

She wouldn't have expressed it like that. She would not have wanted me to think she longed for a way out of her life. She wouldn't have wanted me to feel bad, as if I were holding her back. And I didn't. I didn't question my mother's life. The life she was living must be the life she wanted to live, was what I assumed. Back then I didn't think anything could stop a person from living any life he or she wanted. It was up to the individual, wasn't it? Wasn't it up to you and the power of your mind to focus your thoughts and make your life unfold the way you wanted?

Now I thought, Jonathan Livingston Seagull *is a beautiful, heartbreaking book.*

Now I thought, *What this book says is that there is a way out if only you work hard enough.*

Now I thought, *My mother worked so, so hard.*

....

It was the day before the procedure and I got up early. One more day. Twenty-four hours. I placed the folder that held my will—all my money to the care of my mother, and all my earthly possessions to Sunshine and Brown, and my silver earring to Chris, and *The Velveteen Rabbit* to Eli Chamberlain—on the first rung of the ladder that led to the sleeping loft and my bed of books, and then I turned the key in the lock.

One last hike. Bald Mountain. The fallen leaves were coated with frost that looked like dried salt. Half an hour on the trail and the feeling began to spread inside me, the same feeling that hiking always brought to my body, a flickering sensation that grew until it was me and I was it.

Climbing.

Leaving the world behind.

The sound of trucks and cars on Route 28 receded. The sound of the wind intensified. The bare limbs of oaks and poplars were leafless, and the higher I went, the stronger the wind blew.

Be fearless, Clara. From now on, be fearless.

Long ago I used to hike this mountain with Asa, back when we were teenagers. He used to run down the mountains we hiked up. I would watch him disappear ahead of me on the trail. He laughed when he ran. The way I made my way down was the way most people did, by bracing my knees a little with each step. Fearful, then and now, to run down mountains.

There was so much to fear in this world. Avalanches, sudden blizzards, car crashes, bridge collapses, tunnel cave-ins. Death by freezing, death by fire, death by madmen with assault rifles. Failure. Heartbreak. Gene mutations.

Once, when I was eleven and beginning to understand the world of fear and loss, I looked out the kitchen window of our house in Sterns to see a big black bird on the lawn. The word *raven* appeared in my mind, like a message from poor dead Poe, and fear swarmed up in me. Something bad was about to happen. Someone I loved was in great danger. Was it Tamar? All that day I waited, consumed with worry. Where was the danger, and how could I make it not happen; what were the signs I needed to look for, and where was I supposed to look for them?

Inch by excruciating inch the day passed. Tamar came home from work and we ate beans and corn and pickles out of cans. She was alive. She was alive, and tired, and hungry. She was not hurt.

But *you* were hurt, Clara. That was my thought as I made my way up and up and up, through the bare and muted trees. *You* were hurt. All that worry hurt you, and all that fear. All that wondering how you could possibly stop whatever was going to happen from happening. A foreshadowing of loss to come. But loss came to everyone. The bus careened around the corner, the sheet of plywood fell from the overhead stack, the gene mutation revealed itself.

"It's best to have low expectations," I said once to Sunshine.

"It's best to have *no* expectations," she countered. "Best, but impossible."

I thought about that sometimes. Like now, where the final part of the trail turned to rock. Almost at the summit now. Not far to the Rondaxe Fire Tower. Asa had been with me the last time I climbed the tower. We had stood at the top — it was rickety back then, rusty and neglected, not restored the way it was now — and watched the sun sinking against the western sky. A mile back down to the trailhead but neither of us wanted to leave.

No one else was out today. Too late in the day, too late in the season.

Tomorrow they would thread the wires through my veins and into the heart of my heart, and then they would set it on fire.

The summit. That vast expanse of sky and mountains and trees stretching all around me. The valley spread out below. To the west were the Adirondacks, my home, and to the east, beyond the smoky purple-blue horizon, were the Green Mountains. Beyond them were the White Mountains, where I had gone to college.

Be fearless, Clara.

I turned and started back down. Daylight was fading and by the time I reached the trailhead the sky would be a red glow. I pictured my heart the way it would look tomorrow, lit with fire from the inside in that one tiny, misfiring place. I pictured Asa all those years ago, running ahead of me down the mountain. I heard the sound of my own voice calling to him, laughing but also afraid. Of what? Falling? He had run; why hadn't I? How hard could it be?

Not at all, as it turned out.

Maybe running down the trail felt to me the way flying felt to a bird. I remembered that first airplane flight, back when I was seventeen, from Syracuse to Ohio, how I had looked around for someone who felt the way I did and found the businessman looking at me with recognition in his eyes. *It's a miracle, isn't it?* That was what he had said to me, and all these years later I could still hear his voice in my ears. I flew down the last slope of the trail, arms held out to touch the trees as I passed, and then I signed my name in the ranger's book and called Chris. Heart Surgery for $1600. The Daily Double.

....

Do you have a ride home, and if your ride home is a cab, someone needs to accompany you in the cab. If you notice bleeding from the insertion points, press down firmly using a towel. If there is still steady bleeding after an hour, then have your companion bring you to the emergency room. Avoid sex for at least two weeks. If you notice your heart still accelerating, or trying to, do not worry. Do not panic. Sometimes it takes your heart time to understand what happened to it and that it can't do that anymore, that it no longer has the ability to outrace itself.

"And who are you?" the nurse said to Chris. "Boyfriend, brother, husband, paid escort?"

"Bartender."

"A personal bartender. Now that's something I could get behind. Your name?"

"Chris Kinnell."

He squeezed my hand. The nurse watched us, smiling. "You guys are cute," she said. "How'd you meet?"

"She came into my bar one night," he said, "and ordered a gimlet."

"Did you make her a good one?"

"He did," I said. "Two, actually. Extra lime."

It felt like a long time ago, that night with the high-top table and the martini glass beaded with condensation. The heavy door, opening and closing. The sound of cars and trucks on the gravel parking lot. Gayle with her tattoo. The bartender mixing drinks and pulling beers. The darkness of the bar and the darkness of a day that began early, with the quilt exhibition at the arts center and the children cross-legged on the floor. Blue Mountain and his singular question.

The door opened and the blue-scrubs people herded in with their clipboards and their instruments and their needles and IV pole and their smile-crinkled eyes above masks. The nurse jotted something down on the form. They tucked a blanket around me. "We'll take good care of her," they said to Chris. "You can see her as soon as she's in recovery." And then they wheeled me out.

There were things I wanted to say on that speak-now-or-forever-hold-your-peace ride down the hall to the operating room, things that I would talk to Jack about if it were me and him sitting on the porch, the way we kept doing, even though it was truly cold now. There were things I wanted to say to Asa, and to Eli, and to my mother. To Blue Mountain and to the others who walked among us, their hearts beating outside their bodies. But the drug was trickling through me and the words formed themselves in the air above my head and did not get spoken. *It's short,* I was thinking. *It goes fast. Do everything you can while you can, because it'll be gone before you know it.* The lights overhead, fluorescent tubes of lights, flash-flash-flashed above my eyes as they pushed me along. I thought of the night the bartender dragged the chairs over and lay down so that we could look at photos of Sunshine and Brown together. If I were Blue Mountain's mother I would be proud of him. If I had a baby girl I would name her Grace. If Jack were let out of his bottle he might turn into a genie who held inside him all the secret thoughts I had told him. My thoughts would be big and free then. They would be in the world. They would float from cloud to cloud in a high-white-pine sky. The last thing I remembered was a girl in the trees who looked the way I used to look, and she was looking down at me.

....

There were things I couldn't forget.

Like the feeling in me when I looked up from The Depths and there was Asa at the concession stand, watching me, and even though I didn't know anything that was about to happen, the loneliness started melting out of me.

I went back to that feeling sometimes. That memory. When someone like Blue Mountain appeared, one of the skinless, with his unanswerable question and his shadowed eyes, I conjured up that memory of Asa and I sent it out into the world. *There will be someone for you in this life,* was the message I sent, *someone who will look at you and know you and love you.*

Other things, if only. If only they could disappear.

Like the way Asa still appeared to me, his face contorted the way it was when he told me it was over, we were over. The way he shook his head and just kept shaking his head and telling me he was sorry.

"I'm sorry. I'm sorry."

"Is it because of college? Because we can make it work, Asa."

"I'm sorry."

Asa, who I had never seen cry until that day, stood there before me, crying. It was unbearable, what was happening. I turned my head to the left, toward the edge of the house, where something caught my eye. A curtain, moving. Pulled aside and then let drop. My mother.

"Asa. Why are you doing this?"

"I'm sorry."

Minutes passed, him shaking his head and me crying. "Is there some-one else?"

"No."

"So you just don't love me anymore? Is that it? You stopped loving me?"

His head kept shaking back and forth and it was bewildering. He turned and got into the beater he used to drive around in, that we used to drive around in. How he kept it going nobody but he knew, but he knew that piece-of-crap car like a mother knew her baby, what it needed and how to soothe it, and somehow, always, he could make it work. Ex-cept for that day. I could still see him, grim-faced behind the wheel, fin-gers turning the key and the engine moaning like it was in pain, over and over, quieter each time until it was silent. And there he sat, me standing there, him sitting there, the air between us strange and distant, air that lived in two separate countries.

Then there was the sound of a truck coming through the woods, the shortcut road that only locals knew about, which meant that it was someone I knew, and it was. Eli Chamberlain in his truck. He drove into the driveway and threw it into park before it was ready. He walked up to Asa's dead car and opened the driver's door.

"Come on, son," he said.

Asa got out and Eli put his arm around him and walked him back to the truck and opened the passenger door for him and kept his hand on Asa's shoulder as he put one leg and then the other onto the step and disappeared inside. Eli shut the door and looked at me. What was in his eyes? On his face? Sadness. That was what I remembered.

"Goodbye, Clara," he said, and then they were both gone.

It wasn't true that Asa had stopped loving me. I had felt it then and I felt it now. But the thing I hadn't known when I was young and lacked perspective was that his love would always be with me. It was part of me forever. A room inside a room inside a room, a room that was always warm and bright. I could go and sit in that warmth whenever I wanted.

I hoped it was like that for my mother too.

....

A talisman was waiting for me when I came home after the surgery. She stood on the window ledge where Jack usually kept vigil, a slender, wood-chopping woman carved out of red pine. A tiny ax was gripped between both hands, held high above her head. A pile of miniature split firewood logs was scattered around her, and she wore a lumber jacket painted in a checkerboard pattern of orange and red and black. The carver who had posed her like that, who had taken a pocketknife and drawn the lines of her body so that the grain of the wood became sinew and muscle and bone, who had raised up my mother's arms in the sky, ax clenched between her hands, the master carver of this miniature scene was someone who had seen through to the essence of my mother. Tamar Winter, queen of the northland, in her prime. And off to the side, cradled between the boughs of a miniature white pine, was a girl, watching.

"What kind of wood is that?" I had asked the bartender, that night when my heart went pinballing off the rivers and highways and byways of my body. Woods of the North for $200.

"Red pine."

Chris was already a hundred yards down the rutted dirt road. He had driven me the fifty miles back to the cabin from the hospital in darkness complete but for the sweep of the headlights. He was quiet and I was quiet and my burned heart was quiet in my tired chest. The places where the electrodes had been were smooth now. I put two fingers on the side of my neck, in the familiar hollow where so often a racing heart fluttered. An artery pushed up against my fingers: One. Two. Three. They had found the faulty place and burned it. Part of my heart had died. That was the kind of thought you couldn't say out loud, or write in a book, because it was too dramatic. But that didn't mean it wasn't true.

Chris had gone to get the car out of the parking garage while I waited in the doorway of the hospital. My clothes were back on, my sneakers tied, and on my head for good luck, the same too-big scallion hat that I had been wearing that freezing day we wandered around Old Forge. The tiny silver hammer brushed against the wool and I slipped it out of my ear. Back into the pocket, little hammer. They all said goodbye — the doctor, the nurse, the techs, the receptionist — and out I went.

Age of miracles, I said to the invisible cold air. *We are living in an age of miracles.* The faces of Sunshine and Brown and Chris and Tamar hung in my mind, all of them alive and living in this world, all of us together in the age of miracles.

He pulled up in his big white car and he pushed the door open for me and waited until my seat belt was buckled. Then he put the car in gear and we drove in silence until we were past the Utica floodplain, heading north.

"We get two of so many things," he said. "Two eyes, two ears, two kidneys, two hands, two legs, two feet, two arms. But only one heart. You know?"

I knew. Only one brain too. His right hand stretched across the giant expanse of seat between us and I took it.

"This car feels like a grandmother car," I said.

"That's because it is. She left it to me."

"Did you love her?"

"I loved her completely."

The vast expanse of seat and the pressure of his fingers in mine. The darkness of the night sky with no stars. I remembered the night my mother woke me up and took me downstairs onto the porch, cold cement underneath my bare feet, the aurora borealis pulsing overhead.

"My mother is leaving me," I said. "She's going somewhere and I can't go with her and she's never coming back."

He was steering with his left hand, and his right hand was laced in mine, and he kept nodding and not looking at me, maybe because I was crying. My heart was quiet and beating evenly, even though it was missing a tiny piece of its original whole.

"You'll miss her," he said. "You'll miss her and you'll love her."

"Is that how it is with your grandmother?"

"Yes. She's still with me, though. That's the way it will be with your mother."

"Things get winnowed down," I said, and he nodded. "The less time, the more winnowing. If you're lucky, some peace. Some happiness. Love. You know what I mean?"

"It's like panning for gold at the Enchanted Forest," he said. "Did you ever do that when you were a kid? My grandmother took me there once. You must have gone all the time."

No, I had not gone all the time. But yes, I remembered holding my pan of dirt in the stream of running water and shaking it back and forth, letting the sand wash away. Glints of gold beginning to appear, until gold was all that was left. He and I had been children at the same time. We had both stood at the same stream, strangers on the lookout for treasure.

When we got to the cabin he didn't leave until I had fished out the key and opened the door and flipped on the lamp by the kitchen table. I hadn't noticed the woodcutter talisman yet; that would come later. He put the car in gear and I watched the taillights recede down the dirt road. I wished I had told him about the night my mother woke me up in the wee hours to show me the northern lights. I wished I knew what he was thinking right at that moment, whether he would stop at the bar before he went home, check in and see how the night had gone.

I was past the part of my life where long before now we would have taken our clothes off and flung ourselves onto a bed. That day would come—we both knew it—but it was not now. We pass through each stage of our lives unknowingly, until the day comes when it is behind us.

....

"Do you think you'll write a book about Tamar someday?" Brown said.

"No."

"Why not?"

"Because then that's who she would be. She would be a woman in a book instead of a living, breathing woman."

Or instead of the living memory of a woman who used to live, who used to breathe, who used to be set down so firmly on this earth. That was the danger, if you were a word person. It went with the territory, if your territory was words, and sentences, and paragraphs that turned into chapters that turned into books. When the old man died I built him a house of words to live in, and he would live within its walls forever. He was kept alive in there and yet he was still dead, despite the fact that there were questions I never got to ask him because I hadn't thought them up yet. The world was a place where people were and then they weren't. We remade ourselves so that we could keep living in it.

"You might write about her someday," Sunshine said. "Never say never. You're her word girl, after all."

I talked to my mother sometimes now, in the dark of night, when I was far away from the place where she lived. It was easier to talk to her bundled up on the porch, with Jack next to me and Dog in his urn inside and Sunshine and Brown a mile away. I asked her questions and I waited for the answers to come floating up the hill, from the dirt road, from the huge and silent trees that surrounded me. Answers like fireflies, floating up out of the darkness.

"Ma?"

Sometimes she answered. Sometimes she didn't.

"Ma, I don't know how to handle this."

"Yes, you do."

Immediate and clear. An answer unlike the not-answers she used to give me when I was a child.

"You're already handling it," she said, "even if you don't know you are."

"Handling it how? Driving down to visit you? Watching *Jeopardy!* with you? Talking to Annabelle and Eli? Hanging on to Sunshine and Brown? Reading to you from the seagull book?"

"Yes."

"'Yes'? That's all you got? A one-syllable answer?"

"Yes."

Then she was gone. You could feel when someone was with you and you could feel it when they left. Three yesses in a row. If my mother said I was handling it, then maybe I was. Maybe this was what handling something—something huge and overwhelming, something with no way in and no way out—felt like.

Maybe Sunshine was right, and the day would come that I wrote about my mother. Things that I remembered about her, things that were caught inside me, trapped and wanting a way out. Maybe I would sit here on the porch, with a notebook and a pen, and build a house for my mother. It would be a house for me and her, a house with plenty of

wood for the winter, cupboards filled with jars and cans, Dog curled up
with his stuffed monkey, a place where we could live forever. When my
mother thought I wasn't there she would lie down on the floor and listen
to Len. She would read her seagull book for the thousandth time. She
would think about the dreams she had for her life, the dreams I never
knew she had. Dreams that I still didn't know about, because I never
asked. She would tell me about Eli, maybe, or maybe she would keep
the memory of him for herself alone. When Leonard Cohen sang "Hallelujah" she might start to cry. She might play that one song over and
over again, because she was alone, and who would know? Who would
care?

My mother might think that she was alone. But she would be wrong.
I would be with her, watching over her, in that house made of words.

....

It was a morning of sun so anemic that I kept glancing at the sky through
the window, thinking it was about to storm, but no. Just early winter in
upstate New York. My mother and I were sitting on the Green Room
couch, me massaging her hands, one finger joint at a time. This had
been a recent discovery and so far it was working. Every time she was
bewildered or agitated or asking the same question over and over again,
that brain-fog look of confusion on her face, I would take her hand in
mine and say, "Let's sit down, Ma. Let me work the knots out." And she
would sit down and I would begin, one finger joint at a time, softly and
gently, in hopes of avoiding pain for her. At this stage, we could not tell
if something was hurting, and she herself didn't always know.

Or that was the way it seemed. How strange not to know if you were
hurting, not to know if something was pressing on a nerve or a swol-
len joint or a bruise. But once, months before, something didn't feel
quite right and I looked down to see my fingers kneading a purple-green
bruise on her forearm. "Oh, Ma," I said, "I'm so sorry. That must hurt
like hell. How'd you get that bruise?" But she just looked down at it in
mild interest, as if her arm and its bruise belonged to a stranger.

And the cold. She was always cold, or so it seemed, a condition that
had persisted for months now, despite the layers and layers of clothes

she would keep putting on even after an aide or Sylvia or I persuaded them off. Multiple socks. Her winter coat. A radish hat made for her by Sunshine. I had come upon my mother huddled on her bed under three blankets, propped on all sides by pillows. "Ma? It's eighty-six degrees in here, according to the thermostat. Aren't you hot?" Face pink and hair damp with sweat, she would shake her head no and pull the blankets closer. It seemed impossible that she could be cold, but then who was I to say what was possible and impossible for my mother? Who was I to decide for her? Her world, which might be part of this world but also might not, might be a world filled with chill.

"Ma, I'm going to run to the bathroom. I'll be right back."

Down the hall I went, to the bathroom that I thought of as my bathroom, as *our* bathroom, with "our" being everyone who walked through the doors of this place to visit someone who lived here and then walked on out again to go elsewhere, an else not here, a place called home. This bathroom had handicap rails but was used only by visitors, those like me who strode in and locked the door and did our business and flushed the toilet and washed our hands and glanced in the mirror and strode back down the hall to our parent or grandparent or sister or brother or aunt or uncle or wife or husband. It took me three minutes total.

But when I turned the hall corner, there was Sylvia, standing next to the Green Room doorframe, her hand half covering her mouth.

"Sylvia?"

Panic in my voice, soft, controlled panic because it behooved no one to panic at full volume in the place where my mother lived now. She didn't turn her head, but her other hand reached toward me, fingers spread in a warning that meant *Shhh,* that meant *No need to panic.* So I slowed and approached the way a pioneer girl might have done if she were trying to walk like an Indian guide in the woods, if she were trying to leave no trace of her presence, nothing to give herself away. I stood opposite Sylvia and pressed myself against the wall, angling my head to see what she was looking at, which was my mother, my small, thin mother, with Eli Chamberlain's arms around her. He was rocking her back and forth, there on the green couch in the Green Room, with his face pressed against her dark hair and his eyes closed.

There are times in life when you come across something—a piece of music or a passage from a book or words spoken by a person you love—and something in you responds in an instant, physical way. Your throat swells almost shut, tears spring out of your eyes, your heart draws in on itself in a way that somehow makes it feel bigger. Or broken. Maybe they're the same thing.

The both of us stood, Sylvia and I, one on either side of the doorway to the Green Room, watching someone who was not me and who loved my mother in a way that was nothing like the way I loved her now or ever, gather her in and hold her close.

And she let him.

....

The ship was in Trebek's capable hands and we let him guide it through the calm harbor of the first round. Brown and Sunshine were on one side of Tamar, Chris on the other, and me? On the floor, propped against Chris's legs. Their voices floated in looping, lazy curves in the air just above my head. Winter this and Winter that, Sunshine and Brown telling Chris more stories of back in college, how they used to come drag me out of the piano practice room and haul me downtown for beer and pool.

"How many times you think we've taught Winter to play pool, Brown?"

"Probably as many as we've made her drink beer."

Tamar stayed quiet. Where was she now, I wondered, and what was she thinking about? Was she thinking at all? The day would come when she stopped talking entirely. They had told me that at the Life Care meeting. *Please say something, Ma.*

"There," she said, and I felt her move above and behind me. A small movement, a disturbance of the air. Maybe she was pointing at the port-hole? *Knothole* had turned into *porthole* and we were following her lead.

"There what, Tamar?" Brown said.

"There."

There on the porthole, the sound on mute, Trebek was standing next to the three contestants at their podiums. Time for the contestant interviews. The heinous interviews. Come, first contestant, lean forward and do your best.

Then there was movement above and in back of me again. A hand descended on my head, a light touch, like the touch of a baby trying to understand hair. Sunshine and Brown and Chris stopped talking, all of them, at once. It was as if they had received a signal from the universe: *Be quiet.* Then I understood that the hand on my hair, whispering through it strand by strand, was my mother's.

There might have been nights, when I was a baby, that my mother placed her hand on my head. Maybe there were dark nights, nights when I couldn't stop crying, nights when maybe she couldn't stop crying either, and she sat with me in the darkness and held me and put her hand on my head and cradled me and rocked me. Maybe she sang to me. She must have sung to me, because my whole life was filled with memories of my mother singing. When she was gone from this earth, her voice would still be with me. Nothing went entirely away. Some part always stayed. Like the silent, unseen electricity running its way up and down the walls of the cabin. The shadow world: indivisible from this outer one in which we moved, and drove, and talked and laughed and held hands.

Was my mother scared, when I was little? Did she feel alone? Did she feel as if she were on a path leading somewhere she could not predict, somewhere she would have to go whether she wanted to or not? Was the child in her arms a comfort? Or was I a burden, a responsibility that she had no choice but to take on?

Both. That was the word that came to me, there in the porthole room. *You were both a comfort and a burden.*

On the muted porthole, Trebek was chatting with the three contestants. Their faces smiled and nodded, and so did his. Had I ever really looked at Trebek? Was this what he really looked like, an ordinary person having ordinary conversations with other ordinary people who happened to be good at trivia? Maybe this was who Trebek was, an ordinary, friendly man, and I just hadn't noticed. It was impossible to know the whole story.

Was I still a comfort to my mother? Was I still a burden? Her fingers whispered through my hair, following strand after strand, beginning at the root and moving down and down and down through the length of it, until the length of it ended and her fingers journeyed back up to the top of my head and began again.

"What do you think they're talking about up there?" Brown said.

"Game theory," Sunshine said. "Betting strategy."

Tamar was quiet, but her fingers kept moving. My head felt alive with her touch. Chris was quiet too, his knees solid behind my shoulder blades. Maybe the contestants were talking game theory and betting strategy. Maybe they were talking about the luck of certain shirts, the right tie. Maybe they were talking about their families. Did I know anything about Trebek's family? No. All these years, I had taken him and his show for granted.

Tamar's fingers danced the slowest dance in the world, arranging the strands of my hair in a way that must have made sense to her, because she kept on. She persevered. Then Chris's hands were on my shoulders, and my mother's fingers were light and soft in my hair, and my best friends were talking about what exactly *was* game theory, anyway.

If time could be frozen, that was where I would freeze it. That moment, in that room, with these people, this couch, this floor, that television. Chris's hands on my shoulders, my mother's fingers in my hair. Portal to another world.

The orchids in the corner hung heavily on their long stems, and the porthole kept up its soundless flickering. The third contestant tipped his head back and laughed a silent laugh while Trebek smiled.

....

When the call came I knew what it was about before Sylvia had a chance to say hello.

"She fell, didn't she," I said, and "Yes," Sylvia said, and then I told her I was on my way and I clicked off and then called Chris and Sunshine and Brown. I called Eli too, and left him a message. It was late in the evening and I waited on the porch with the quilt wrapped around me over my coat until headlights came flickering through the darkness and wound their way up the hill. Chris got out and opened the door for me, and Brown drove and Sunshine sat next to him.

She had fallen while trying to cross the black abyss. She was trying to get outside, through the glass door into the bare, pre-snow stalks of the back garden, invisible at night. She was trying to get to her daughter, lost out there somewhere.

I pictured the swatch of black paint in front of the locked sliding doors. The aide might have been asleep on the couch, or taking a bathroom break, or watering the orchids, or adjusting the volume on the porthole. The alarm had sounded and Sylvia had gotten there within seconds but not soon enough. My mother had left behind her walker, jumped the black hole and fallen into the abyss.

I undid my seat belt and slid across the big back seat to Chris, who wrapped his arms around me the way Eli Chamberlain had done the day I went to tell him how sorry I was. The headlights pierced the darkness of Route 28. Soon we would be at the junction of 12. It was a bad fall, Sylvia had said, and the tone of her voice filled in the meaning of *bad*. Soon we would be on the outskirts of Utica, at St. Luke's, where they had taken my mother. She was going down a road and I could not follow her.

I thought about the bartender, how he had pushed those chairs together and lain down next to me the night my heart wouldn't stop hammering in my chest. How, when it finally calmed, he had taken my hand in both of his and held it all the way to the car. I thought about my mother's fingers, how in these last months they had described curves and shapes in the air. Her fingers had traveled ahead of her to the land of words and phrases, the place where all her lost words and phrases lived now. They waited there for her.

I thought about Blue Mountain and pictured him asleep somewhere in a house in the high peaks. I pictured him waking in the darkness of that house, maybe from a bad dream. Or maybe from a good dream. I conjured up a nightlight in a corner of his room, a nightlight shaped like a star. I conjured up glow-in-the-dark stars glued to the ceiling of his room. I pictured him counting stars, counting himself back into the land of sleep.

I thought about Asa, the day things broke between us. I thought about Eli, how he had laced his arms around his boy and guided him into the truck and driven him away. I thought of before that day, how Asa used to put his arm around me and hold my far hand and, if he thought I was cold, sneak it into the pocket of his jacket. How he alternated first one arm and one hand and then the other arm and the other hand, so that neither of my hands had a chance to get too cold. I thought about the baby I might have had with him, how he might have waved his hands in the air when he cried, searching for comfort. For someone to help him. Someone to feed him, change him, soothe him, rock him. Someone to take the hurt away.

If ever I made it to the contestant interview, maybe I would tell Trebek about the Adirondacks and the Green Mountains and the White Mountains, how even though they were low and old mountains, they were my favorites. Maybe we would talk about books, and the people who lived inside them. Maybe I would ask him which books he loved as a child.

Whatever questions came my way from now on, and however I chose to answer them, I would hold a night in my heart. I was four years old and my mother was a girl of twenty-two. She woke me in the middle of the night and took my hand and guided me downstairs and out onto the porch.

"Look up, Clara," she said, and I looked up.

Red and yellow and green and blue, soundless and unearthly.

"It's the northern lights," she said. "The aurora borealis."

The dark night sky had glimmered and pulsed with light. I hung on to my mother's hand.

Now the four of us, in Chris's big white car, rounded the final curve of Route 12. The valley spread out before us, shimmering with city lights like a sky fallen to earth. It came to me that my mother had staked her life not on travel, or adventure, or school, or work, or a man to love, but on me. I was the great gamble of my mother's life, and she had not held back. She had bet it all.

Acknowledgments

No book writes itself, and I have many to thank in the writing of this one. Julie Schumacher, whose typically brilliant take on an early draft propelled the book forward, and whose encouragement was, and is always, solace. Nevin Safyurtlu Marino, for so generously sharing her experience; the lovely Margaret Miller, for advice on details of nursing home life; and Rebeccah Berry, Jeremy Moberg and Aria Dominguez, for their kindness. Kathi Appelt, dear friend and fellow writer, whose early enthusiasm and feedback were invaluable. The Alzheimer's Foundation and related forums on which caregivers write with such honesty and love in the face of great challenges. Several artists known to me only through their haunting and beautiful work, which accompanied me throughout the writing like lamps in the darkness: photographer Todd Hido, painter McArthur Binion, and poet William Stafford, in particular his poem "Remembering Brother Bob." My inimitable parents and their continuing examples of hard work and good cheer. My beloved agent, Doug Stewart, and his enthusiasm, smarts, Manhattans and all-around awesomeness. My wonderful, funny and keen-eyed editor Helen Atsma, whose insights were so perspicacious and wise that I sat right down and began revising. My copy editor, Amy Edelman, whose brain works in such mysterious and marvelous ways. My three great joys of children, who crack me up and also inspire me with their courage and determination to make the world a better place. And finally, Mark Garry, a.k.a. The Painter, who has lived with this book and others for years, and whose endless reserves of patience, artistic insight and listening ability are matched only by his humor, steadiness and love.

About the Author

Alison McGhee writes for all ages in all forms, from novels to poems to books for children. Her best-selling novel *Shadow Baby* was a *Today* Show Book Club pick, and her picture book for adults, *Someday,* was a number-one *New York Times* bestseller. Her work has won many awards and been translated into more than twenty languages. She has three grown children and lives a semi-nomadic life in Minneapolis, Vermont and California.